CW01660831

Playlist

everything i wanted - Billie Eilish
Obsessed - Olivia Rodrigo
we're not alike - Tate McRae
The Fall - The Weeknd
Blind - SZA
Dear Society - Madison Beer
Looping - Charlotte Cardin
Oui ou Non - Angèle
7 rings - Ariana Grande
Cancelled - Taylor Swift
How Does It Feel To Be Forgotten - Selena Gomez
Without me - Halsey
Who's Laughing Now? - Ava Max
Piece of Me - Britney Spears
Gifted - French Montana
All my girls like to fight - Hope Tala

Out Of Touch

Elle Grand

Content Note: This story includes references to eating disorders, self-harm, bullying, and suicidal ideation, as well as some mild adult language. Please take care while reading.

Cover design by Noemi De Feo

ISBN 978-2-8399-4885-2 (paperback) | ISBN 978-2-8399-4886-9 (ebook)

For the ones who made their own doors
when none would open

1

The first time I see Birdie Bay in real life is the day she moves into the apartment across the street, directly facing mine.

Our buildings in the 11th arrondissement are draped in typical Parisian charm: creamy stone, wrought-iron balconies, the whole clichéd package. But the area is more artsy than posh, without the romantic luster tourists are on the hunt for.

In short, this isn't the kind of neighborhood that would attract a multi-million-follower influencer like Birdie Bay.

Now, Birdie, she's everything you'd expect from her curated Instagram grid. Ethereal as hell, with a tanned, slender frame, a face shaped like a heart, and that platinum blonde hair cascading down to her belly. And her smile? It's got my own mouth doing a tug-of-war from across the street.

Behind my curtain, I watch her settle into her new space, curiosity piqued each time she opens a new box and retrieves an art piece or a pack of hangers, or her fancy-ass golden cutlery. The girl's got nicer stuff than a Kardashian (well, almost). Makes me consider tossing my own things and indulging in a little Amazon splurge.

"What are you doing?"

Daniel's voice comes out of nowhere, and I startle, binoculars in hand. His gaze flits from the binoculars to the window and lands on Birdie's new place.

"You are not going to believe who just moved into that apartment. Look," I say, handing him the binoculars.

Daniel complies, his eyes narrowing as he focuses across the street. I wait for the lightbulb to flicker on.

"Hmm, a living, breathing Barbie doll?" he deadpans, shooting me a quizzical look.

"She's Birdie Bay!" I snatch the binoculars back. Men, I swear, they're hopeless, and my boyfriend is no exception. "She's like—a star!"

"Never heard of her," he says, shrugging, and I have to remind myself that Daniel wouldn't recognize Justin Bieber if he were literally head-butting him. The man treats social media like it's toxic waste.

I place the binoculars to my eyes again. A recent post on Birdie Bay's profile had served as an announcement that she was moving back from LA to Paris, to "reconnect with her culture and motherland." Her followers had freaked out at the news. Would she keep publishing weekly training sessions? Did this mean she would move her jewelry brand production to Europe?

The picture she used was an old shot of herself from when she was a child. She was shyly posing by the Seine River, with the Eiffel Tower in the background. I had shrieked when the post popped up in my feed. One like wasn't enough, so I left a comment, "Paris better get ready for you!" and shared it with everybody I knew. Admittedly, there were only a handful of followers on my own small profile. The news was exciting in itself, but I never would have dreamed she'd become my neighbor. Suddenly, I'm the luckiest girl in town.

"Don't you think it's a bit wrong to snoop on her like this?" Daniel asks, bringing me back to Earth.

I keep the binoculars pressed to my face. "Wrong? How is it wrong? She's a public figure—it's literally her job to be seen. And it's not like I'm a freak or a stalker."

Daniel's quiet. I don't have to look to know his brows are drawing together.

"Come on," I coax, softening my tone. "I'm just having some fun. Isn't that what these binoculars are for?"

It had started as a joke between us. Parisians are so private, so walled off, that we figured we'd have to spy a little to get to know them. "Like a safari, but with people," Daniel had said, grinning. Through our lens, we discovered that the old woman on the first floor had a suspicious number of "guests"—probably illegally renting her apartment on Airbnb. And the polite, bespectacled boy downstairs? He'd pace by the front door every weekend. One day we caught him handing off a little plastic bag—weed, most likely. Mystery solved.

Daniel lost interest after a week. I didn't.

People fascinate me. The way they hide behind carefully built façades, shaping themselves to match what others expect. That old woman who looked too proud to greet a foreigner like me, or that boy who seemed the model student, each revealed something truer when they thought no one was watching. Those unguarded moments feel like tiny secrets of humanity, and I think they're beautiful.

But with Birdie Bay, it's different. In the words of Olivia

Rodrigo: *I know her star sign; I know her blood type*. Daniel doesn't get it. I *know* her, even if she doesn't know me yet.

"Well, that girl better get some curtains soon," he says after a beat.

I shoo him out of the room. Birdie Bay has started unpacking her shoes, and as a seasoned follower, this is not something I'm willing to miss.

In the days that follow, I morph into an inconspicuous spectator, watching Birdie Bay's daily routine unfold like a curious researcher who just stumbled upon a new breed.

I discover she strums her guitar with closed eyes, watches YouTube videos on her phone while applying makeup, and receives dozens of parcels daily that she doesn't even bother to open.

But more interestingly, I learn that Birdie Bay is a creature of unyielding routine.

Every morning at the crack of nine, she emerges, sipping a glass of water before sliding into one of her many Lululemon jogging sets—perks of being a brand ambassador, no doubt. Then, with clockwork precision, she embarks on a forty-minute run.

It's good to have routines, and guess what? She influenced me to do just the same.

So this morning, I take off the tags from my newly purchased Lululemon leggings and jacket. Then I lace up running sneakers that have long languished in my closet. Staring at my reflection, I note how the leggings complement my figure, and the dark red shade I've chosen makes my pale complexion pop.

Best hundred bucks spent.

I pull back my long, chocolate brown hair into a ponytail, add a touch of mascara to enhance my hazelnut doe-shaped eyes, and gently apply sunscreen over the freckles scattered across my cheekbones.

Sure, I might not exude the West Coast allure that defines Birdie Bay, but I'm rather satisfied with what I'm seeing in the mirror. She and I share the same stature and body frame, a thought that prompts a self-amused smile. With a touch of blonde and tan, we could pass off as sisters, or at least cousins.

I wink at myself; I look like a runner. A few selfies later, I'm outside my building, pretending to scroll on my phone.

True to her schedule, Birdie Bay steps out of her building at nine-thirty. She doesn't see me. Doesn't look, in fact. AirPods in, she makes a left turn, and I mimic her movements, keeping a safe distance. Together, we traverse the urban morning hustle, sidestepping delivery cars and weaving through a city awakening to its daily grind. We pass a charming park adorned with blooming flowers and the quaint photography store where I procure film for my cameras. The summer morning is already heating up, and the sun is casting a warm glow over the neighborhood.

Fifteen minutes into the run, I find myself gasping for air. By the time Birdie pulls the brakes, I'm a sweaty, panting mess, and I don't feel *that* sexy anymore in my Lululemons. I lean against a tree to catch my breath. Unfortunately, that's all it takes for Birdie to slip away from my sight. *Crap.* I look around, hoping to spot her pink set, but all I see are grumpy Parisians and a few homeless souls still deep in sidewalk slumber. I jog a bit further down the boulevard, and I'm almost tempted to ask passersby if they have seen a gorgeous blonde run by.

That's when a flash of pink catches my eye inside the bakery—Birdie, at the counter, paying for what looks unmistakably like a croissant. I shift my angle just enough to see better. Ham. A ham croissant.

Wait. She's vegan.

The thought blinks like a warning light, but I brush it off almost immediately. Maybe it's for someone else.

I stay nearby and wait for her to exit, and when she does, she eagerly bites into her pastry.

A smirk plays on my lips. Birdie Bay, the vegan evangelist since age ten, caught red-handed with a ham croissant. Human, after all. And now we share a secret. Emboldened, I close the gap between us.

"Hello, Birdie!"

Birdie Bay jumps slightly, startled. "Hey..." she mumbles, all embarrassed, as she attempts to hide the contraband croissant behind her back. "Sorry, I'm not really up for a picture right now. I feel kind of gross with this sweat."

She does look sweaty, unlike in her videos, where she always seems put together. Standing close, I notice subtle differences from her online persona. Still beautiful, of course, but somehow less polished, a touch younger perhaps, and a bit... realer, I suppose. It's like meeting your favorite princess at a theme park photo booth: the magic is still there, but the sparkle isn't quite the same as on screen.

"Oh, it's fine; I just wanted to say hi," I chirp, my tone sweet like honey on bread. "I'm your neighbor!"

"Yeah?" Birdie's blue eyes roam over me, a touch confused. "I guess I haven't met everyone in the building just yet."

"Oh, not in your building. I'm across the street."

She blinks at that, doesn't say anything.

"I jog too!" I say, gesturing to my mimicry of her outfit. "Thought we could grab coffee sometime. I know how lonely it is to move to a new city, not to know anyone..." Drawing from my own journey relocating from London to Paris three years ago, I feel a certain assurance in this part of my pitch. I can still remember how challenging the initial year had been in terms of adaptation: from wrestling with French to mastering the art of not looking bewildered when people started sipping wine at 4 pm.

"I was born here," she answers flatly, flicking her hand dismissively to check the time on her nonexistent watch. "Um, I'm sorry... What did you say your name was?"

"I didn't say, but I'm Chloé. Chloé Warner."

"Nice meeting you, Chloé Warner, but I'm afraid I must go now."

"Of course," I mutter. "I'll message you on Instagram!"

But Birdie Bay is already running the other way, tossing her empty bakery bag in the trash.

Back in my apartment, I bide my time for a couple of hours before mustering the courage to shoot Birdie Bay a friendly DM through her Instagram account. As soon as it sends, I anxiously station myself by the window, binoculars in one hand and my phone in the other.

As the day wanes, I find myself compulsively refreshing her profile so often that I've memorized all her recent pictures. Then it hits me—Birdie Bay, with her whopping three million followers, is likely inundated with a deluge of

DMs every day. A small laugh escapes me at my own naivety. Of course she hasn't seen my message! Without missing a beat, I copy and paste it, then dispatch it to the email address listed on her profile.

The night rolls on, and another full day passes. I keep observing her from my window perch. She indulges in yoga sessions in her living room, basks in the glow of the golden hour on her small balcony, and shares a couple of snapshots featuring her new Roche Bobois "Bubble" sofa on her profile.

And she keeps running every morning.

"Birdie Bay still hasn't answered," I tell Daniel over lunch.

We're sitting on the terrace of our favorite café near the school where Daniel works as an English professor.

He sighs and adjusts his glasses on his nose. I'm team contact lenses, but even I have to admit that Daniel wears them well. It adds to his character—this touch of nerdiness. Without them, he'd just look too good for a professor, with his curly auburn hair, chiseled jawline, and athletic build. Think Romain Duris with olive skin and a tendency to smile even when something isn't funny.

"Did you really think she would?" he asks, smiling (of course).

Suddenly annoyed, I stuff the remains of my avocado toast into my mouth, then reach for Daniel's muffin while still chewing.

"Well, of course. You weren't there. She said, 'Nice meeting you, Chloé.'"

"Are you really going to eat that?" Daniel asks, pointing at the pastry in my hands.

Peeling away the foil, I shrug like it's no big deal, even though it is. "I'll get you another one."

"It's just that you're always so funny with food that..."

"That what?" I challenge him, then take a big bite of the muffin, instantly feeling the familiar heaviness creep in. Taking another bite, I muse, "Maybe I should just hit her place. Give her a neighborly knock and a hi."

Daniel gives me a worried look, then appears to be choosing his battles carefully. "*Mon cœur,* she was being polite. People like her probably get stopped on the street all the time, she can't have coffee dates with everybody."

I battle a wave of frustration. The food feels heavier than it should in my stomach. "We're neighbors; it's not like I'm just a random follower anymore. I told her I would write her, so she must be wondering why I didn't reach out."

Daniel raises his eyebrows ever so slightly. "If you're so sure of it, you should send her a message when you see she's on her phone. This way, you'll see if she gets it or if you're just sending bottles into the ocean. But if I'm being honest, I think you should forget about her and focus on your art. How's that selection of pictures coming for the photography contest?"

I shake my head and quickly rise. "Going to the loo," I say over my shoulder as my mind wanders to his idea. That might actually be a good one.

The next day, I'm parked by the window, waiting for Birdie Bay to kick off her morning routine. She's on the floor, legs crossed, messy bun in place. Her phone goes horizontal on a tripod next to her mirror, and she hits play on a video. She once told *Elle* magazine that she never used her phone before noon to avoid distracting her brain. Something about beta waves and mental performance.

Some sort of bullshit, I guess, since she's now fully engrossed in what must be a makeup tutorial.

Through the binoculars, her screen's a blur, but her face is clear as day.

I pick an emoji—the one with a smiley and raised hands. It's friendly, open for a reply. I hit send and grab the binoculars. Birdie Bay tilts her head, snatches the phone, glances at the screen, and... rolls her eyes.

My jaw drops so wide a fly could move in.

For the briefest moment, her hands hover over the screen, and I draw in a breath, afraid that exhaling might alter the course of what's about to happen. How many rejections can one take before it damages them beyond repair? I think of my childhood, my mind wandering to places I wish I'd never have to visit again. My mother's face looms before me. It always does. And then, as if in slow motion, I watch Birdie as she swiftly replaces her phone on the tripod and returns to the video, crushing my hopes, dreams, and the remnants of my pride in one fell swoop.

That's it. Birdie Bay read my messages and *chose* to ignore them. Cheeks on fire, I toss the binoculars into a drawer.

The following morning, I get up at seven and put on my running outfit. I wait for Birdie Bay to come out of her apartment and follow her on her run. What is it that they say? Don't meet your heroes. She doesn't even know me!

She's unaware of the fun and loyalty I could bring to the table. I would have been her friend no matter what.

We cross the park that smells of dog shit, then pass the shabby photography store. We could have been besties, she and I. I could have shown her the best parts of the city, and she would have benefited from my photography skills. We could have been such a power duo.

A little part of me is relieved that she follows the same route for her jog. That only proves I was right to tail her today. Call me petty, but I want her to pay for making me feel so insignificant. No, scratch that, it's not about vengeance. I don't want you to think it is. It's about making things right.

As we near the bakery, though, Birdie Bay doesn't stop and keeps running. I furrow my brows and hasten my pace, ignoring the growing pain in my side. She charges down the boulevard, runs through the Sunday market, and disappears into a side street. Unable to follow without risking being seen, I linger on the corner, stealing cautious glances.

There, I see our neighbor, the middle kid from the family living in the apartment below mine, take a hundred-euro bill from Birdie Bay's hands and search his pockets for something.

I don't hesitate; the world has to know that Birdie Bay isn't who she pretends to be.

So I take my phone out and snap a picture.

2

"What time was Diane supposed to get here?" I ask Daniel, polishing the Leica's lens with slow, steady circles, mostly to keep my nerves occupied.

"Seven," he says, flicking his wrist to check the Cartier Tank gleaming in the late-afternoon sun. "Which means it's currently seven-thirty... and we're realistically looking at seven-forty-five."

Our eyes meet, and the corner of his mouth lifts. Despite sharing a face with Daniel, Diane didn't inherit a shred of his obsession with punctuality.

We order another round—Pinot Noir for Daniel, Rosé for me—and settle into one of our favorite games.

"Would you rather," Daniel begins, with that coy smile of his, "have to sing your order to the bartender or dance for your drink every time you order?"

I laugh, considering. "I'd go with singing. You?"

"Oh, I'd totally pull off dancing moves." He swirls his glass like it's a grand cru and takes a sip. I smirk, picturing it.

He's right. If anyone could turn random dancing into an art form, it's Daniel.

"Would you rather..." I continue, scanning the bar's terrace for inspiration. The place is low-key, with wooden benches and Ikea string lights that don't do much for illumination but add a cozy touch. The crowd is young, mostly students in casual outfits. It's one of our favorite spots to chill after a busy day. Tonight, though, the plan is to meet here for drinks and use the location—great lighting and a prime view of the cute rooftops—to snap some pictures for Diane's new job's website.

I'm about to ask something trivial when my eyes catch a glimpse of a blonde with her back to me. My heart skips—but it's not the right shade of strawberry blonde or the right height. Despite everything that happened, I can't shake the feeling that if Birdie Bay were actually here, the gravity of the place would shift.

The blonde enlists her bored friend to take pictures of her while she pretends to sip her cocktail. *Lower angle, zoom in x2, pull the brightness slider down to -0.7. Yeah, that's it, no wait, can you take another one where I pretend to look over my shoulder?* I don't hear them, but I know the drill. It's what we all do, trying to mirror our online idols.

If only they knew.

"...I were somebody else?" The words escape my lips before I can catch them.

Daniel blinks at me, caught off guard. "What do you mean?"

I feel my cheeks flush. "I don't know, like, taller? Blonder? More successful? French, maybe?"

He chuckles. "*Ma belle*, I like you just the way you are. A bit of a weirdo, sure, but determined. And so, so talented."

I'm about to argue about the 'weirdo' comment when he adds, "And you have the cutest accent when you try to speak French."

"*Merci beaucoup.*"

Daniel's hand finds mine, his thumb brushing my knuckles. It feels right, like he's just inflated a balloon inside me. It's surprising how he still manages to make my heart flutter after two years.

"Your turn," I say, grinning like an idiot.

Daniel straightens up. "Would you rather take one mega-hit picture that makes you famous but then be stuck with a creative block and never take another successful photo again, or..."

I cut him off with a single laugh. "Damn, your 'Would You Rathers' are so much better than mine. Do you prepare them in advance?"

"Of course," he says, winking. "That's all I do—grade papers and come up with torturous questions for you." He gets all serious again. "Or would you rather steadily publish dozens of shots that fly under the radar but keep you consistently getting published?"

I part my lips, ready with a retort, when Diane suddenly drops into the empty chair between us. Her long chestnut hair spills over her shoulders, and a rosy flush colors her cheeks.

"I know, I know. I'm late!" she says with a grimace. The church bells nearby are ringing—it's definitely past eight.

Diane pulls off her glasses and buries her face in her hands. "I've had the worst day ever."

Ever the considerate twin, Daniel is already flagging down a waiter. "Let's get you a glass of Bordeaux."

Diane peeks out from her hands and scrunches her face.

"Mmh, I don't want to sound un-French, but wine's not gonna cut it today. I'll need something stronger."

Trying (and failing) to hide a smile, Daniel makes a sound that's half-laugh, half-sigh. "Told *maman* you were moving to Paris?"

"Told *maman* I was moving to Paris, and she totally freaked out." Diane shakes her head, blissfully unaware of the setting sun and our golden hour photo plans. I shift in my seat. The news of her accepting a position as an associate at a small law firm in the second arrondissement came two weeks ago, and that's roughly how long it took her to break the news to their mother, Julienne.

"I did tell her," Diane adds, lighting a cigarette and letting out a dramatic puff, "that besides the obvious upgrade of being in Paris instead of the suburbs, it comes with a sweet pay raise."

Daniel snorts. "As if money were a decisive factor for her."

Perks of never having to worry about it, I think, biting my tongue just in time.

"True that," Diane sighs, then flashes a bright smile at the waiter. "*Je vais prendre un negroni s'il vous plaît.*" Her attention shifts back to us as she draws another breath from her cigarette. "Long story short, she spent the whole lunch lamenting about how I'm abandoning her friends' practice to, and I quote, 'rub shoulders in the stinking metro with all the homeless and left-wing supporters.'"

"I wonder if she's ever even taken the metro herself," Daniel grins, "or if her views come exclusively from TV dramas."

"Hah! That's exactly what I told her while she was serving dessert."

"Let me guess." Daniel tilts his head with a smirk, "You never got that blueberry tart?"

Diane scrunches her face in mock exasperation. "It was apricot, and yes, she did send me to my room."

Daniel bursts into laughter, clearly enjoying every second of the story.

"Well, it's not like I'm twenty-seven and a hotshot attorney or anything," Diane says, continuing over his laughter. "But ever since her favorite son"—she gives Daniel a playful elbow jab—"moved out, she's been pouring all her maternal energy onto me. It's exhausting."

Daniel rolls his eyes, but there's a fond smile on his face. "Oh, please. You know you secretly love the attention."

Diane laughs. "Sure, if you count the constant unsolicited advice as love."

I catch Daniel's gaze across the table, and his amused smile fades when he notices my discomfort. I shift in my seat, trying to ignore the twinge of envy gnawing at me. I've gotten better at handling the subject of mothers over the years, but it's still hard to sympathize with Diane's complaints about her mom making a fuss over a move that's only 30 minutes away.

"Anyway, I..." Diane's eyes fall on my Leica, and she quickly puts out her cigarette. "Shit, the pictures. Do we still have time?"

The topic shift is so welcome, I could hug it. "It should be fine," I tell her, forcing a smile as my shoulders finally loosen. The terrace is now bathed in soft, golden light, making even its shabbier corners look lovely. "You might want to..." I gesture vaguely at my face, implying a quick touch-up.

"Right, give me one more minute," Diane says, jumping up from her chair and hurrying toward the bathroom.

I whip my gaze toward Daniel, who gives me an apologetic smile. Our previous game is all but forgotten.

"Sorry about that," he says. "I know conversations about mothers must be tough for you."

"Oh, that," I shrug, trying to downplay it even though it stings more than I let on. "I barely even thought about it." *About her*.

Daniel's eyes search my face, moving from the look I'm trying to hide to my slightly pinched lips. He's about to say something, I can tell, when his twin reappears from the bathroom, her hair combed and a touch of blush applied.

"Let's get this done," Diane says.

CAMERA IN HAND, I direct her to her spot, and everything falls into place, like a well-rehearsed dance between the shutter button and me. The angles, the light, it all comes naturally. My craft is honed by years of practice, and I can already envision how stunning these photos will look once I've edited them. To be fair, aside from a little tone-softening and some added grain, they'll need almost no work.

"One more where you smile," I say.

Diane obliges instantly, her face shifting with ease. She *is* pretty. Not in a glossy Vogue-cover way, but with that effortless French allure, the kind that can't be taught. Her face is long and elegant, her lips always painted a perfect crimson, her Bambi-wide eyes framed by round glasses. To a stranger, she might seem light, frivolous even.

But through my lens, the truth sharpens into view.

The late-afternoon light wraps around her, catching the confident tilt of her chin, the steadiness in her gaze. Beneath the breezy charm is steel. Diane knows who she is; she understands the currency of perception. Let people underestimate her—it gives her room to move, to observe, to strike when it counts.

It must be handy in her line of work.

I snap a few more photos even though we already have the perfect ones. My camera is steady, but my mind drifts to the other pictures stored in my phone. The ones of Birdie.

Two days have passed, and they're still sitting there, untouched. At first, taking them felt righteous—like capturing proof that what I saw wasn't just a feeling, not some jealous fantasy. A vindication. Evidence that the cracks in her polished world were real.

But now?

Now the rush is gone, and all I'm left with is a knot in my stomach and a question I still don't know how to answer: *What am I even planning to do with them?* And... do I really want to do anything at all?

Part of me loves the idea of sending them to a gossip paper just to watch the fallout.

Another part wants to delete them and pretend none of this ever happened.

And then there's the petty voice whispering: *Send them to her. Tell her you don't want to be her friend anymore.*

As I said, I haven't decided yet.

"You're a godsend, Chloé," Diane exclaims, scrolling through the shots I've taken. "Without you, I'd have ended up with some dreadful iPhone selfies."

I laugh it off, giving a small shrug, even though the compliment is appreciated. The truth is, I'm grateful for any work, however small. My camera is always within reach, but the opportunities to use it haven't exactly been flooding in.

When I first moved to Paris, I arrived armed with a diploma, a camera, and the kind of naïve confidence only fresh graduates possess. I was convinced I'd become *someone*. You know, the brilliant young photographer everyone suddenly discovers. A few striking shots, a charming apartment with an ivy-covered balcony, exhibitions, interviews...

I cringe just thinking about it.

Reality was swift and merciless in correcting me. Paris didn't roll out a red carpet; it handed me humility and told me to get to work. And honestly? I've been learning that lesson ever since.

Whether my feelings are written all over my face or Diane's just perceptive, she takes a sip of her drink and casually asks, "How's work?"

"Chloé's been looking into photography contests around town," Daniel chimes in for me. "There's one with a deadline in, what, two weeks?" I nod, throwing him a grateful glance and mentally noting not to miss the submission deadlines.

Diane snaps her fingers. "That's a good way to get your name out there; I like it."

I take a sip of my wine, now lukewarm, and she adds, "Are you still doing those gigs on Fiverr?"

And that's where my UAL degree hangs its head in shame.

My dad, wanting me to focus solely on photography, has been covering my rent and other essentials since I moved to Paris. But I can't expect him to fund my coffee dates and shopping sprees, so I picked up small gigs on Fiverr—mostly kids' passport photos, which I particularly hate doing.

Although it's below my pay grade, for sure, at least it helps cover my expenses.

"Yep, still gotta eat, right?" I answer, tucking a lock of hair behind my ear, trying to sound nonchalant.

Diane raises her glass. "No shame in that."

I nod, desperately wanting to believe it myself.

"I was thinking of maybe," I take a deep breath, "becoming more active on social media."

"Like Instagram?" Diane prompts, all curious.

Daniel cuts in. "What, like that girl who moved into the apartment facing ours? What's her name again?"

"What girl?" Diane asks.

I clear my throat. "Birdie Bay. But no, not like her."

"Oh, I follow her on Instagram!" Diane exclaims. "Wait, she's your neighbor?"

"You follow influencers now, Di?" Daniel lifts a brow.

"Yes, Daniel. I'm participating in modern society instead of living like a cave troll," Diane replies, folding her arms. "And don't call me *Di*."

Daniel shakes his head, eyes heavy. "Social media is a trap many of us underestimate."

"Social media is a ladder," his twin counters. "And Chloé is right to use it. Might as well try to get some attention from galleries."

Daniel sits back in his chair, a little thrown, a confused smile on his face. His eyes won't meet mine, and I know why. It's a sensitive subject for him.

"But," Diane straightens up, "don't you think that train has already left, though? I don't say you can't do it, of course, but I feel like today's big names were those who started at least a decade ago."

"My goal isn't to be famous," I say, bright enough to make

it sound true. "All I want is a bit of recognition. And..." My gaze locks with Daniel's at last. "A few paid projects?"

He presses his leg against mine under the table and sighs. "You know I'll always support you. But you have to be realistic. The people who make a lot of money off their images, who go *viral*—they're different from us. It takes a lot to make it out there."

I glance at Daniel and remember how I would have seen it just two days ago, believing that people like Birdie Bay were special, almost god-like in their superiority.

But I've seen through the façade now. It's all just a performance. If they can do it, why can't I?

"You realize it's not real, right?" I say, shaking my head. "All those perfect lives online—it's all a lie."

I'd checked Birdie's Instagram earlier today. She'd posted a selfie in the exact same workout set she wore during the drug run. *"A healthy mind in a healthy body,"* the caption read. I could've laughed if it weren't so absurd.

Influencers rely on a kind of silent contract. We trust that the life they sell us is at least tethered to reality. That the person behind the camera isn't a complete fabrication. But those pictures ... they make me question everything I know about Birdie Bay.

It's not even the vegan thing. Or the drugs.

It's that none of it matches who she was in real life.

Fuck—she isn't even *nice*.

"I get it," Diane cuts in, voice slipping into her courtroom cadence. "Influencers are essentially glorified salespeople. But right now? They move markets. You can't deny the visibility they bring."

Daniel doesn't answer. He just twirls his empty glass between his fingers, gaze distant.

"Grass is always greener on the other side, right?" he murmurs. There's a sadness in his tone—wistful, maybe—and it tugs something tight in my chest. I glance at him, hoping for a shared spark of understanding, but his thoughts seem far away.

The disappointment sits heavier than it should. Outside, the last light bleeds out of the sky, Paris slipping into evening.

"No," I say softly, almost to myself. "Nothing about it feels right." My mind drifts back to the photos still tucked away in my phone, a tiny piece of proof that something isn't what it pretends to be.

And then I think, *maybe the grass seems greener because it's fake.*

3

I sit in front of my computer, staring at Diane's photos—stunning, if I do say so myself. The lighting, the subtle eeriness in the atmosphere around her... these might just be *the* breakthrough I've been waiting for. Without wasting a second, I upload them to my Instagram profile, which still hovers stubbornly at 300 followers. Gotta start somewhere, right?

Fueled by the ambitious plans I rambled about last night, I do my homework: the right hashtags, a few key photography accounts that might repost, and two Parisian galleries I'd die to be featured in. Then I hit publish.

It's not my first post, but it's the first since Birdie, without meaning to, showed me that "fake it till you make it" actually *works*. Funny how I never saw it before.

You know, over the years, I've followed my fair share of influencers.

It all started with beauty gurus. As a teenager, I'd spend hours watching YouTube tutorials and product reviews, soaking up words like *contouring* and *highlighting* with the eagerness of a kid learning to talk.

Then my attention shifted to the wanderlust-inducing world of travel influencers. I loved their vlogs, sure, but it was the photos on Instagram that really hooked me. There was something so satisfying about scrolling through snapshots of beautiful places captured from a fresh perspective—not the polished perfection of *National Geographic*, but the view through the lens of girls with affordable cameras, just like me. Maybe that's part of what inspired me to pack my bags and move to Paris the moment I graduated. It's not Bali or Alaska, sure, but the idea of starting fresh somewhere new thrilled me.

Over time, my interests changed again. I stopped following so many travel accounts and found myself drawn to lifestyle creators instead. Some people say they just sell aesthetics—pretty places, curated outfits, the glossiest parts of life.

But for me, it was about *achievability*.

With beauty and travel influencers, there was always a distance between their world and mine. I knew I'd never master a flawless evening makeup look or take off backpacking through Mongolia on a whim. But I *could* buy a pair of Lululemons and a gold-plated bangle from Birdie Bay's latest collection—and somehow, that felt just right.

Now Birdie Bay—she's what you'd call a wellness influencer.

Her whole image is that of the effortlessly clean, vegan girl who only buys sustainably sourced products and clothing, swears by yoga, pilates, and sunrise runs, sips on fancy kombuchas, and wouldn't be caught dead at a fast-food joint.

I liked that about her. It resonated with me, despite my non-vegan, non-sporty existence. I always watched her content with a sense of admiration, striving to be just like her. She's like the big sister you always try to emulate. There is a sense of satisfaction gained each time you consume something Birdie Bay consumes; it's like she's floating someplace over you, winking at you, like: *good job, girlie.*

I could do with some encouragement right now, but that boat has sailed.

The Fiverr orders waiting on my computer aren't going anywhere, yet I can't seem to concentrate. Every few minutes, my hand reaches for my phone. *Have I made it yet?* I refresh the page obsessively—only to be met with the same twelve likes from five minutes ago, staring back at me, mocking.

It's maddening and disheartening to have such beautiful content and feel like it's going unnoticed. I'm tempted to delete the post and try again—maybe the algorithm will favor it this time.

But a small voice in my head nags me: you really thought you had it all figured out, didn't you?

Self-doubt seeps in, chasing away the fragile optimism I had just found. Despite all the skills and years spent curating my Instagram feed, it never seems to gain traction. My photography, my one true passion since I was six, feels like it pales in comparison to other girls' selfies. I'm stuck at forty or fifty likes, trapped in a cycle of disappointment that feels like it will never end.

It's not for lack of trying everything to crack the code of Instagram success.

First, I tried editing my photos with overpriced filters—back when filters were *a thing*. Then I swung the other way, chasing "authenticity", following advice like "use natural light only" and "don't overthink it". I even splurged on an online workshop, where a local, duck-lipped Instagrammer named Victoria Thoumieux swore that "the key is confidence."

But you know what the unfiltered truth is? Gatekeeping.

Those successful influencers want you to believe anyone can make it—that it all comes down to creativity. And maybe that's the cruelest part: the way they make you think your lack of virality is your fault.

Here's the real question, though: would they actually benefit from another girl rising on social media? Are they really here to help, or just putting on a show to cash in? They say there is a place for everyone, but let me ask you something: if everyone's on stage, who's left to applaud?

Time in the spotlight is limited. That much, I can tell you for free.

And no one's ever going to teach you how to steal theirs.

TEETH GRITTED, I reach for my phone again, this time heading straight to my photo library. Scrolling down, I find the pictures I've been looking for and just stare.

There she is. My role model. Hands busy buying drugs.

A few shots are a bit blurry, but most are crystal clear. Birdie Bay, the poster child of America's anti-drug crusade two years in a row—what a farce.

Hard to believe her face used to be plastered across billboards. I remember that campaign so well; it was everywhere. Birdie Bay, posing all serious, arms folded across her chest, dressed (for once) in plain clothes. I even thought it was clever marketing—the muted colors, the artfully blurred background. The photographers made sure we'd focus on the celebrity and her message to the masses: *Drugs Are Cringe*.

I get up and walk to the living room's window, catching a glimpse of movement in her apartment. Yoga time.

My thoughts spin out. All that talk of clean living, sustainable choices, mindful living. All those *namaste* captions. Lies. Every last one.

I look at the pictures again; I feel like it's all I've been doing for the past three days. On the last one, bless her heart, we can clearly see the white powder in that little transparent bag. I had read somewhere that cocaine helps you stay lean; is that how she always stays in shape?

Call me naïve, but the feeling of betrayal gnaws at me, and the longer I stare at the photos, the angrier I get. I trusted her with what I put into my body, with what I spent my hard-earned money on. And I'm not alone. There are millions of us—followers who take her word as gospel.

I'm done hesitating. Selfishly, I don't want to be alone in feeling this way. People have the right to know.

I open Instagram again, but this time I don't waste energy lamenting my lack of exposure. Instead, I create a new account named @FauxEver. In the bio, I write: *Sometimes the grass only seems greener because it's fake.* A bit recycled, but catchy.

These shots of Birdie—I bet they'll get more likes than anything I've ever posted. The realization surges through me, quick and hot, and my heart races. If I hadn't seen this as an opportunity before, I do now. I might finally have something valuable in my hands. A chance to throw my two cents into the game and show that even the untouchable can be brought down.

With a deep breath, I upload the pictures to a carousel album. I tag several people-magazine accounts. I tag the anti-drug campaign profile. Lastly, I tag @BirdieBay.

And I hit the publish button.

The post uploads, and I watch the little circle spin until it's done. Then... nothing.

You'd think virtual fireworks would burst from the screen and serenades would be sung about you the moment you post something, but it's not true. Nobody's waiting for you out there.

I cannot help but refresh the page after a few seconds, but there is still no activity. A couple of minutes later, I only have two likes, and to add insult to injury, they're bots. I almost laugh at myself here; for a fleeting moment, I let myself believe that something I did could actually matter. Pathetic.

I glance at my computer and the editing I still need to do. Maybe that's the only thing I'm truly good at. Sighing, I capitulate and put my phone away.

"*Mon cœur*, why aren't you dressed? We're going to be late."

I whirl around in my chair. "What?"

"At my parents'," Daniel says. His white linen shirt and matching beige pants suddenly remind me—it's brunch day today. "You forgot?"

I totally forgot. "No, of course not," I quickly say. "It's just that I'm not feeling very well. I'd rather stay home today. Say hi for me?"

Daniel steps closer. "Are you sick?"

"Just the drinks from last night still messing with my head." I pinch my lips, then give him my sweetest smile. "You were right; that fifth glass of rosé was definitely one too many."

"Oh, right," he says, though he doesn't look convinced. "It has nothing to do with my mother, does it?"

The wince crosses my features before I can rein it in. In the two years we've been together, I've been to countless brunches with his family in their fancy house in Versailles. While his mother has mostly been polite, there's always been an edge in her tone, as if Daniel and I were just a fling, a mere phase before he found a good French girl. It didn't matter that he'd told me he loved me, that we moved in together, and began making plans. To her, I'll always be the future ex-girlfriend. I've voiced my suspicions to Daniel, but he dismissed them as my imagination. "French women just don't let strangers in that easily," he'd say. So, missing brunch with his *maman* is not something I'm going to regret—and the feeling's mutual.

"Of course not," I say softly, rubbing my temples for effect. "Maybe Julienne's got some fancy aspirin she'd be willing to share?"

Daniel nods and kisses me on the forehead. "I'm sure she does."

Something's buzzing.

I only hear it once the front door closes behind Daniel, and the apartment falls silent.

My eyes catch my phone sprawled face-up on the desk, screen busy with notifications. Heart pounding, I snatch it up and rush to open Instagram. Holy shit. Like the virtual fireworks I'd half-joked about earlier, the post is on the verge of hitting two thousand likes, with over a hundred comments and the numbers blur upward with every refresh.

Four hundred followers.

The comments range from mean—I always knew she was too good to be true—to hateful: The bitch should die.

I check out mentions and see that @SocialTea has reposted the content in their stories. Their profile boasts a staggering 3.7 million followers. Their caption is: *What's in the satchel, little Birdie?* And @FauxEver is tagged.

"Wow," I say out loud and keep scrolling. My phone morphs into a micro-bomb, ticking away with likes, comments, and shares.

My DMs are exploding, too, and I'm flooded with messages like:

Who are you?

Please post more!! They need to be exposed.

Do @kendalljenner next.

I respond to some comments, claiming to be an anonymous truth-bearer here to unveil the reality behind our influencer gods (feeling pretty inspired, I must say). I assure them I'll keep the revelations coming and clarify that I have no issue with Kendall. I backtrack and delete that last comment; personal vendettas aren't the aim.

It's about them, the influencers.

More notifications flood in. People are sharing the post, tagging friends, spreading the word. It's like watching a ripple turn into a tidal wave. My heart races as I refresh the page over and over again, each time seeing the numbers climb higher.

I only stop refreshing and answering when my fingers start to ache; then I just lie there, staring at the intricate moldings on the ceiling.

The irony kind of stings—my polished, carefully edited photos barely make a ripple, yet the blurry shots of a girl buying drugs are exploding online.

And still, with every buzz of my phone, that same electric jolt of validation runs through me.

Is this what Birdie Bay feels every time she posts? Powerful, intriguing, *heard*? I've never tasted this level of attention in my life, this much love. Suddenly, I'm no longer Chloé Warner, the aspiring photographer who has never sold a single piece. I'm the hero of the masses, here to dismantle the influencer lie.

At some point, the jingling of keys interrupts my digital awakening. Daniel is already back, which means that—shit, it's 4 p.m. already. Time seems to have slipped away in the whirlwind of scrolling on my phone. My boyfriend walks into the room and takes me in. "Well, it's as if you haven't moved since I left."

I haven't. I blink, slowly coming back to reality. My computer screen is in Screen Saver Mode, but I'm still seated behind my desk. Damn, how long have I been sitting here? My throat feels dry, and I don't even remember having a glass of water.

"So," Daniel slurs, handing me a white paper box. He's always a bit tipsy when he comes back from brunch with his family. "My mom didn't have any aspirin. But she packed you some tarte Tatin. Said you had to eat more—said you'd have fewer headaches."

Hah, of course she did. Julienne never misses a chance to comment on my eating habits. But you know what? I'm in a good mood today. "How nice of her," I say, leaping to my feet to take the box, earning another wry look from Daniel. Not that I plan to eat it; my stomach's still not over the muffins I gorged myself on three days ago. I'm just being the bigger person here.

"How was brunch?"

Daniel runs a hand through his hair. "Tense. Mum and Diane are still not talking and..."

I nod along, feigning interest, but my focus snaps back to my phone. It's still buzzing with notifications. I wonder how many followers I have now and if I can make it to a thousand.

It's funny how suddenly that little device has become my most valued possession.

"Daniel, it's not that I don't want to hear all about the fight with your matriarch," I interrupt him, joking without *really* joking. "But first I have to show you something."

FauxEver. It's the first time I'm going viral, and it's exhilarating. Granted, this isn't the type of photography I dreamed of, but it's a start. I can't wait to see his reaction when I show him the number of shares!

Daniel smirks, more amused than annoyed. "Okay, give me five minutes to shower and I'm all yours."

He starts walking toward the bathroom but abruptly pivots. "Oh, before I forget, do you know who I bumped into just now?" he asks, unbuttoning his shirt.

That's a view that can distract a girl. "Hmm, who?" I say, my eyes wandering down his perfect abs.

"That famous girl you're obsessed with. She seemed in a hurry. I saw her punch the building door."

My gaze jerks up. "She punched our door?"

Daniel's eyebrows knit for a second; he chuckles. "No, her door, of course. I think she was in quite a mood."

"Oh, of course," I repeat, feeling a bit foolish. Birdie has no way of knowing it's me who posted these pictures.

Still, she must have seen the post by now.

And the comments under it.

As soon as Daniel heads to the bathroom, I race to the window, binoculars in hand.

Birdie's lights are on. I don't spot her immediately; my eyes flit from the artworks on her walls to the red guitar on her couch. But then I see her. Birdie's lying on her wooden floor in a fetal position. My stomach drops.

I've killed Birdie Bay.

4

I've not actually killed Birdie Bay.

She's on the floor, yes, but she's moving. Her shoulders rise and fall in rhythmic shudders. I think she's crying, but I can't be sure as she's facing away from me. My brief relief is hijacked by a pang of guilt so intense that I start shaking too.

I want to look away, but I can't. Every sob feels like a tally mark against me.

I did this.

Have I ever made someone cry before? I don't think so. I've never had a fight, never even had heated words with anyone. And now my actions are causing someone so much distress that...

My train of thought is interrupted by a text. It's from Diane.

I just saw the post!

My face flames. How could she...?

Another text pops in:

> Do you mind sending me the pics today? I'll ask them to be uploaded on the firm's website asap, make it official before my mother finds a way to sabotage it

Right. She's talking about her pictures, her post. I reply with a winking emoji and check my own profile. Thirty-nine likes and a comment from my dad—my biggest fan. Zero new followers. Zero DMs from art galleries.

I scoff. If I weren't so offended, I might laugh. And if I didn't have @FauxEver and the support of thousands of strangers just two clicks away, that scoff might have turned into one of those hysterical laughs that dissolve into a whimper.

But I do have online validation now. I won't say it justifies what I did. Still... is it wrong that it makes me feel better?

Daniel comes out of the bathroom, and for some reason, I don't want him checking on Birdie right now. I don't want this to overshadow the exciting news I'm about to share. So I step away from the window—not fast enough for him to miss the binoculars in my hand.

"Jesus, you look a bit stalker-ish, babe."

I laugh it off, stretching the time before telling him. "It's just that she's been making the news today," I say, turning my phone screen to show him Birdie's pictures on @FauxEver's account.

He lets out a long whistle, thumb scrolling through the post. "Whoa, when was that?"

"This morning," I say, fighting the urge to blurt out that it's *mine*. That it didn't take me that long to go viral. But I want him to fully grasp the scale of it first, so I add, "I mean, it was posted this morning."

"Hah, the pictures must have been taken on another day because that's not the way she was dressed when I saw her entering her building." He pauses and gives me a quizzical look. "Wait, do we have paparazzi now?"

"Hmm, it's this new account..." I start, going back to @FauxEver's page and suppressing a smile as I silently note the follower growth. Now, I'll tell him now. "Isn't that..."

Daniel cuts me off. "It's so nasty."

"Right?" I snort. "Birdie Bay's doing drugs. I guess it's true what they say about all celebrities secretly being addicts."

He shakes his head. "No, I mean the pictures. Exposing her like that. That's such a shitty thing to do."

What? I blink, thinking I misunderstood, but Daniel's oblivious to my shock.

"Reminds me of when that kind of shit went down at the school..."

I freeze, instantly knowing what he's talking about.

"It's not the same situation," I say quickly. And it's not.

The scandal at Daniel's workplace involved a colleague caught in one of his student's online vendetta crusades. From what I heard, the student decided her grade wasn't good enough and accused her teacher of sexual harassment. It all turned out to be fake, and apologies were issued, but once the story hit the internet, that teacher's name was ruined. He quit, and no one ever heard from him since.

Daniel swore off social media soon after.

I tighten my grip on my phone, pressing it against my stomach, away from him, as the truth settles in.

I can't tell Daniel. He wouldn't understand—he's too

damn righteous for that. He'd judge me, blame me, probably make me delete the account. The thought is like a cold shower.

No, I can't tell anyone about the coolest thing I've ever done.

The risk is too big.

"...it feels like bullying," I hear him say now, my eyes focused on that little drop that falls from his wet hair to the floor when he shakes his head, all inspired.

"Come on," I manage to say, my throat suddenly like sandpaper. "It's not like that."

"Online bullying is still bullying." Daniel's not smiling now. "There's just no excuse for it."

My shoulders slump a little; this is not how I expected this conversation to go. "Of course, but... I kinda feel like Birdie Bay has a responsibility towards her followers, and they have the right to know."

"To know what?"

"That she's not who she pretends to be!" I retort, thinking of how she looked at me when I came over to say hi, and then her eye-rolling when she read my messages.

It's Daniel's turn to look at me with disbelief. "She's just a girl making a bad decision. But that person who knowingly put her there... well, that alone speaks volumes about them. I mean, it could have been you."

My eyes roll by themselves. "I'm not famous."

Daniel stares over at me.

"Yet," I add as an afterthought and instantly regret it. It makes me sound like I don't give a fuck, but I do. I swear I do.

"I don't think it's the point here, *ma belle*."

I clamp my mouth shut and glance back at the pictures. I've always seen Birdie Bay as this larger-than-life figure, and somehow, over the past few days, she's gone from role model to nemesis. I never thought of her as just another girl my age. Someone who can screw up. Someone human.

Is Daniel right? Am I bullying her?

Can a former victim become the torturer?

I've known my share of bullies. I've spent plenty of time curled up on the floor, just like Birdie is now. High school memories don't fade, they linger, like bruises under the skin. Petite, motherless, with food issues and a stammer that showed up whenever I felt cornered—that was one hell of a cocktail. Add braces and a few extra kilos, and I went from invisible to a target overnight.

It's frightening how easy it is to slip into self-loathing at that age. If I hadn't retreated behind a camera, if I hadn't found safety in the lens instead of in myself... I don't even want to imagine who I'd be now.

I shake off the memories. I'm not unique; high school sucks for everyone.

Or maybe not everyone. High school's pretty great when you're the bully.

Bullies, I've realized, tend to be the same. A little prettier than average, a little louder, a lot less introspective. Definitely not smarter—but does intelligence even matter when it comes to having a good high school experience? Debatable.

I try to remember mine, but the faces blur together until they all start to look like Birdie Bay. Blonde divas with radiant laughs, striding down the hallways as if to say: *We're better than you.*

Daniel's wrong. I'm not a shitty person. I'm not a bully.

People like Birdie Bay are.

They move through the digital world, flaunting their

dazzling, flawless lives, oblivious to the insecurities they spark in the rest of us. We scroll past their curated perfection and suddenly feel inadequate for enjoying the simplest things: a greasy burger, an unglamorous couch, a steady 9-to-5. We start believing our skin isn't good enough because we don't splurge on the same five-hundred-euro creams or book weekly facials. Bit by bit, they chip away at our self-esteem.

So tell me—who are the real bullies?

Influencers are just the grown-up version.

"Is someone trying to reach you?" Daniel asks, leaning in to look at the screen again. "Your phone's been buzzing ever since I came home."

He's right—alerts from @FauxEver keep flooding in, to my equal delight and dismay. I really need to figure out how to turn them off.

"Just my dad," I reply hastily, swiftly sticking my phone inside my back pocket. "He's seeking some gardening advice."

Daniel nods, then goes to get dressed, leaving me standing alone in the middle of our living room.

Part of me wants to grab the binoculars and check on Birdie—because despite all her faults, I can't help but wonder if I went too far. Which, inevitably, leads to another thought: should I take the post down? Maybe even apologize?

But something stops me. Greed, maybe.

I try to put things in perspective. What can I do now? The deed's done. Those pictures aren't really mine anymore. The moment I hit "post," they became public property. Even if I deleted them, the screenshots would live on, reposted by someone else.

And I'm not about to let anyone steal the attention that should be mine.

5

In the following days, @FauxEver reaches eight thousand followers, and I stop counting likes. I voraciously read all the comments, though, and after even Birdie Bay's hardcore fans quiet down in the face of undeniable proof, all messages go my way.

Only ugliness beneath the filter

Thank you for your service!

The end of the influencer era

It feels ominous, and I'd be lying if I said I didn't take pleasure in the way they validated my initiative.

Validated me.

I don't check on Birdie. I haven't touched the binoculars since the day I created @FauxEver, and I can't really explain why. Maybe I'm busy monitoring the account, or maybe I don't want to see her suffer from the consequences of my actions. Because it's one thing to throw a bomb and hide, but it's another to face the person you hurt.

Go on, judge me. Call me a coward all you want because

while you do, I'll be feeding on the applause and scrolling and scrolling and scrolling.

THE FIRST BLOW lands while I'm having breakfast with Daniel in our cramped little kitchen.

The space is tiny: just the table, two chairs, and us. Still, for reasons only he understands, Daniel insisted on squeezing in a compact wine fridge. Its constant hum drives me crazy, but I've learned to tolerate it; it doubles as a footrest anyway.

I'm scrolling on Instagram, checking for anything new about Birdie or @FauxEver, but the news is stale. Every day, the post gets less traction—fewer likes, fewer comments. The follower count has flatlined. I'm just about to reply to a few comments to bump engagement when I spot one that stands out: longer, sharper. Nothing like the usual praise.

My eyes narrow as I read it. It's from a private account, some @AnnieRevel girl from Kansas City:

What Birdie's doing is obviously bad, but don't you think it's almost worse to have taken these pictures without her knowledge and shared them with the world like that? Who do you think you are? Gossip Girl? I give this sad little account a few more days before everyone forgets about it, as they should.

I stare at the comment, unsure of what to do with it. The audacity of this girl—probably one of Birdie's fans—to call me out, when I'm the one telling the truth! Still, there's a tiny pang of discomfort, a voice in the back of my mind whispering that maybe, just maybe, she has a point.

Technically, @FauxEver has already served its purpose. I exposed Birdie Bay for the liar she is. Mission accomplished.

But along the way, I've found something I didn't expect: a platform. An audience. People who actually listen to what I have to say, who look forward to what I'll post next. Something I've been chasing, and failing to find, for years.

Sure, the whole anonymity thing is a problem. But it doesn't feel like something I can't eventually work around.

Diane was right: social media is a ladder, and I've only just started to see how high I can climb.

But now... what else is there to post? Catching Birdie buying her stash had been pure luck—well, luck for me. But lightning doesn't strike the same place twice, or whatever.

I let out a loud, involuntary sigh. Daniel looks up from his newspaper, frowning.

"That bad?" he asks.

I know he means the news. He's reading about wars, recessions, immigration. Real problems. And here I am, sulking over followers. I set my phone face-down on the table and drag my hands through my hair.

"No. Yes. I don't know," I say. "I just feel... stuck with something."

He raises his eyebrows, silently nudging me to go on.

"I had this... opportunity the other day," I say carefully. "A good one. The kind that could actually open doors for me."

Daniel folds his newspaper, suddenly interested.

"A photography opportunity? You didn't mention anything about that."

"Mmh, yeah," I say. Technically not a lie. There *is* photography involved. "I don't want to jinx it, but I'm kind of stuck. It could really pay off, but it also comes with a lot of challenges. And honestly, I'm not sure I can pull it off."

"Well, if avoiding *jinxes*"—he makes air quotes—"is

what's keeping you from asking for advice, I guess I'm out of luck."

I roll my eyes. I hate it when he gets all teacher-y with me.

He keeps going, unfazed by my irritation.

"Come on. Knowing you, I'd be shocked if you gave up that easily. Remember when we first saw this apartment?"

I do remember. About a year ago, Daniel had just started working at the private language school down the street, and I was thinking about applying to another art program nearby. So yeah, location was everything. I wanted something new—white walls, an open kitchen, double sinks in the bathroom. But Daniel, being the true Frenchman he is, went all in for creaky wooden floors and paper-thin walls. I could appreciate the charm; Paris does that to you. Still, I'll never understand how I agreed to a bathtub shower. And the fourth floor—no elevator.

"You didn't even like it at first," Daniel says. "But when the landlord mentioned he had a pile of applications and our chances were slim, you basically harassed him—"

"I did *no* such thing!" I protest.

Okay, maybe I sent a few emails. Made a couple of calls to his mobile. Stopped by his office once or twice to "check in." But honestly? The housing crisis in Paris is no joke.

Daniel chuckles and picks his newspaper back up, giving me that amused look. "Exactly. You chased him down until he gave us the apartment. When you want something, you don't back off."

I smile, because he's right. I'm not a quitter.

Out of habit, I check my phone again. @AnnieRevel's comment is suddenly getting traction with likes piling up fast. Zero to fifty in just a few minutes.

I believe in free speech. I really do.

But I also believe in *deleting and blocking*.

And just like that, @AnnieRevel from Kansas City, and her little comment, are gone.

SWAPPING my blood-red Lululemons for my trusty old black leggings from the pandemic era and a simple gray T-shirt, I feel like Joe-fucking-Goldberg, but I don't care. I'm blending in; I'm being subtle.

Birdie leaves her apartment on time, and the first thing I notice is that she's not wearing colors either—just a low-key black running outfit, the kind you wear when you don't want to be recognized. Being canceled does not suit her style.

I settle into a trot at a safe distance from her, and we quickly fall back into our routine, as if nothing had happened.

Want to know something about me? I hate running. The sweat, the waste of time. Runners' high is a myth promoted by people who don't want to run alone. Believe me. But I'm willing to make the sacrifice today. I tell myself it's only to check on her, see how she's coping, make sure she's not too much of a mess. And if I happen to catch her in the act of doing something worthy of being posted on @FauxEver, well, that's not really on me, is it? Happy coincidence.

I pat my phone in my pocket and try not to focus on the stitch in my side. Damn, she's fast today. It's almost like she's running to purge something—anger, sadness, maybe both.

She hasn't posted a thing since I dropped the pictures. Comments turned off. Radio silence.

And it's not hard to see why. Within hours of my post

going viral, Sephora, Nike, and Revolve all dropped her. The anti-drug campaign released a statement "wishing Birdie the help she needs," and every ad featuring her vanished from their site.

The number of YouTubers and TikTokers who've shared it is mind-blowing. It's like everyone's racing to share it first, to prove they're on the right side of things—to scrub their own hands clean.

And still, Birdie doesn't respond. She just... runs.

But she can't outrun her problems.

And she sure as hell can't outrun me.

We pass the photography store—that's one good sign. It means she hasn't changed her route. And that route, I know by heart. In less than a minute, she'll stop by the fountain for a drink, stretch her back on the bench, and then...

Bingo.

"Come on, Birdie... I know you want it," I whisper, a spark of delight creeping into my voice.

She hesitates—I can see it in her expression. Then, in a moment of defiance, she mouths *"fuck it"* and strides inside. *Yes*.

I dart forward, heart pounding, ducking behind a tree for cover. She's at the counter now, pointing at the ham croissant. This time, my hands are steady as I lift the camera and snap the shots. It might not be cocaine, but to her army of vegan followers, it might as well be.

I swipe through the photos, and they are perfect. *Take that, @AnnieRevel. @FauxEver isn't going anywhere.*

I turn to head home when Birdie steps out of the bakery. I move fast, half-hiding my face—but it's too late. She's seen me.

"Hey, you're the neighbor, right? From across the street? I'm so sorry, I forgot your name." She walks closer.

"Chloé," I manage, forcing a faint smile.

"Chloé, right. Like the brand. I had it right on the tip of my tongue." She mirrors my smile. "Funny how we always run into each other here."

"It's the best bakery in the neighborhood," I lie. It's definitely not. "I see you're a fan of the ham croissant too."

The accusation slips out before I can stop it, and I scramble to hide it behind another smile. From Birdie's expression, I can tell I failed miserably.

"Yeah, well..." she starts, glancing down at the paper bag in her hand. Her shoulders drop as she tightens her grip on it.

I try to look away, but it's like watching a tightrope walker lose balance—you can't look anywhere else.

"Fuck." She lets out a small laugh, but it breaks halfway into a sob. Her eyes meet mine, glassy with tears.

"Oh, Birdie..." I step toward her, and before I can react, she throws herself into my arms, crying. For a moment, I freeze. Her body pressing against mine feels like the hardest slap imaginable. I don't dare move.

I glance around but no one pays attention. It's perfectly normal to cry in the middle of the street in Paris at 10 a.m.

"Hey, it's gonna be okay," I murmur, because what else can I say?

And before you judge me—I know what you're thinking—I'm not a two-faced bitch. I can be the voice of reason online *and* still act like a decent human being when someone breaks down in front of me. Which I do, as I pat her back.

Birdie loudly sniffs and straightens up, wiping her red eyes with the back of her hand. "Ugh, shit. I'm so sorry. We don't even know each other..."

Can't quite explain it, but that one lands. *Well, I certainly know you.*

"...and I've been kind of a bitch to you the other day."

Yeah, you were. "No, you weren't!" I say quickly. "Don't worry about it, really."

She pulls out her phone and snaps a selfie, her bottom lip sticking out. I try not to look appalled that even now, she's using her tears for future posts. But I definitely am.

"Now I feel like I owe you a coffee," Birdie says, oblivious. "Do you know a place that serves alternative milk? It's such a pain to find in Paris. I'm fine with coconut, but I prefer hazelnut."

My phone burns in my hand. I'm about to tell her I need to head home when our eyes meet again, and hers are still shiny, still raw. Guilt hits me square in the gut. It *is* my fault she's crying. And now that she's seen me here, I can't exactly post those new photos without raising suspicion.

"Sure," I say, pretending to be chill, even though I'm both annoyed and kinda stoked. "It's not far."

I PINCH my hand for the umpteenth time, but somehow, I don't wake up.

Birdie and I sit in my favorite coffee shop, one of the few terraces in Paris that doesn't reek of exhaust, tucked instead in a quiet square overlooking a small garden.

"Mmh, girl, you have no idea how grateful I am right now," Birdie groans after taking a sip of her vanilla matcha. "I thought I'd sworn off matcha the moment I landed in France, but this one—this one's a revelation. Not that usual grass-tasting crap. This place is going to be my new hideout."

I hate how pleased that makes me. I take a quick sip of my cold brew to hide the grin threatening to give me away.

"So, tell me about yourself, neighbor. How long have you been in Paris?"

"About two years now," I say. "Feels like yesterday, though..."

"Hah! I get that," she cuts in. "It's wild how fast time flies once you're after twenty. When I was a teen, months used to drag forever, and now I blink and entire seasons disappear."

I frown slightly. "But your life must be so interesting—all those trips, events, parties... They say time only drags when you're bored." *Like I am.*

"Of course," she says, then hesitates. "I mean, I'm grateful for it all, don't get me wrong. But... it comes with a price. Some days I wonder if a simpler life wouldn't be easier."

"Mmh, sure?" I say, a bit too quickly, unsure whether she's joking or not. Because if that's irony, I'm the punchline. "I guess there's more than meets the eye."

Okay, maybe I'm a *little* two-faced.

Birdie pauses, lips pressed together.

"It's just so hard, you know?" she says, staring into her drink. "The pressure of always looking perfect, spotless. I never asked for this. All I wanted was to make videos and pay rent, you know?"

I nod as if I understand, though I couldn't possibly.

"But now people have this image of me, and whenever I slip, I'm crucified like a fucking witch," she groans, biting into her cookie.

I keep nodding, resisting the urge to point out that witches were burned, not crucified, and that buying cocaine is more than just a *slip*. But something tells me that's not what friends do. And we almost look like friends right now, don't we? Sitting on a terrace, sipping coffee, talking about feelings. Life is weird.

The moment shatters when a kid—there's really no other word for her—walks up to our table, clutching her phone nervously.

"OMG, are you Birdie Bay?" she asks. And, OMG, is that what I looked like the other day when I ambushed her myself?

Birdie sniffs, then smiles, her polished persona sliding neatly back into place. "I am."

"Oh wow, I've been following you on Insta since forever," the girl gushes in broken English. "Can I take a picture with you?"

I brace for Birdie to decline—her eyes are still glassy, her forehead shiny—but to my surprise, she nods. It stings a little, I'll admit.

"Only if you promise to post it in black and white," Birdie says, forcing a laugh. "I'm not exactly at the top of my game today."

The girl nods solemnly. "I promise." Then she turns to me, thrusting her phone forward. "Could you...?"

"Yeah, sure," I say, a little too eagerly. And just like that, I'm back behind the lens, taking yet another picture of Birdie Bay. Funny how life always finds a way to put you back in your place.

"Thanks!" the girl chirps, not even glancing at me. "You're amazing, Birdie Bay. My friends are gonna die when they see this."

"Gotta work on that affection ratio, right?" Birdie says as the girl walks away. I can tell from her smug smile and the way she sits up straighter that the encounter has revived her, though her voice still carries a hint of tiredness.

"Does that happen often?" I ask.

She hums. "What, people recognizing me? All the time. I guess it comes with the job, though no one really warns you about it."

"Must be nice," I offer.

Birdie huffs.

"Some days it is, really," she says. "My audience is what keeps the lights on, after all. But there are other days when..." Her face tightens, closing off a little. "When I'd rather just be invisible."

I blink. It's written all over her expression—she's thinking about my @FauxEver post—and for a second, I'm afraid she's going to cry again.

I take a slow breath, then leap.

"You can always text me if you ever want to talk, or..." I shrug like it's nothing, even as I feel the heat creeping up my neck. "Or if you need more coffee recommendations."

Birdie studies me with those ocean-blue eyes, then takes a slow sip of her matcha before turning her phone toward me.

"Can I have your number?"

6

Birdie Bay calls me the next morning.

"Want to go for a run?" she asks. I really don't, but I still say yes. And so we run together, like we've done before —though she has no idea.

A few days later, we're having lunch. By the end of the week, we're renting bikes to explore Parc des Buttes-Chaumont.

When Daniel sees me that day, all ready to head out on our little adventure, his eyebrows shoot up, and not just because of the Alo Yoga biker shorts Birdie had gifted me, which, by the way, fit like a dream.

"How did you two get so close all of a sudden?" he asks, clearly puzzled.

"She finally replied to my message," I lie with a casual shrug, as if it were nothing. "I guess that whole drug scandal made her realize real support isn't so easy to come by."

Daniel crosses his arms, giving me a skeptical once-over. "Is that so?"

"Don't be so surprised!" I laugh it off, already inching

toward the door. "I always knew we'd vibe. We're practically best friends now."

And this time, it's not a lie. Because it actually happens: Birdie Bay and I become friends.

It's not instant, of course. I do have to push my luck some days, keeping a close eye on her routine to make sure we "coincidentally" bump into each other on the street or at cafés. *Quel hasard!*

Do I go as far as scheduling a manicure at the same time as her pedicure (a bit of bribing involved, obviously)? Absolutely. But it pays off when, just two weeks after the whole @FauxEver story, I finally cross the threshold of her apartment, gawking as if I haven't already studied it from across the street.

It's definitely bigger and prettier than mine. I do my best to hide the flicker of envy as I follow her inside. The high ceilings and squeaky wood floors are similar to my place, but the comparison ends there. Her apartment looks straight out of a design magazine—or a Pinterest board titled *Dream French Apartments*.

An enormous white marble fireplace anchors the room, crowned by a massive mirror. Around it, colorful paintings by local artists, oversized green plants, and sleek Swedish lamps give the place that effortless, curated charm influencers pretend comes naturally. I catalog every detail, not just because it's beautiful, but because I want to remember it later. Maybe even recreate it.

"Home sweet home," Birdie says, lounging on her cream sofa and nudging a stack of Assouline books aside to make room for her feet on the marble coffee table. A Diptyque candle teeters dangerously close to the edge, but she either doesn't notice—or doesn't care.

"Wine?" she offers.

I'm about to point out that it's two p.m. on a Tuesday when she adds, "It's always apéro time somewhere on Earth."

What can I say to that?

While Birdie rummages through one of her many shelves in search of a bottle opener, I ask where the restroom is, and take the chance to explore. I'm eager to see her kitchen, bathroom, and bedroom: all the corners I can't spy from my apartment.

The hallway is cluttered with unopened boxes—not exactly her most photogenic space—so maybe that's why it's been left undecorated. The walls, though, are lined with framed magazine covers, each capturing a different moment in Birdie's life. I lean closer to one I recognize: *American Teen Vogue*. I remember buying that issue with my pocket money the week it came out. She must've been sixteen.

"They let me keep the Burberry poncho after the shoot," Birdie says, appearing beside me with two glasses of rosé. "I was so thrilled I didn't even care that I was the only one on set who didn't get paid."

I turn to her, smiling as I take the glass. I'd watched her unpack these very glasses last month, and now here I am, holding one in my hand.

"It's nice, having these framed," I say.

Birdie tilts her head, eyes still on the cover. "Yeah. Some people have childhood photos, and I have... whatever this is."

"You don't have pictures of yourself as a kid?" I ask. What I mean is *normal* pictures, but she gets it anyway.

She shakes her head. "Nope. Maybe a few from when I lived with my mom here in Paris, but after she died, my dad took me to LA, and... well, he wasn't exactly the scrapbooking type. No albums, no keepsakes."

Her expression hardens. We both take a sip of wine to drown the awkwardness of such sudden intimacy.

"I kind of know what you mean." The words slip out before I can stop them, and when Birdie looks at me, curious, I rush to clarify. "Not my dad—he's great. It's my mom. She went out for a hairstyling appointment one day and never came back."

"Shit..." For a brief second, something flickers across her face—a glint of recognition, or maybe empathy. "How old were you?"

"Oh, I don't really remember," I lie. I remember perfectly. I was six. One month shy of seven. But I've already said too much, and suddenly I want to steer things back to safer ground, like those glossy magazine covers.

"Shit," Birdie repeats, softer this time. Then, as if to match the level of confession, she adds, "My mom's family never got over her falling for a penniless American. The fact that he was a musician was the final nail. They cut her off completely, and... now it's all too late to fix."

So, no family at all. Funny how someone can be adored by millions and still be utterly alone. For the first time since I started following her, I don't feel envious.

"Music, huh?" I say, seizing the chance to shift gears. "I'd love to hear you play sometime."

Her mouth curves into a faint smile. "Let me grab my guitar."

Birdie is far less skilled than she thinks, but what she lacks in talent, she makes up for in enthusiasm. Every few minutes, she pauses to sip her rosé, and I do my best to silence the small, insistent voice telling me to grab my phone and snap a photo. *"I don't drink alcohol,"* she always claims online. I shove the thought deep into the same mental drawer where I keep the @FauxEver password, reminding myself that Birdie and I are friends now.

The afternoon drifts by in a blur of off-key strumming and nonstop doorbell rings. DHL, FedEx, private couriers—one after another. They bring her offerings of free makeup, clothing samples, and jewelry—gifts she didn't ask for and probably won't use, but that brands send anyway, praying for a mention in her Stories.

"Wow, is it your birthday or something?" I ask, aiming for casual, though everyone knows her birthday's in October.

"Ah, no." She shrugs and tosses another parcel onto the growing mountain of unopened boxes. "It's like this every day, from morning till evening. So annoying."

Receiving free stuff is *annoying*? It takes everything in me not to roll my eyes.

She resumes playing some cover of Tate McRae's *Greedy*, but I can't take my eyes off the boxes. Now that she's mentioned them, I see them everywhere. Towering piles by the entrance, bubble envelopes shoved under tables, smaller stacks creeping across shelves. How many valuable things are just lying around here? And how can she not tear into them the second they arrive? I know I would.

Birdie catches my stare and laughs. "Take whatever you want."

I bite my lip, shaking my head too quickly. "No, I wouldn't dare..."

"It's fine," she says, rolling her eyes. "I don't need all this stuff anyway. Half the time it's the wrong shade, wrong size, wrong everything. You know? So don't be shy."

I get up from the couch and head toward the pile, my eyes gleaming with more excitement than they probably should. I pick up a large fuchsia box and glance at Birdie. She gives me a little nod of approval.

Inside, there's a smaller, heavy plastic container.

"A mini beauty fridge!" Birdie fake-gasps. "Groundbreaking. As if there's anyone left who doesn't already own one."

"I don't have one," I say.

"Oh." Her mouth tightens, a twinge of guilt flashing across her face. "Well, then keep it."

I should refuse. Our tiny bathroom is already bursting, and I have no clue where I'd even put it. But if Daniel can have a wine cooler in the kitchen, I can damn well have a beauty fridge.

Birdie sets her guitar down, a spark returning to her face. "You know what? This is fun. Open another one."

I laugh, a little too high-pitched, like a kid in a candy store. A slightly tipsy kid. I grab a smaller box this time and peel it open to find dozens of identical peach lip oils. I hold one up, raising an eyebrow.

"Ah, those I can't give you yet," she says, taking a sip of rosé. "I'll need them soon."

"Need them for what?"

"For a campaign. It's on hold for now, but once that silly drug drama blows over, I'll announce to the world that my…" She lifts her fingers in air quotes. "*All-time favorite* lip oils are from Summer Fridays."

I set the product back down, a thought dimming my excitement. Isn't it wild how, in Birdie's mind, it's unthinkable that her digital storm won't just blow over? That she might actually stay canceled and not claw her way back to influencer royalty? To her, it's just a temporary glitch—nothing worth learning from.

"About the drugs," I start, hesitant. We haven't talked about it since we began hanging out. "Are you...?" I trail off, unsure how to finish. On one hand, I'm her friend now, and I want to be supportive. On the other, I did watch her buy cocaine, so...

Birdie meets my eyes. "An addict? No. God, no. It was all a huge misunderstanding."

She stretches, as casually as if she were talking about the weather. "It just helps me focus when I'm under pressure, that's all."

I don't tell her that the whole thing is messed up, or suggest that if she needs help focusing, there are simpler fixes—coffee, vitamins, sleep. Instead, I just nod and say it's a shame she's catching all this heat over five grams of coke.

"Right?" she says, her voice all needy. "You know, I have this rule about not getting too close to followers, but I'm really glad I broke it with you. I like you for never judging."

All I hear is that Birdie Bay likes me. *Me,* Chloé Warner from the south of Kent. The girl who stood by her when everyone else turned away. She won't forget that.

I take a sip of wine and savor being that person for her.

Then Birdie pops my little bubble.

"Oh, and I can't wait for you to meet Gabrielle!"

My radar pings. "Who's Gabrielle?"

"My best friend since childhood," she chuckles, like I'm being cute. "You're going to love her."

7

There is nothing to *love* about Gabrielle de Terron.

I know it the second she waltzes into Birdie's apartment like she owns the place, her Amina Muaddi platform mules (I Googled them; they cost as much as my rent) clacking across the floor, stomping unapologetically all over my fragile new friendship with my idol.

"Gabi!" Birdie squeals, jumping to her feet. Within seconds, they're tangled in an embrace, shrieking like hyenas.

Gabrielle looks at me over Birdie's shoulder without a word. Dirty-blonde hair brushing her collarbones, sharp jawline, big dark eyes framed by even bigger brows, and lips to match—everything about her is oversized, dramatic. She's not beautiful, not really, but she fills the room like she is. And God, she's tall.

"Birds, I can't believe I wasn't here with you while you were going through this mess," she says.

"It's been a literal nightmare, Gabi."

"How did you manage without me?"

"Oh, I've been so lucky to have Chloé here to support me. She's been precious."

Gabrielle finally gives me a curt nod. That's it. And somehow, that tiny, dismissive gesture irritates me more than outright hostility ever could. As if I need *her* gratitude for being Birdie's friend.

"I heard your bikini project with Revolve is on hold because of it," she says, her tone all concerned.

"It is, imagine that. After six years of partnership! I lowered my rates so much for them that I was basically working for *free*, and they dare drop me in the middle of this stunt."

"Scandalous," Gabrielle purrs, rearranging a lock of Birdie's hair behind her ear.

From where I sit, the dynamic is glaringly obvious, but I try to convince myself it's all in my head. Still. The familiar ache of being sidelined creeps in, cold and sharp. I push it down, but it sticks. Abandonment issues run deep.

Summoning a smile, I rise from my seat and approach Gabrielle, planting a kiss on her cheek, the French way.

"Love your dress," I offer as an olive branch.

"Alaïa," she replies coolly, her gaze flicking down to me without returning the compliment. Nice.

I bite my lip, scrambling for something to say. "Do you want some wine? We're having this lovely rosé—"

"Gabi only drinks champagne," Birdie interrupts me, and I don't like the tone. Like I am being silly or something. "I'm gonna pop a bottle open."

Gabrielle turns on her heels and plops onto my spot on the couch, a smirk on her face.

———

From that moment on, my one-on-one time with Birdie turns into trio encounters. I try not to let it bother me—Birdie genuinely enjoys Gabrielle's company, and I can be a girl's girl, I swear I can. Still, something about Gabrielle just doesn't sit right with me.

See, Gabrielle is *tall*. And not just "a little taller than average" tall. No, she carries her height like a performance, flaunting it the way a peacock shows its feathers. She claims she hates being the tallest in every room, but I've never seen her in flats. She laughs as she pretends to bump into things—"I'm just not used to narrow spaces"—as if the world were inconveniently built too small for her.

She's always touching Birdie, too. A hand on her shoulder, a tap on her arm, the kind of casual physical claim that says, *mine*. "You're adorable," she tells Birdie, like she's a little pet rather than a person.

At the crux of it all is how effortlessly Gabrielle shifts the dynamics. Suddenly, it's Birdie who seems grateful to be around *her*—Birdie Bay, the girl with millions of followers, acting lucky just to share a table with Gabrielle de Terron. I can't wrap my head around it. I keep waiting for someone else to notice. Surely I'm not the only one who can see right through her act?

Gabrielle is not a good person. That much I'm sure of.

And she doesn't like me, either. I see it in the flicker of her expression when Birdie laughs at one of my jokes, in the way her thick brows knit when our eyes meet across the room. If she could erase me from Birdie's life with a snap of her manicured fingers, she would.

A WEEK HAS PASSED since Gabrielle hijacked my friendship with Birdie, and now the three of us are huddled around Birdie's computer, watching the rebroadcast of last night's Tony Awards.

"I hate Michelle Williams's dress; looks like Zara," Gabrielle snorts.

Birdie nods, reaching for another handful of corn chips. "She should fire her stylist."

"Jodie Comer looks incredible in Thom Browne, though."

"Yeah, Jodie's a queen." Birdie leans over to offer me chips, but I shake my head. She arches a brow, then looks back at the screen. "I saw her at Erewhon once, and even in washed-out Pangaias, she was fabulous."

I scan the screen, searching for something clever to say, but honestly, I think everyone looks beautiful. And the smell of food is making me queasy.

"That dress on Jennifer Lawrence would look amazing on you, Gabrielle," I offer, instantly regretting how eager I sound.

Gabrielle crunches into a chip. "Everything looks good on me."

"Be nice," Birdie murmurs, nudging her with an elbow.

I doubt she could be nice, even if her life depended on it.

Gabrielle turns to Birdie, voice honeyed. "Why aren't you invited to the Awards? Aren't you big enough in the States?"

"Influencers rarely get invites to those things," Birdie says, eyes fixed on the screen.

"Yeah, that makes sense." Gabrielle purses her lips, pretending to think. I know that look by now—she's winding up for the kill. "If they can have real stars, why settle for you guys, right?"

Wow.

Birdie says nothing, so I jump in. "They'd be lucky to have Birdie, actually. She'd bring a bit of youth to the lineup."

My friend flashes me a thin smile, but Gabrielle gives me a long, assessing look that makes my skin prickle.

"Do you only wear neutrals, *Chloey*?" she finally says, stretching out the ending like a taunt. I hate how she does that—even though Birdie's corrected her, what, five times by now?

I glance down at my white romper, heat creeping up my neck. My wardrobe isn't exactly extensive, and ever since I started hanging out with Birdie and Gabrielle, I've come to the humbling realization that most of my clothes belong to the "garbage" category. So lately, I've stuck to neutrals, hoping simplicity might pass for intention.

"Gabrielle..." Birdie sighs, shaking her head.

"What? Every time I see her, she's in white. Are you one of those *Sad Beige girls*?"

"What's a Sad Beige girl?" I ask, though I can already guess it's not a compliment.

Birdie shoots Gabrielle a warning look. "Someone who only dresses in neutrals. You'll never catch a Sad Beige girl in anything but black, white, or beige. Maybe the occasional brown."

"That's... convenient?" I say, weakly defending myself. Truth is, every piece still hanging in my closet fits that exact palette.

"It's lazy," Gabrielle says, smirking. "Means you don't have the guts—or the style—to pull off color. So basic."

I want to shrink into my chair, but Birdie steps in. "Neutrals *do* look good in pictures, and good basics matter," she says quickly. "But some people make it their whole thing —never a hint of color. Safe, but boring." She stands and stretches, then adds, "Chloé's not a Sad Beige girl, though. She was wearing a red Lululemon set the first time we met."

My head snaps up. She remembered that?

A small smile breaks through before I can stop it, the validation washing over me like sunlight after a long, gray day.

Gabrielle rolls her eyes. "Whatever." She pops another chip into her mouth and sits up straighter. "Oh, by the way, Papa got us tickets to the Beyoncé concert next Friday. VIP lounge and everything. Even Jay-Z won't be that close to the stage."

"Geez, that's insane! I'm obsessed with her last album," Birdie says.

I hate to admit it, but a thrill runs through me. Beyoncé! "Wow! What does one even wear to a VIP lounge?"

"Uhm, sorry, *Chloey*," Gabrielle says, dragging my name like it's sticky on her tongue. "I only have two tickets. Besides, bestie time's long overdue, right, *Birds*?" She flashes a smile that doesn't reach her eyes.

Heat creeps up my neck. "Oh, yeah, sure," I mumble, wishing I hadn't opened my mouth like some overeager kid.

But Birdie's eyes flick between us, her mouth tightening. "Gabi, can you come with me to the kitchen?"

All those childhood memories of being left out flood back as they vanish down the hall. I hover a few seconds, pretending to scroll my phone, before doing what any rational adult would: tiptoe to the bathroom and press my ear to the thin wall separating it from the kitchen.

"...inviting me in front of Chloé..."

"And when is that? You've been glued to her ever since I came back."

"Stop it. She's in the living room, I don't want her to hear."

"I *want* her to hear. I don't give a fuck about this girl. There's something weird about the way she looks at you."

My stomach drops.

"You're imagining things, Gabi. You always do."

"Okay, but don't you think it's strange she showed up in your life *right* when those pictures came out to ruin your career?"

I freeze. That's not good.

"She didn't 'show up' anywhere," Birdie snaps. "She's lived here since before I moved in. And my career is not ruined. Everyone goes through a scandal. It's normal."

I press closer to the wall—too close. My shoulder bumps the shelf, and Birdie's *Tom Ford Lost Cherry* bottle teeters. I grab it midair, heart hammering, and exhale a shaky sigh of relief.

Then, shouting.

"...not your place to advise me on my future!"

"For fuck's sake, all I meant was you don't *have* to keep doing this influencer thing. *They* can—"

"Don't talk to me about *them!*"

"Oh my God, *Birds,*" Gabrielle groans. "You know what? Call me when you've opened your eyes."

A door slams. The sharp click of her sandals echoes down the hall, then silence.

I count to ten before stepping into the kitchen. Birdie's half-sitting on her marble counter, eyes fixed on the tiny backyard window.

"Hey," I say softly, "so, um, I might've overheard a bit..."

She cuts me off, finally looking at me, her voice flat. "It's fine. If I really wanted to see Beyoncé, I'd buy my own fucking ticket."

IT'S SETTLED—GABRIELLE needs to go.

Not because she doesn't like me; that's her right. And not because she basically implied I was behind @FauxEver (not ideal, but hey—no body, no proof).

No, she has to go because she's toxic for Birdie. And Birdie's my friend.

When I get home that evening, I switch into full investigation mode. Time to dig.

I know my way around the internet. As my dad likes to remind me, it's where we Gen Z practically grew up. Navigating it is second nature—don't want to brag, but it's true. Ask anyone born after 1997 to find dirt on someone, and they'll have a full report ready in ten minutes. Millennials don't quite get it the same way.

Still, after an hour, I've got nothing.

No Instagram, no TikTok, no Twitter. Not even a LinkedIn.

All I manage to find is a blurry, watermarked Getty shot of her after a Dior Couture show, walking through the Tuileries in knee-high platforms and a fully beaded blazer. Even with the oversized black sunglasses, you can tell from the downturn of her burgundy lips that she's pissed at the photographer.

I try Googling her family, but there's no trace of the De Terron clan. A few companies, yes—a private bank in

Switzerland, a notary office in Paris—but nothing that tells me who she actually is.

"You've got to be kidding me," I mutter, glaring at my screen.

As far as the internet goes, it's given me nothing to bury the bitch with.

8

When the internet fails you, there's always old-school detective work. So I decide to track down Gabrielle's place.

She's been dropping her street name more times than would be considered normal in a healthy conversation, so I hop on the subway to Neuilly-sur-Seine—the fancy side of Paris.

Two things about that neighborhood. First, it's a trek from my arrondissement: a subway ride, the usual métro funk, a dodgy encounter with a homeless guy, and two train swaps. Second, when I arrive, it feels like a different city entirely. Clean streets, swanky cafés, gorgeous facades. In short, it's Paris, Disney edition.

I'm not judging, just taking in the kind of environment that could've birthed a creature like Gabrielle de Terron.

As I walk to her building, I pass kids lugging tennis rackets and see more Birkins than I can count. Birdie hasn't said much about her friend beyond the obvious—she's loaded with family money. Which means private schools, unlimited allowances, personal drivers. A life of privilege. Shit, does she have surveillance? *No. Don't even go there.* Breaking into an apartment once was enough of a lesson. My heart still kicks faster remembering that scare... not my proudest moment, and a story for another time.

I'm closing in and doubt creeps up with every step. What did I expect to find? A confession taped to the concierge's door? It's not like she's going to hand me her darkest secrets from the stoop. I inhale sharply, noting that the air seems clearer here. Who am I kidding—of course I'd briefly considered breaking in, just to see how she lives, maybe snag a laptop or a hard drive.

I slow down as I read Gabrielle's street name on the brass plaque. My eyes wander in search of the street numbers and land on—her. Gabrielle is on the terrace of an expensive-looking café on the corner, a slim Vogue Menthol between her fingers, chatting with someone. Lucky me, I guess. I slip around the building, approach the terrace from behind, and ease into a seat far enough away not to be obvious but close enough to catch every word.

The woman Gabrielle is speaking with looks much older. Her grandmother, maybe? The first thing I notice is the pearls: dozens of them looped around her neck, so many it's a miracle she can move her head. When she turns slightly, her face comes into view, sharp and severe, the kind of face animators give to villains in old Disney films. And yet... her eyes look strangely familiar.

"*Je sais, Catherine...*" Gabrielle says, flicking ash into the tray. Then something else in French—something about *travail* and maybe *argent*? Work and money, I think. I really need to start taking those French lessons seriously.

"*Il faut lui laisser le temps,*" she adds in a tone I have

never heard her use before. It's almost like respect, which is so out of character for Gabrielle that I almost forget to focus on translating what she's saying. "*Elle est têtue, mais elle n'est pas stupide.*"

Is she speaking about Birdie? I lean in but miss the end of the sentence because of a loud ambulance passing by.

"*...aussi ce que je pensais de sa mère,*" the old woman interjects with a venomous tone, caressing her pearls as if they were living things. "*Mais il se trouve qu'on peut être têtue et stupide. S'amouracher de ce clochard américain...*"

I frown; it's obvious that they are talking about Birdie, but how does she...

"Excuse me, *Mademoiselle*, this table is reserved." The waiter's voice slices through the terrace chatter, startling me so badly my chair scrapes against the pavement. My bag slips from my lap. Murmuring an apology, I bend to grab it, keeping my hair curtained over my face. The world feels too still, too quiet. Is Gabrielle watching me? I can almost feel her gaze burning between my shoulder blades.

Without looking back, I stand and head for the street—fast but not quite running.

My pulse doesn't settle until the city swallows me underground, the roar of the subway drowning out my own heartbeat.

Did I hear someone call my name while I was fleeing? Did Gabrielle see me? It's highly probable. Knowing her, she's likely firing off messages to Birdie as we speak. Damn. How could I explain my presence there? The journey home zips by in an agonizing blur as I rack my brain for a plausible escape plan.

I decide I'll flat-out deny it. Say she's imagining things. Swear I never even set foot in Neuilly. Birdie won't question me—she knows I've always been loyal. Not like Gabrielle.

I almost growl with frustration; today's given me nothing on Gabrielle. I wish I'd been braver and slipped into her apartment to find something, anything, to prove to Birdie that her so-called best friend isn't as perfect as she seems. Something like—

Oh.

The next métro stop is mine. I step off with a smile. Maybe I just thought of the perfect thing to use against her.

The following day, Birdie and I go for our morning jog, followed by our ritual park rendezvous by the fountain, complete with ham croissants and iced lattes. It's been nearly a month of this comforting routine, and I usually savor these quiet moments when it's just the two of us. But today, I can't stop watching her too closely, scanning every smile, every laugh for even the faintest trace of suspicion. There's nothing. She's her usual bright self, chatting about a new photoshoot idea and a podcast she can't stop listening to.

We haven't mentioned Gabrielle since *that* scene in the kitchen. While it was initially a relief, now it feels... dangerous. I can practically see Gabrielle's tall, smug silhouette reappearing out of nowhere, cutting in with some barbed comment before I've even had time to brace myself.

I decide to test the waters.

"So, is Gabrielle still mad at you?" I ask, swirling my straw through melting ice, eyes fixed on Birdie's face.

"I'm the one who's mad at her, not the other way around," she responds, then takes a sip, ice clinking against plastic. "But we're family, so it'll blow over."

Well, that is something new. I feel my shoulders tense, and the croissant suddenly feels like lead in my stomach. "Really?"

"Not family-family, like in the classical sense of it," she explains. "We've known each other forever. We went to the same preschool, and braided each other's hair and stuff—before my mum died."

"Oh." I nod slowly. I guess that explains how they've known each other for so long, even though they clearly don't move in the same circles. "Funny, though, I've never seen any pictures of you two together on your profile."

"Gabi's not on socials," Birdie sighs. "She actually hates anything to do with the internet. She's... private."

As if I didn't already know that, I think, trying not to let the irritation show. But this—this is my in. I arch my brows, feigning curiosity. "So, what does she think about your career then?"

Birdie looks down at her hands, something I've learned she does when she's sad and trying to hide it.

"She knows about my dad, and how I first started vlogging just to afford makeup and Abercrombie T-shirts. I think she respects that, in her own way. But it's different for people like Gabrielle. She's old money. She grew up riding horses on family estates across France, just for fun, and dropping thousands on designer clothes without even glancing at the price tag. She'll never understand what it's like to hustle, or to wonder if you can afford your next electricity bill."

I nod. That was exactly my impression from that little field trip to Neuilly-sur-Seine.

"Her family actually knows mine," Birdie continues. "I mean, the rich side—my mum's side. I told you it was because of my dad, but it's also because... well, they think I'm an embarrassment."

"You? An embarrassment?" I exclaim, genuinely indignant. "But you're a star!"

She plucks something from the corner of her eye and pretends to examine it, her voice flattening. "That's the embarrassment, actually. They're ashamed of the way I spill my life online. Privacy is sacred to them. It doesn't matter how much I make doing this. I'll always be cheap in their eyes. Living proof that society's gone to hell. Like a joke, they mention only at cocktail hour. *Listen up, people, a relative of ours is actually being paid to cry on camera; how fun is that?*" She drops her voice into a mock drawl, but the bitterness lingers long after the impression fades.

The old woman from the café flashes in my mind—the pearls, the sharp eyes. Could she have been Birdie's grandmother? It would explain the eerie sense of recognition.

"I'm so sorry they're so—" I begin.

"Mean? Heartless?" Birdie interrupts with a brittle laugh, folding her legs beneath her on the bench.

"I was going to say *close-minded*," I counter softly. "Only fools don't see how the world's changed. That a girl's voice from the LA suburbs can carry as much weight as *Vogue* now." I mean it, every word of it. Whether all that power in the hands of teenagers is a blessing or a disaster... I'm not so sure. But I keep that thought to myself, watching Birdie's shoulders slump under the weight of people who should've loved her better.

"But those people from your family," I press gently, noticing the tiny flinch that ripples through her at the word *family*. "They don't try to see you now that you're back in Paris?"

"No," Birdie mutters, the word landing heavy. "They're waiting for me to crawl back, probably. That's how it works with them—you have to need something before they'll even look at you. It would never cross their minds to reach out first. Not for something as simple as love."

"I'm sure Gabrielle's not like that," I say, baiting her, trying to steer the conversation back where I want it.

Birdie pauses, thinking. "She's not," she admits softly. "Gabi's... different. I know she loves me, and I know she doesn't think exactly like them. But sometimes I get the feeling she wishes I'd just drop everything—quit social media, make peace with my mother's family, and come play the part of the rich, mysterious heiress with her."

There. Showtime. I pinch my lips together and try to look thoughtful. It works.

"What?" Birdie asks, tilting her head.

"It's just that..." I let the pause linger, pretending to weigh my words. "You say Gabrielle hates it that you're an influencer. That she thinks the internet's toxic."

"Thank you for the recap, Chloé." Birdie rolls her eyes and takes another sip of her iced latte.

I feel her slipping, so I go straight for it. "How far do you think she'd go to make sure you got canceled? To make sure you stopped being an embarrassment to your family?"

What if Gabrielle were behind @FauxEver? Of course, I know she wasn't, but let's entertain the thought for a second.

If she were, it would make getting rid of her almost too easy. Not that I need it to be true; I just need Birdie to *wonder*. It's a small tactic borrowed straight from Gabrielle's own playbook—she accused me without proof, didn't she?

And just like that, I've got her. Birdie's eyes go unfocused for a moment as the idea sinks in. I can almost see the gears turning, tracing the breadcrumb trail I've laid out for her.

She's thinking about how Gabrielle knew about the drugs.

She's picturing her following her that day, snapping those photos.

She's remembering how fast her so-called friend jumped on the hate wave and told her to quit.

If there's one thing I've learned about Birdie, it's that her career—her online self—is everything. Maybe it's fear of slipping back into that trailer park with her drunk father, or maybe it's just the awareness of how fragile her empire really is. Either way, the second I plant that seed of doubt, I see her face close up like an oyster.

Birdie slides on her cat-eye sunglasses. "Let's not talk about her anymore." She stands, brushing crumbs from her lap. "I need to get back and film. It's time for Birdie Bay to return to her people."

Her tone is light, but it doesn't land that way. I know I've succeeded.

And she's right—it *is* time. Time for her to reclaim her spotlight. And time for me to delete @FauxEver once and for all. Because when she finally realizes Gabrielle was never her friend, I'll be here to catch her.

9

I log into @FauxEver with one goal: shut it down.

I should've done it weeks ago, back when Birdie and I first started hanging out. It doesn't feel right to keep the account alive while growing closer to her.

I haven't posted in almost three weeks, not since those infamous drug photos. Still, the numbers have climbed: over nine thousand followers, sixty-eight thousand likes on that single post. Guess @AnnieRevel was wrong after all.

Who knew people were this thirsty for *truth*?

Although... maybe it isn't truth they want. Maybe it's just gossip, dressed up as virtue.

Either way, I need to erase every trace linking me to the thing that broke Birdie. No account, no guilt.

But before deactivating it, I take one last look—just a quick peek at @FauxEver's DMs.

Most of the new messages come from nosy followers asking why I've gone silent or trying to unmask me. Still, a few stand out: messages with photos, screenshots, confessions.

Look at that—he's married.

Please post these.

LMAO, some people are shameless!

And that last one's right. My screen floods with dozens of images and clips—familiar faces from my own following list caught in compromising situations. Illicit affairs. Offensive jokes. Influencers mistreating fans.

Mostly, it's just proof of how spectacularly out of touch they all are.

I lean back in my chair, my thoughts colliding. A few minutes ago, I didn't know what to do with @FauxEver. I never meant to become some online vigilante hunting down content creators for sport.

But if people are sending me material... doesn't that make me a kind of platform? A media outlet?

Couldn't this serve a greater purpose? Something beyond that first jab at Birdie?

If I pivot the mission—to holding influencers accountable, to exposing hypocrisy—maybe I can still justify keeping @FauxEver alive.

Before I can talk myself out of it, I start typing. A quick post about a girl from Marseille who somehow gained three hundred thousand followers in a week.

Then I hit Post.

"Surprise!" Birdie sings as I open the door.

And it *is* a surprise—to see her standing there, beaming on my doorstep. She's in a ripped Billie Eilish T-shirt and slouchy jeans that make her look like a kid who raided her older brother's closet.

"What are you... doing here?" I force a smile, my brain scrambling for an excuse to make her leave. I'm caught between mild panic and a flicker of delight that she's crossed that invisible line in our friendship—the one where you can just show up, unannounced.

"Well, we've been hanging out at my place nonstop, so I figured it was time I saw where *you* live," she says, already breezing past me and stepping inside.

My stomach drops. The place is a disaster. Too many coats crammed behind the door, shoes (mostly mine) spilling across the floor. I've been meaning to clean, but it's summer now, and somehow I still haven't gotten around to it.

Birdie pauses in the entryway, taking it all in, and suddenly I'm seeing my own apartment through her eyes. How narrow it is. The chipped turquoise paint. The hideous rug Daniel insisted on keeping from his parents' house.

Her gaze drifts to the wall, where a few of my old photographs hang.

"These pictures are beautiful." And I can tell from her face that she means it.

There are four of them, all from my final year at university. Each captures some small, ordinary corner of my dad's house, with him always there at the center—blurred by long exposure, like a ghost caught between moments. The stillness of the room versus his movement. Presence and absence, coexisting.

My professors called it a meditation on time and identity and gave me the highest grade, but what really stayed with me was the way my dad's face lit up when he saw the finished series.

"Thanks," I say, smiling at the memory.

"Wait—hold on." Birdie squints at the wall, then back at me. "You took those?"

I nod, suddenly self-conscious.

"Chloé, you're *so* talented!" She leans in, examining the prints more closely. "I mean, I knew you did photography, but I didn't realize it was, like... *real* photography."

I can't help but laugh. "What kind of photography did you think I did?"

"I don't know, the Instagram kind?" She grins sheepishly, biting her lower lip. "But seriously, this looks like gallery stuff. Shouldn't you be doing exhibitions or something?"

"I'd love to. It's just..." I shrug. "That world's hard to get into without the right contacts."

I don't add that when I first moved to Paris, I went door to door through the galleries in Le Marais, portfolio in hand. Not the fancy ones, of course, just the smaller spaces that showcased emerging artists. In all honesty, after seeing some of the work on their walls, I knew I could do better. But the owners only offered me tight smiles and polite dismissals, and not one of them ever called back.

"Really?" Birdie says. "Weird. Every photographer I know is always booked solid."

I press my lips together, forcing a small smile. "Well, I never tried *fashion* photography, so I wouldn't know."

"Right," Birdie mumbles before continuing her tour of the place. "Your apartment is so similar to mine," she observes, her blue eyes drifting around the room. "The high ceilings, the moldings... Don't you just love those creaking floors?"

"Mmh, sure." I steal a quick glance toward the window. The binoculars are lying on the floor, in plain sight. While

Birdie gushes about the *timeless charm of Parisian architecture*, I casually stroll over and nudge them under the curtain with my foot.

Birdie joins me at the window, oblivious.

"Oh wow," she breathes. "I never realized you had such a good view of my apartment."

I force a laugh. "I actually just noticed that the other day. Funny, huh?"

"Funny—unless you're a stalker, of course."

We both laugh at that, because we don't live in a world where it could be true.

"Do you want to drink something?" I attempt to divert her from the window. "I have coffee, some infusions..."

"Anything stronger?" Birdie offers with a grin. "Sorry, it's just that I could really use a drink right now."

"Uhh, yeah," I mutter, thinking of what I might offer her. "I might have some vodka and ginger beer if you like Moscow Mule?"

"Sounds great!"

I head to the kitchen to dust off the old vodka bottle Daniel and I bought back when we thought we were the kind of couple who hosted dinner parties with other grown-ups. One painfully awkward evening with his coworkers was enough to prove otherwise. The bottle's been living unopened under the sink ever since.

When I get back into the living room, Birdie's standing by the bookshelf, one of Daniel's history books tucked under her arm.

"There is a shit ton of books; are you that passionate about Ancient Egypt, or do you have a roommate?" she asks, snagging her Moscow Mule from my hands.

"These are my boyfriend's."

"Sorry, what?" Birdie gives me a quizzical look. "Boyfriend or *boyfriend*?"

"Boyfriend," I answer, carefully.

She presses her free hand to her heart in mock drama. "Excuse *you*! How come you never told me about him?"

How come I didn't, indeed? I guess we've spent the past three weeks talking about all things Birdie—a topic I was more than happy to indulge. Being with her felt like stepping into a parallel universe where I wasn't Chloé Warner anymore but someone far more intriguing. Someone who nodded knowingly at words like *engagement ratio, cross-media repost*, or *exclusivity offer*.

And Daniel? He was too real, too personal for the Birdie bubble.

"I guess he just never came up," I say, dodging, but Birdie's attention is already hooked. She flops onto the couch with a grin.

"Then we'll just have to make him come up, won't we? Tell me everything about your...?"

"Daniel," I supply.

"Daniel the," she looks down at the book she's still holding. "Archeologist?"

I let out a single laugh. "He's a teacher."

"Uhh, a professor. Makes sense. So what does he think of your impending success as a photographer?"

"Well, he's very supportive of that, of course. But I think he's starting to wonder if it's really gonna happen for me."

"I see." She suddenly looks thoughtful. "You should post more on Instagram—not just the pictures, but the process, the behind-the-scenes of your photographer's life. That's what people want to see now. Maybe Mr. Professor could help you shoot those."

I chuckle. "I doubt that. Daniel still takes pictures in landscape mode. That's how far away he is from anything digital."

Birdie pulls a face. "Okay, that's not great. But hey, at least you don't have to worry about some hot pastry chef with doe eyes and daddy issues sliding into his DMs to offer her hot buns."

"That's a disturbingly specific example," I say, raising an eyebrow.

"Yeah, well, they say the best stories come from life. And my love life? Let's just say it could've been a very sad limited series."

"I remember that one guy you used to date, though..." I pretend to think, tapping my temple, though his name is burned into my brain. "...Brad? Benson?"

It's Bellamy. *The* Bellamy. Model, singer, influencer, demigod. I used to be obsessed with that face—liked every photo, every video, every grainy mirror selfie, each click carrying my quiet little hope that he'd somehow notice me. He never did, of course.

Birdie freezes for a beat before giving me a small smile—half sad, half embarrassed. "Bellamy and I never really *dated*," she says, and for a moment I wonder what story sits behind that. "It was... whatever."

She rolls her eyes, takes a sip, and lets out a low hum. "Mmm, very good mule. Anyway, did I ever tell you about the actor who saved my number as *Friday* in his phone because that's when he'd hook up with me? Such a jerk. But he did teach me to surf on his private Malibu beach, so I guess that's something."

I stare at her, horrified.

She bursts out laughing. "Oh, come on. What did you expect? In social media, there are only three kinds of men." She lifts her hand and starts ticking them off with her fingers. "One—the self-absorbed men-fluencers. You'd have to hate yourself a little to date one. Believe me, I've been there. Two —the gays. Absolute gems. They're the reason I haven't sworn off men entirely."

"And the third?"

"Predators," she says, matter-of-factly, before taking another sip. "Where there are young, impressionable women, there will always be sick agents, brand reps, or investors waiting to pounce."

I want to ask her more. I love when she goes off about social media. But Birdie's cheeks have taken on a pinkish glow, and I know that once she's tipsy, she only follows her own train of thought.

"I just wish I could meet a kind guy with a normal life," she sighs, glancing at the book in her hand. "Preferably one who reads something other than DMs. But no, I have the worst luck with men. You wouldn't believe it."

She leans forward, animated. "Like, I really thought I'd found a decent one two weeks ago—right after I moved in. Think Prince Harry, but blond. So hot. Imagine the babies we'd have had? Ugh. Anyway, we went on a few dates, and then he started replying... sporadically. One night, when we were supposed to go out, he texted that he couldn't make it because his *buddy* wanted to hang out. His buddy, Chloé."

I chuckle. "Tragic. So, you dumped him?"

"Well, we weren't exactly dating," she says with a smirk. "But I texted back, 'No worries!' Waited two minutes. Then sent, 'Actually, my night just cleared up,' followed by, 'Oops, wrong person.' He tried calling after that, but he was already dead to me."

I blink, processing. "Oh. That's..."

"Petty?" she finishes for me, grinning. "Yeah, well—I'm a petty bitch. No shame. When someone disappoints me, I cut ties clean. Learned that the hard way."

10

Daniel and I met through acquaintances a few months after I moved to Paris.

I've never been great at making new friends, and days in a foreign country without a job or any real purpose can really drag. So when a girl I knew from university came to visit from London and got invited to a party in Le Marais, I practically begged her to take me along.

Daniel was the quintessential movie nerd: dressed like he was twice his age, a pen sticking out of his blazer pocket, and social skills that could make a silence stretch for miles, especially around women. (For the record, he can discuss wine-tasting notes for *hours* if you let him.)

But I've always had a vision. Where others might have seen Tom Hanks in *The Terminal*, I saw Ian Harding from *Pretty Little Liars*. Glasses included, obviously.

So I made sure to hover nearby until one of us would "accidentally" bump into the other. It didn't take long. Daniel tripped over his own feet and spilled white wine all over my sneakers.

After an onslaught of apologies and a frantic napkin routine, he confessed he was chronically clumsy.

I told him it was fine—that we British people were famous for our awkwardness too.

He said he loved London and was fascinated by Shakespeare.

I'd read *Macbeth* once in school (thought it was fine, if a bit overrated), so I nodded like we'd found common ground.

Back in the UK, my friends used to joke that I never fell for the guy himself—just his potential.

And Daniel had plenty of that. Beneath the hipster cardigans and awkward charm, he was actually handsome. Then there was the vintage gold Cartier Tank watch—probably an heirloom, and a dead giveaway he came from good stock. And while I stood nearby, pretending not to listen, I overheard him describing the food from his sister's wedding in such loving detail that I knew right then he was husband material.

We exchanged numbers, and predictably, he called the next morning, inviting me on a tour of Paris's best English bookstores. I wasn't much of a reader, but I was already halfway smitten, so honestly, he could've suggested the catacombs and I'd have said yes—it's a thing here, apparently.

We met outside Brentano's, and I could tell right away that Daniel had made an effort. He was clean-shaven, wearing a crisp white shirt and what looked like brand-new beige sneakers. He smiled at me, that slightly awkward, earnest grin that reminded me a bit of my dad. How Freudian.

At Galignani, he caught me admiring a book by one of my favorite photographers, Peter Lindbergh, and when he thought I wasn't looking (I definitely was), he bought it for me. Then the sky broke open, and we ducked into a café for shelter. It should've been one of those cinematic Paris moments—rain, shared glances, the beginning of something—but it turned out to be *Angelina*, the most tourist-infested place in the city. We ordered overpriced drinks (a hot chocolate for me, a café noisette for him) and tried to talk over the constant hum of chatter and clinking cups.

"I'm the youngest of four. My twin sister beat me by six minutes," he said.

"Lucky you," I replied, keeping my tone light. "I always wanted siblings." No need to unpack my own family history just yet.

When the rain stopped, we picked up where we left off, crossing the bridge to Shakespeare and Company. Somewhere between the Seine and the bookstore queue, I realized Daniel wasn't just potential. I genuinely liked him. There was something so easy about him. So steady. He held doors open, laughed at my jokes (even the mediocre ones), and made me feel... special.

He was a keeper.

By the time Daniel's keys jingle in the lock, both Birdie and I are positively drunk.

"Is it the professor?" Birdie whispers, because it's her fourth Moscow Mule.

It's my third, so I giggle like a schoolgirl. "I certainly hope so."

"*C'est moi, ma belle,*" Daniel sings as if to dissipate any doubt, which, for some reason, makes Birdie crack.

"You're never going to believe what Diane—" His eyes

settle on Birdie, bypassing me entirely. "Oh, hi!" He blinks, jaw hanging a bit.

"Birdie, this is Daniel. Daniel, meet Birdie," I slur.

Birdie tilts her head up and flashes him that blinding, starlet smile. "Hello."

"Well, that's a surprise," he manages, giving an awkward little wave before glancing down at his outfit—creased shirt, mismatched socks. "Had I known we'd have company, I'd have..."

"Oh, it's all on me," Birdie says smoothly, cutting in. She sucks briefly on her thumb, a tipsy habit, then grins. "I sort of roped Chloé into this impromptu party. How long's it been, Chlo? An hour? Two?"

"Looks more like two or three," I chuckle. "But we've had some enlightening conversations."

"Terrific talks," Birdie echoes. "Very... astute."

"Unlike Birdie's exes," I tease.

She forms an "O" with her mouth, then scrunches her face. "True enough."

"O-okay," Daniel says, and I can tell he's trying a little too hard to play it cool. "May I join you, or is this a girls-only soirée?"

"Be our guest," I reply.

As soon as he disappears into the kitchen, Birdie leans in and stage-whispers in my ear, far louder than she thinks. "Handsome! Good for you, bitch."

I try not to smile, but the compliment lands anyway, fizzing pleasantly in my chest. So when Daniel returns a moment later with an open bottle of red and three glasses, looking all shy and domestic, I can't help it—I smirk, dizzy with wine and my own ridiculous luck.

"So, why are you this drunk?" he asks us, but really, he's only speaking to Birdie.

She bats her eyes. "Me? I'm having a rather shitty day. Or a rather shitty week, actually. And when you think of it, the entire month's been crap too. The barista down the road used the wrong milk in my cappuccino twice, and the Russian girl who's been doing my nails went to open her business in Geneva, and I actually gained three kilos eating all these croissants in the morning. Am I forgetting something? Oh yes, everybody thinks I'm a drug addict, and I'm losing what is the most important to me: my fucking career."

Daniel nods earnestly. "Right, Chloé told me about the... you know. I'm really sorry that happened to you."

"It's okay," Birdie answers, a little amused, maybe a bit embarrassed. "I'm not here to mope."

Daniel's watching Birdie the way you'd stare at a Christmas tree in the desert—half in disbelief, half in awe. I follow his gaze, trying to see her the way I used to before I really knew her, before Birdie Bay became just Birdie. She's still magnetic, still impossible to ignore, but the spell has worn off. The shimmer's there, yet it doesn't reach me anymore.

"So, professor," she says, taking Daniel's book that's been lying next to her for the past few hours. "Have you ever been to Egypt?"

Daniel shoots her a surprised look. "Not yet. I want to, but Chloé's afraid of the terrorists."

I huff. "Of all the things I'm afraid of, terrorists are probably the least embarrassing." Both of them look at me with wide eyes. "What? They're a real threat in Egypt; Google it."

"I've always wanted to go," Birdie says, running her fingers over the book's cover. "I was invited to an event there once—right before the pandemic—but when everything shut down, the trip was canceled."

Daniel and she exchange a look, and I wonder what's happening there.

"Do you travel a lot for work?" he asks.

"Mmmh, yes. But mostly it's the same places. New York, London, Milan... This is where fashionable stuff happens. What I really want to see is the Great Wall of China, Machu Picchu, the cathedrals in Saint Petersburg. And the Northern Lights—God, I'd die to see them in Finland."

Daniel's face brightens. "Me too! A friend of mine went last year and—"

That's my cue. I scoop up our empty cocktail glasses, using them as the perfect excuse for a graceful retreat to the kitchen.

With all that drinking, I haven't checked how my latest @FauxEver post is doing in hours. I log in and can't help smiling at the screen—three thousand likes and forty comments. Not bad at all, especially given the subject: a mid-tier influencer from Lyon caught on video brawling with a homeless man twice his age. Hardly headline material, and nowhere near Birdie Bay's level of fame, yet the engagement's impressive. I scroll down eagerly, ready to savor the comments.

lol humanity garbage

Anyone else is bored of these people?

Straight to therapy

Two comments don't go my way, though.

Taken out of context for likes

@FauxEver by posting this you're just part of the problem

I hesitate before deleting them. Lately, comments like these have been cropping up more often, and I don't want to look like I'm censoring dissent. But leaving them up feels riskier. It opens the door for others to pile on, turning @FauxEver's comments section into a digital free-for-all. After a moment's deliberation, I do what I always do: block both accounts, quietly, efficiently. Then I grab a bottle of water and three glasses and head back to the living room.

Neither Daniel nor Birdie seems to have noticed I was gone. I ease back onto the couch, trying to tune into their conversation, which has drifted from dream destinations to—of all things—Birdie's stalker.

Interesting.

"It's the not knowing that gets to me," Birdie says, tracing her finger around the rim of her glass. "Just realizing someone's been following me at some point. Now, every time I leave home, I feel like I have to look over my shoulder. And when I do, and someone happens to glance my way, I can't help wondering if it's them, you know?"

Daniel rubs the back of his neck, shooting me a quick, uneasy look before focusing back on her.

"Have you talked to anyone about it?"

"What, like a therapist?" she asks dryly.

"Like the police," he says.

I struggle to keep my expression neutral. Could he just mind his own business?

Birdie shakes her head. "And tell them what? That I bought drugs in an alley and got caught? *Please, officer, find that person who exposed me?* Nah," she presses her hands against her eyes. "The worst is that they caught me at my lowest; I don't do drugs that often, and when I do, I know it's wrong. But seeing it online and getting all this hate for it... It makes me wonder if I am indeed all those things they say."

I lean forward to take her hand, but Daniel beats me to it, resting his over hers. "I don't know what people are saying about you right now," he says gently, "but I can tell you with absolute certainty—you're a good person, Birdie Bay. Everyone makes mistakes."

She gives him a soft, drunken smile. "Thanks... Thanks to both of you, really." Her gaze drifts to me, and I'm relieved to finally be included in the frame again. "You're good friends."

"Anytime, babe," I murmur, forcing a smile that feels tight around the edges.

"Of course," Daniel adds, his voice a touch too quick, too eager, cutting right over mine. "We're here if you ever need to talk."

I can see what's happening; I'm not dumb, in case you're wondering. She's chocolate spread on warm toast, and he's eating her up. It's painful to see him trying that hard, I admit, and I wonder if that's how I looked just a few weeks ago. She has the power to make you feel like a million bucks, and who wouldn't want to be that to somebody as dazzling as her? But she's Birdie Bay; she's as unreachable to Daniel as Saturn, so why bother with jealousy?

"May I ask you something?" Daniel swirls his wine in his glass, all pensive.

"Sure, professor."

"Is it worth it?"

Birdie arches a brow. "What, the drama?"

Daniel nods, and I lean in closer because I'm also interested.

"When I started posting on YouTube, it wasn't about

fame or money. It was about connection—finding people who got me, who made the world feel a little less small. I grew up with that attention, got used to it. It's my oxygen. But the game's changed. Now everyone wants a piece of it. There are thousands of creators chasing the same air, treating it like it's easy money and instant fame. So, to keep breathing, you've got to weather every shitstorm that comes your way. And you ask me if it's worth it? Tell me—how much is your oxygen worth?"

I cannot help but feel that punch of sadness, and if it's only a fraction of what Birdie's going through, I might need to worry about her more.

Daniel stays silent for a moment, jaw tight.

"You shouldn't beat yourself up for something that happened online. It's social media; it's not real life," he says in a strained voice.

Birdie shoots him a sad smile. "I take it you're not on Instagram, professor. If you were, you'd know that it's, in fact, realer than life."

11

I guess I shouldn't have worried about Birdie after all; this girl rebounds from depression like a softball. One day she's sobbing on my couch, reliving childhood traumas, and the next she's off to a glamorous dinner cruise on the Seine, celebrating Dyson's latest hair tool launch with Paris's finest influencers.

"I need someone to take a few pictures of me, and I thought of you if you're free Thursday night," she says in that Birdie way that isn't really a question. "There'll be food, drinks, styling sessions—though no one gives a damn about those. I mostly just need to show my face, you know, shut down the whole *Birdie's in rehab* rumor."

"You want me to photograph you at an event?" I repeat, just to make sure I'm not hallucinating.

"Well, not *officially*," she clarifies. "You'll just be my plus-one. But it'd be great if you could grab a few shots on my phone, and maybe rescue me when I get cornered by someone I can't stand."

"Birdie, wait, that's so cool!" I try not to squeal, but my voice betrays me anyway. "Of course, count me in!"

Her eyes narrow at my excitement. "You do realize it's not paid, right?"

I shrug, beaming, probably looking like a cartoon character with starry eyes. A real influencer event. Me. There. Questions tumble in my head:

What do we wear? — *Dress code's all white. We'll go shopping.*

Who'll be there? — *Everyone who matters, plus a few desperate TikTokers.*

Can I take photos with celebrities? — *Absolutely not.*

We arrive at the quay more than fashionably late, but Birdie doesn't care.

"They're not gonna sail off without their VIPs," she says.

I expect a regular tourist boat, one of those glass-roofed cruisers filled with families in baseball caps. Instead, I'm greeted by a gleaming, full-sized yacht emblazoned with the Dyson logo. It looks like something out of *Emily in Paris*. The air hums with lively chatter, laughter, and the pulsating beats of music. Some random people film us while we approach the boat as if we were stars. Well, Birdie is, but I'm still chuffed.

Just before boarding, she plucks a glass of champagne off a tray and downs it in one go.

"It's the only way to survive these things," she says, handing me a glass.

I don't think I've ever had free champagne in my life— unless you count the prosecco from Aunt Zelda's 50th, which, honestly, you shouldn't. I take a tentative sip and follow Birdie up the gangway.

A woman dressed head-to-toe in Dyson gray and pink greets us with a tray of designer sunglasses.

"Birdie Bay! So nice to see you again!" She air-kisses Birdie three times, French-style, before turning to me with a polite but puzzled smile. "And you must be...?"

"Chloé," I say brightly, extending my hand.

"My plus-one," Birdie cuts in smoothly. "Thanks for having us, Tara. Love the idea of a cruise in the city."

Tara beams. "Right? Maybelline did something similar last summer, so we thought—why not? Different crowd anyway," she adds with a conspiratorial wink.

"Yeah," Birdie murmurs, the corner of her mouth twitching.

I keep smiling, nodding as if I know what they're talking about, though I have absolutely no clue.

"I'll let you discover all the little surprises we have in store tonight," Tara chirps, holding out her tray of sunglasses. "Here's a little gift to get you started. And don't miss the photocall on the front deck—it's stunning at sunset!"

I grab a pair—classic Ray-Bans with the Dyson logo neatly engraved on the arm. *Freebies.* My inner student does a tiny fist pump.

Birdie, however, barely glances at the tray. She spots someone behind Tara, waves, then smiles politely. "Thanks, darling. I'll skip the shades, though. See you around."

As soon as we're out of earshot, she mutters under her breath, "As if I'd give them free brand placement. No money, no honey."

The boat starts to move away from the quay, and I feel the gentle sway beneath my feet. I let myself be carried inside, where the party is already in full swing. The DJ is blasting *"I Can Do It With a Broken Heart"* by Taylor Swift, and the room hums with chatter, laughter, and the clinking of glasses. Guests crowd around trays of hors-d'œuvres, snapping photos and exchanging air kisses. A sleek Dyson display showcases their newest product, while in another corner, hairstylists demonstrate its power on volunteers.

The moment we step into the space, Birdie is immediately ambushed by two girls wearing identical white tube dresses.

"OMG, if this is not my favorite LA babe!" the first girl, a tall redhead with the prettiest blue eyes I've ever seen, says by way of greeting, her French accent coming through.

As they exchange cheek kisses, it hits me—she's Ania Thommens, one of France's top influencers. I recall scrolling through her profile once: a curated blend of old-money aesthetics and "how to be effortlessly elegant" reels.

The second girl, all sharp cheekbones and glossy black hair, leans in and brushes my cheek with hers. "So nice to see you, love," she purrs, though I've never laid eyes on her before.

"Thanks, you... too?" I manage. Her perfume is familiar —*Gris Dior*, I think, from a tester at Galeries Lafayette.

Birdie clinks glasses with Ania, fighting a smirk. "Melinda, please don't scare Chloé; she's my friend."

"Ah, a plus one?" Melinda gives me a wry look and steps away as if I had Covid.

I hear someone chuckle behind my back. "As if Birdie Bay had friends." I whip around, but whoever said it has already melted into the crowd.

"What's up with the matching dresses?" Birdie asks the girls.

Ania rolls her eyes. "Courrèges sent it to me for the party..."

"But they didn't mention they'd sent the same one to me," Melinda cuts in, arms crossed.

"Rude," Ania whines.

Birdie nods. "So rude."

A server glides past with a tray of champagne, and the three of them snag glasses mid-conversation.

"Loved your makeup video from last week," says Melinda, who's practically glued to Birdie at this point.

"Aww, *merci*." Birdie's mouth tugs upwards, not quite reaching her eyes.

It was her first upload since the drug scandal. The backlash had been so vicious she'd disabled comments within an hour. She hasn't dared to post since.

"*Oui*, so nice," Ania adds, "But hey, how's been ... life?" A sparkle lights her eyes, and I find them less pretty all of a sudden. Pretending you don't know what everybody knows to get some juicy first-hand gossip? Oldest move ever.

Birdie senses it too. She shifts uneasily on her heels. "Um, it's amazing. You know what? Let's catch up soon, girls. I have to—"

That's my cue. "I think Tara's been looking for you—to talk about that project, remember?" I cut in quickly.

"Oh, yes," Birdie says, flashing me a grateful look.

Melinda, however, is less appreciative. Her glare could cut through steel. "Wait," she says, flagging down a photographer, "we *have* to take a picture first."

The girls set down their champagne glasses and huddle together, instinctively tilting their faces toward the best light. I'm just about to flash my brightest smile when Ania taps me lightly on the shoulder.

"Um, influencers only for this one? No offense, okay?"

Heat shoots up my neck, blooming across my cheeks. I force a tight smile and glance anywhere but at Birdie. "Yeah, of course," I mumble, stepping back.

One photo turns into a whole impromptu shoot—different angles, different poses, laughter that sounds just a little too loud. Before long, the photographer is herding them toward the deck for photocall shots by the sunset. Birdie follows, her smile stretched thin. I can practically feel her fuming from here.

Taking the opportunity, I drift toward the Dyson product stand, eager for something to do. It's sleek and spotless, lined with perfectly arranged displays of gadgets I know by name but could never afford. I pick up a heatless straightener, turning it over in my hands, half-imagining it's mine.

"Could you do that again for me, please?"

I startle. A man with a massive camera has appeared out of nowhere.

"Excuse me?"

"Just... pretend you're looking at the product for the video, yeah?" he says—and immediately starts filming.

I oblige, awkwardly rotating the straightener. He vanishes as abruptly as he appeared, without so much as a thank you.

"Having a great time?" says a voice behind me.

I pivot to face a man around Daniel's age. The comparison ends here since he's bald, with honey-toned skin and an arm entirely covered in tattoos. Next to all those fashionable people, he looks surprisingly *normal* in his brandless white t-shirt and beige chino pants.

Sighing, I cross my arms around me. "I'm not an influencer; don't feel obligated to waste your time on me."

He eyes me curiously. "Yes, I know. Saw you coming in with Birdie Bay earlier. What's your name?"

"Chloé," I answer.

"I'm PM," he offers. "And before you ask, I'm not an influencer either. I'm a creative director at a magazine, and I only got invited because my friend is working at Dyson."

"I wasn't going to ask," I lie, though I definitely need connections like that to kickstart my career as a photographer.

Suddenly, a streak of blonde cuts across my vision, and Birdie launches herself straight into PM's arms.

"Ah, Pierre-Marieee!" she squeals.

The guy's whole face lights up.

I blink, taken aback by the display. Birdie isn't exactly the touchy-feely type—at least not with anyone other than a camera. I'm just about to file the scene under *things I'll never understand about Birdie Bay* when I notice her eyes flickering around the room. It's so quick anyone could have missed it, but I'm not just anyone, and now I understand that at least a bit of it is for show.

She wants everybody to see her as friendly and surrounded by cool people rather than as the drug addict she's been labeled as for weeks now. An afterthought pops into my mind: is that why she invited me tonight?

"You are the only one allowed to call me that, darling," PM says as they fake-kiss.

"That's because we knew each other *before* his big personal rebranding," Birdie explains with a hint of teasing in her tone. "Back when I was just starting to grow on socials, and he had zero tattoos and had just landed his first creative director gig at... what was it again? *Grazia* magazine?"

"It was Tatler, and you should know; you were on the cover!"

"I forgot," she muses. "So many covers..."

He pinches her arm playfully. "Oh, you were already a star. Had to book you first-class plane tickets, or you wouldn't come, remember?"

"I'm still shocked somebody thought I'd fly from LA to Paris *anything but* first class." Birdie tilts her head and eyeballs him.

PM sniffs a smile, then shakes his head.

"I heard you're at Vogue now," she presses on, but before he can answer, a gorgeous girl with curly black hair appears at his side.

"Am I too late to join in?" she bats her dark eyelashes, and I want to ask her where her mascara is from because: wow.

PM beams again and locks the girl in a tight embrace. "Ladies, may I introduce you to Jess?"

"Hey, I love your dress," Birdie says, and I know she doesn't mean it. Jess is wearing a long boho sleeveless dress that makes her tan skin look extra tan, and Birdie hates anything boho. She says only Coachella gets a boho pass.

"Thanks," Jess smiles brightly. I wasn't sure whether to wear heels since it's a boat party and all..."

"We can't even see your shoes under that dress," Birdie says, her tone sweet as vinegar. The air instantly cools—PM and Jess exchange polite, brittle smiles.

I clear my throat, trying to salvage the vibe. "So, Jess, do you work at *Vogue* too?"

"Uh, I used to intern there," she says, clearly relieved for the distraction. "That's how PM and I met—I was his assistant."

"But she was destined for greater things," PM cuts in, grinning proudly. "Jess has been blowing up on Instagram lately. Even *Vogue* couldn't compete with all that attention."

Jess amicably slaps him on the arm, and he chuckles.

My interest is piqued. "What's your handle? I'll follow you."

I can practically feel Birdie's long look on me as Jess types her name, @JessDreams, on my phone.

"I'm nowhere as big as you," Jess tells Birdie, handing me my phone back.

Indeed, she has 180k followers, so compared to Birdie's millions, it's not a lot. But her content is fire, and mainly videos. I quickly scroll down, promising myself to watch everything more in detail later on.

Next to me, Birdie plucks another glass of champagne from a waiter and takes a bored sip. "Everyone seems to be an influencer nowadays."

I throw Jess an apologetic look, who just mirrors mine.

"What about you? I don't think we have met before," she asks, setting her clear eyes on me.

"Oh, you wouldn't have. It's actually my first influencer party. Birdie invited me."

"Well... It's a good first event to dip your feet into the digital world, right?" Jess smiles.

I hear Birdie snort. Is she drunk? I rush to say something, anything, before whatever unfiltered comment she's about to make slips out. "Definitely! I'm actually a photographer. At least, that's what I studied. So I should probably ... get into the boat and start posting more." I cringe at the unintentional pun, but I'm grateful when Jess laughs, stepping closer to me.

"So true. Well, don't hesitate if you need any help; social media is a tough world to navigate alone."

"Chloé has all the help she needs," Birdie slurs, locking her arm into mine and I throw her a look. *Do I, now?*

PM's eyes swing between Birdie and me. "Wow, you two actually kind of look alike."

Birdie erupts into laughter as if it's the funniest joke ever, and I can only manage an embarrassed smile.

"No, I'm serious," he insists. "Same height, same style..." PM turns to me. "You're like a brunette version of Birdie."

Birdie gives me a once-over as if seeing me for the first time.

"Damn, you're right. Crazy, I had never noticed..." she says, batting her eyes a lot. "We should take a picture together!" She scans the surroundings and spots a mirror, which she promptly pivots to face the Seine River. "Here, come."

She snaps a couple of pictures, and it's all so eerie that, for a moment, I feel detached from my own body.

When I first fell in love with photography, it was about the magic of preserving a fleeting moment—making it matter, holding it still in time. I liked being the one behind the lens, the silent observer. Being in front of it, though, always felt like giving up control, like letting someone else decide how I should exist.

But what I see on Birdie's phone screen isn't the shy, background version of me I'm used to. It's something else. Two stunning girls, laughing under the last light of day, at the party everyone will be talking about tomorrow. Birdie glows, her hair catching the sunset like molten gold; even in a simple white dress, she looks effortlessly polished.

And me—wearing the white sleeveless jumpsuit she picked out—I look different. Poised. Sun-kissed. At ease.

I look like I belong next to Birdie Bay.

I look like her equal.

"Ugh, we look amazing! I'm posting these," she declares, eyes gleaming as she scrolls through the shots.

Maybe it's the champagne fizzing in my veins, but a rush of giddy warmth floods through me.

"Let me tag you..." she says, energetically typing on her phone. "Wait, what's your Instagram handle?"

I open my mouth and almost let @FauxEver slip, but catching myself in time, I mumble. "It's @ChloéTakesPictures5."

Birdie blinks before letting out a single laugh. "Oh, we'll have to work on that handle, babe."

I smile back, unsure of what to do with the comment.

The sun is rapidly setting, casting a golden glow across the boat's deck. In the distance, the silhouette of the Eiffel Tower looms against the fiery evening sky, and everyone is now snapping pictures, either of themselves or the breathtaking view.

"Nobody's dancing," I observe, feeling bubbly. Some Britney remix is now playing in the background, and I sway my shoulders a bit. "The DJ's pretty good, though..." My enthusiasm fizzles as soon as the words escape my lips, noticing Birdie's rapid blinking.

"Dancing? Oh no, babe, nobody dances at these things. Imagine you do something embarrassing, and it gets caught on camera," she pulls a face. "We do drink, though, so I'm gonna grab us more champagne, ok?"

Before I can respond, she pivots on her heels and disappears into the bustling crowd.

All around me, conversations ebb and flow, and laughter echoes against the backdrop of the sparkling water. I close my eyes for an instant, letting myself soak in the atmosphere. But then, a conversation on my right catches my attention.

"...some nerve coming here after that @FauxEver post."

"Yeah, I wouldn't have shown my face in public for at least a year. But I guess when you have 3 million followers, you just don't give a shit."

"I think she dropped to 2.6 million now."

"Lol, karma's a bitch."

Trying to remain inconspicuous, I discreetly glance in the direction of the girls talking. With their backs turned to me, I can't see their faces, but I edge closer to catch more of their conversation.

"Amen... Do you think the girl behind @FauxEver is here among us?"

"How do you know it's a girl?"

I pinch my lips; indeed, how does she...?

"I don't know. It's such a girl thing to do, don't you think? I mean, I'm all for feminism and everything, but when it comes to drama, men just can't keep up. My money's on another jealous influencer—why else would someone go out of their way to sabotage Birdie, if not to steal her spotlight?"

"You forget Dan Humphrey; he was a man."

"Gossip Girl's ending is controversial! I'm still not convinced it could have been him all along."

"Well, maybe..."

I stop listening to them as I clench my teeth. Jealousy? Do they truly think that? Then, the purpose of @FauxEver is totally lost on them.

I try to look around for Birdie, Jess, or PM, but I think they might have been taken upstairs for a photoshoot. Anyway, I need to pee, so I weave my way to the loo, trying to shake off the gnawing sensation suddenly gripping me.

There is only one toilet, so unsurprisingly, there is a line of about six people ahead of me.

"What's in the goodie bags?" says a guy in an oversized suit, which seems way too thick for the current weather.

A dark-haired girl answers without turning back. "I think it's the Airwrap set."

"Ugh, they couldn't have chosen another product? I already have, like, three of them."

Another guy behind me jumps into the conversation. "Right? And it's so heavy. I'm dining at LouLou later, I don't want to carry that all the way to the Jardin des Tuileries!"

I close my eyes again, and this time, I'm not enjoying myself at all.

12

By the time I make it back home, Daniel is already asleep, which is a relief. If he had asked how the party went, I wouldn't have known what to say.

I sit in the dark living room, staring at the oversized goodie bag I brought back with me. Part of me wants to unpack it, to chase that flicker of excitement I'd felt earlier on the boat. But the aftertaste of the night lingers—sourer than I'd expected. This world I'd spent years yearning for is finally within reach, and yet it feels so out of touch. Both literally and figuratively.

My head tips back against the couch, and I let out a sigh. What would Dad have said about the spectacle I just witnessed? All that extravagance, and not a shred of joy. He would've laughed, probably—called it ludicrous—and changed the channel, the same way he did when we watched the last royal wedding together.

I pull out my phone and send him a photo Birdie took of me at sunset, the Eiffel Tower glowing behind me.

He replies right away. It's not like him to be in bed by eleven.

You look beautiful Chloékins! A true princess!

A small smile tugs at my lips.

Thanks, it was an interesting night

I see that he starts typing something, deletes it, and starts over in a minute or so. I steel myself for the message because I know already what he'll ask.

I'm happy for you. But tell me, are you eating well?

Were he in front of me right now, I'm pretty sure I'd see that familiar twinkle of concern in his eyes. I type back hastily:

Have a good night, Dad

He's not here, though, and I don't want to talk about it right now.

On Instagram, I open my personal account. My pulse skips when I see the flood of new followers and likes. For a split second, I think I've accidentally logged into @FauxEver, but no, it's just @ChloéTakesPictures5. Birdie's right, though. I really do need to come up with a better handle.

Both Birdie and Jess have followed me back, and I'm surprised to see a DM from Jess:

Was lovely meeting you today! We should grab a coffee sometime xx

I don't miss a beat and shoot back immediately.

It was great meeting you, too. Your content is sick ☻

Might be a stretch, but I have two tickets for the new exhibition at the Bourse de Commerce tomorrow, and the person I was supposed to go with kind of dropped me. Wanna join?

Satisfied, I hit send and switch over to @FauxEver, diving straight into the DMs. I scroll until something catches my eye—a message from some young TikToker, a guy I don't recognize. He's sent me a video of Ania, filmed earlier at the boat party. I press play. At first, the sound is a blur of laughter and music, but then the camera steadies, and Ania's champagne-soaked voice cuts through.

"...he'd buy me anything for a lingerie shot, anything! ... What? Um, well, for an apartment, I'd have to lose the clothing, maybe, but what's a couple of pictures in exchange for real estate, right?"

I can't see who she's talking to, but her red hair is unmistakable. The video keeps rolling.

"Yeah, but I don't care about her, really. She can stay the wife as long as he keeps spoiling me."

My jaw drops. Ania—an escort? And a married guy involved? I can't say I'm shocked. Influence pays well, but Ania's always lived like royalty: draped in Hermès, floating from one mansion to another. Now the jig's up.

It could be good for @FauxEver, actually. Exactly the kind of video that could turn the profile from a one-off stunt into something bigger. But the girls' conversation on the boat keeps echoing in my head. Am I jealous? Maybe I was, once—of Birdie, especially. The fame, the gifts, the travel—Who wouldn't be? But that's not it anymore. What stings is that everyone thinks my mission is just petty sabotage.

I'd like to believe I was wrong to expose Birdie and the others, but the evidence keeps proving otherwise.

Let me give you a simple example.

A couple of days ago, right after her comeback video flopped, Birdie called me and asked if I'd come with her to an American food store.

"I'm having withdrawal issues," she groaned over the phone, and I couldn't help finding her choice of words ironic, given her current situation. "I need to eat some junk food real quick. Come with me... for the plot!"

Of course, I gave in. The fear of missing out on anything "for the plot" really should be studied.

We wandered the aisles, commenting on random products. For a moment, I felt oddly comforted, like we were real friends, just grocery shopping together. Birdie was picking up some questionable American cheese (ew) when I spotted an industrial pumpkin pie on the bottom shelf.

Birdie had endorsed that brand a few years back, swearing on Instagram that their store-bought pumpkin pie was "unparalleled." There'd even been a charity tie-in, something about raising money for children. I remembered reading that the campaign had been a success—millions collected.

I grabbed the pie and ran to her.

"Hey, look what I found."

She wrinkled her nose. "Mmmh, I hate pumpkin pie."

"Really?" I stood there, unsure what to do with it. "I thought you were *obsessed* with it," I said, quoting her own caption.

Birdie stopped browsing and frowned. "Ah, that old campaign? You've got a dope memory." Her eyes narrowed, and I froze. Remembering things about her was cute in small doses, but I didn't want her thinking I was some obsessive fan.

She blinked, then let it go. "It was just a gig. Good marketing, if you still remember it."

"Oh," I said, feeling stupid. "But... what about the charity?" I knew I was poking the bear, but curiosity won out.

"What charity?"

I gave her a look. "You know, the part where the company promised to donate a percentage of sales to orphanages? The money for the orphans?"

Birdie looked away, back to the shelves. "I guess."

"What do you mean, *you guess*? You're not sure?" My voice came out colder than I intended.

She looked up, startled. People didn't usually talk to her like that. "What's with you, Chloé?" she snapped.

I blinked, forcing a smile. Definitely not a fighter. "Sorry! It's just—I remember that campaign. It seemed so genuine."

Her expression softened. "Yeah, well, all I know is that I was supposed to visit the orphanages myself to hand over the checks. But after it ended, no one ever contacted me again. So I don't know if they followed through."

The charity thing.

I stared at her. "And you don't think that's... problematic?"

"Of course it is," she said, shrugging. "But so are a lot of things in marketing. I was just a pawn to grab attention. What can I do?" She reached for a jar. "Let's get some Marshmallow Fluff before we leave."

You see now? That's the kind of deception I'm talking about. It has nothing to do with envy. Hell, it even has nothing to do with me.

I grip my phone so tightly it almost hurts, type a quick thank-you to the guy who sent me Ania's video, and upload it as a reel.

They're fake. They're rotten. And that's the story I'm trying to tell.

I tag @AniaThommens and hit *publish.*

I SLEEP SOUNDLY, in case you're wondering. Deeply, like an innocent. I doubt Ania does.

When I wake up, the first thing I notice is that her video has gone viral—fast. By the time I'm sipping my first coffee, it's racked up over ten thousand likes and six hundred thousand views, which, in turn, brings me thousands of new followers.

I wouldn't say I'm surprised, but maybe I underestimated Ania's reach. Judging from her profile, I honestly thought most of her followers were rich men. I mean, who else would follow a white, skinny girl who claims she "only sleeps on silk pillows" and keeps *"be nice to everyone—you never know who has a boat"* in her bio? Turns out—a lot of people.

The wave of hate that hits her is even worse than what Birdie got because, in her case, nobody has a single nice thing to say about her. It's like her audience had been waiting for her to stumble just so they could tear her apart.

By noon, Ania deletes her Instagram account.

Around that time, Jess finally replies to my last message—which, honestly, is more than I expected.

So sorry! Last night's afterparty was wild. I'm free all afternoon. Does your offer still stand?

I smile at my phone, buy two last-minute tickets to the exhibition, and text back:

No worries. Let's meet at 3 p.m. in front of the museum's metro entrance?

She sends a thumbs-up emoji.

I GET THERE EARLY, but Jess is already waiting, which gives me a moment to observe her before she spots me. She's smaller than I remember, though still a head taller than me. Her style leans boho—something I'd already gathered from scrolling through her Instagram last night. My research also revealed that she's great at lip-syncing and dancing, classic Gen Z stuff, but what really sets her apart is her dedication to replying to every comment. It makes her seem approachable—and conveniently boosts her engagement rate.

Today, she's wearing a flashy pink linen dress with side cutouts—a sharp contrast to my modest, sand-colored Zara mini. For a second, I regret not choosing something brighter and silently pray I don't look like a Sad Beige Girl.

Jess's face lights up when our eyes meet.

"Chloé!" She kisses me on both cheeks. "I was so happy you suggested this little cultural moment. So original!"

I frown slightly, unsure what's so original about going to a museum in Paris.

Inside, I instantly feel lighter. I always do around art. The Bourse de Commerce has that effect on me—it's easily my favorite museum in the city.

I've walked through the permanent collection dozens of times, and as we move through the building, Jess mentions she's been here a few times, too. We silently agree to skip the central rotunda and head straight to the temporary exhibit. The museum itself is a masterpiece—restored over a decade, its dome floods the space with soft natural light.

As we wander, I pull out my Leica. I brought it along mostly to live up to the claim I'd made to Jess last night—that I'm a photographer. When she isn't looking, I capture a shot from a low angle, her hair blending with the fresco above. I can see it before I press the shutter: the muted tones of the dome, Jess in the center, a vivid burst of pink.

When I show her the photo, she lets out a delighted shriek.

"Damn, Chloé, that's gorge!" She studies it for a moment longer. "Do you think you could send it to me? I'll tag you, of course."

After the exhibition, Jess suggests heading to Madame Rêve for a cocktail. The manager recognizes her and offers the first round on the house.

"We're so lucky, aren't we?" she says, cradling her Gin Fizz. "To live the life we live. My parents both work nine-to-five, every day, and still make less than I do. They think Brasserie Lipp is peak sophistication. They have never stepped inside a five-star hotel for fear they might get charged something just for breathing the air." She laughs, tipping her glass toward me. "And here we are, drinking for free and getting paid for it."

I don't tell her it's not really *my* life—that I was Birdie's plus-one last night, and now I'm hers.

"Influence seems like a full-time cruise," I offer with a shrug.

Jess chuckles into her drink. "I wish! But honestly, I feel like I'm late to the wild years of influence. You know what I mean."

"Hmm." I purse my lips. "Do tell."

She hesitates, then leans in a little.

"Well, people always say it was easier back then—the first wave of influencers had no competition. Followers were new to the idea, and they didn't question anything. Just pure admiration."

I get the sense she's talking about Birdie. I fight the urge to defend her, even though part of me agrees.

"And that's not the case anymore?" I ask, though I already know the answer.

Jess snorts softly. "Oh no. Now, we're held accountable for everything."

I blink, and she quickly adds, "Which is good, of course. I know Birdie's your friend, but girls like her aren't used to limits. They grew up with millions worshipping them and never stopped to ask if it was deserved."

I nod—partly because it's true, partly because I want her to keep talking.

"So now," she continues, "followers question everything. Every brand deal, every caption. You can't just post an ad anymore; you have to make it *authentic*, on-brand, ethical, sustainable. And even then, someone comments, 'It's all for money anyway,' and that one gets the most likes. People get off on hating creators now. As if making money was something we should be ashamed of."

I take a sip of my spicy Margarita. I only ordered this because the hot waiter recommended it, but the burn in my throat instantly makes me regret it. I say nothing, just listen, filing away her every word.

"Don't get me wrong," she adds. "I'm grateful for the first generation. They walked so we could run."

Birdie's words echo in my head—*the game's changed.*

"I never realized there was so much drama in this world," I say carefully. "From the outside, it all looks so perfect."

Jess clicks her tongue. "Welcome to the other side, baby." Then she leans closer, lowering her voice. "Speaking of drama—did you see this morning's video of Ania?"

I posted it last night, but whatever. I nod.

"Classic first-gen privilege," Jess says, swirling her glass. "She built her following when no one else was around, and now she's milking it for all it's worth. I'm not judging—but honestly, she could stand to be a little quieter. Especially with that creep following us around."

Her choice of words catches me off guard. I cough.

"Spicy," I say, holding up my drink.

Jess grins. "Let's get you something else," she says, flagging down the waiter.

She orders two Gin Fizzes, insisting that I *must* try it, but what I *must* do is get back to that conversation.

"You know," I say, taking a long sip of my drink (she was right, it's good!). "On the boat yesterday, I overheard some girls saying it might be another influencer behind the account."

As if!

Jess gets pensive before shaking her head. "Um, I doubt it's another influencer. Nobody would risk their reputation like that. Imagine if word got out that you're targeting fellow content creators. It's social suicide."

I listen intently, though her words don't sit well with me. Still, I press on, feigning indifference. "So, who then?"

"A random nobody who is jealous," she answers, resigned.

I take another deep breath, forcing my expression into neutrality, though the term burns like acid.

"You'd be surprised what jealousy drives people to do," she adds, running a hand through her curls. "It's basically currency in our world. Whoever's behind @FauxEver is just an outsider looking in. Give them the opportunity, and they'll emulate everything Birdie and the others do, but ten times worse."

I can't help but snap. "Why would you think that? Not everyone wants to be famous."

Jess tilts her head, smirking. "Really? My mistake."

Unable to defend myself without exposing myself, I change tack. "You know, what you think about the industry, that's something you could share. I mean, not only with me but with your audience. It's such good insight and..."

Jess laughs and places a hand on mine. "Chloé, I don't feel like being canceled today."

Fair enough.

Later, scrolling through Instagram, I see her post: Cultural afternoon, shot by @ChloéTakesPictures5.

Three hundred new followers appear on my account. I guess that's something.

13

"Happy ten thousand followers, babe! May these be the first of many!"

Birdie bursts into the living room, grinning from ear to ear, carrying an extravagantly pink cake topped with ten flickering candles.

It's been two weeks since the boat party. To some, they might have felt like just another blur of ordinary days, but to me, they've been like beads on a string—each one a tiny, self-contained life, threaded carefully into a necklace of small joys.

First of all, my Instagram game has been on point. I revamped my personal username to @ChloéLeWarner (because @ChloéWarner was already taken, and Birdie insisted the "Le" added a French touch). And I've started sharing glimpses of my daily life as if I were an influencer myself. Fake it till you make it!

Me on my balcony during golden hour.

Me in my Lululemons before my run.

Me and Birdie at Café Marly, posing with the Louvre pyramid.

Me and Jess making goofy faces in selfies.

Photos with Birdie or Jess always pulled the most engagement, but lately, my solo shots have started to hold their own.

People often think that posting a few pretty pictures from beautiful places is enough to make them famous, and then they're shocked when nothing happens. What they don't realize (what I've finally come to understand) is that the ones who make it treat it like work from day one. They show up every single day, creating and posting, even when no one's watching. Success isn't luck; it's endurance.

And I've been showing up on the app like my nine-to-five.

This morning, it paid off: ten thousand followers.

Compared to the two hundred fifty-five thousand followers on @FauxEver, my ten thousand feels almost laughable. But @FauxEver is still a secret, while this account—my name, my face—represents something I can finally claim as my own.

"Aww, you shouldn't have," I tell Birdie, even if I'm stoked she did that for me.

"Nonsense! Any excuse for red velvet cake is a good one," she says with a grin. "Besides, milestones deserve to be celebrated. I remember hitting my first 10k like it was yesterday, and I totally failed to make a big deal of it."

"You didn't?"

She makes a face. "Please. That was the year my dad sent me to stay with some friends of his in Phoenix. Six months of a Christian school nightmare. No celebration in sight."

I nod, remembering that old vlog where she reinvented

her school uniform into something borderline scandalous. I must have watched it a dozen times.

"At least it gave you some good content," I say lightly.

She smirks. "True. It sucked big time, but the audience loved it." Her smile falters for a moment. "I joke, but honestly? Sometimes I wish I could go back. Things were simpler then. Enjoy being at the start, babe. You still have everything ahead of you—no reputation to maintain, nothing to prove."

For a second, I think I see it: a flicker of envy crossing her face. She moves to slice the cake, but I stop her with an excited cry.

"Wait! We've got to snap some pics of it first."

Birdie sniffs a laugh. "You're a fast learner."

I smirk. "*If it isn't on IG, did it even happen?*"

And I think of the people who claim they're not addicted to social media. They'll never understand the rush of posting something and watching the likes pour in within minutes—the instant validation, the jolt of energy that makes you want to create more, post more, just to keep riding that wave of approval every single day.

Sitting back, I publish Birdie's cake on my page with the caption Thank You Soulsister @BirdieBay. These are words I might blush saying in person (and I most likely wouldn't), but it's just a caption, and it's cute, so it's okay.

Birdie's the first one to like.

"Soulsister, heh? Next, people will call us besties."

She says *besties* like it's a cringey word, but I can see on her face she's pretty thrilled about it.

"You look nice," I tell her after a beat, partly to switch topics and partly because that Helsa mini dress she's wearing is gorgeous. "Do you have a date later or something?"

"Well, first of all, I don't dress *well* for men. I dress well so I can stare at myself in every window I walk by," she says with a smirk. "So, no, I don't have any date planned. Although, to be fair, I wouldn't mind attracting the attention of a guy like your professor."

Surprised, I turn to her. "Daniel? Really?" A strange flicker of satisfaction runs through me—as if it somehow validates my relationship. "Didn't peg you for the nerdy type," I tease.

"Me neither!" Birdie laughs. "But hey, it's not working well with pretty Instagram boys, so if the professor has a brother..." She winks.

The image comes to my mind uninvited. Birdie and I being more than friends; family. How cool would that be? I shake away the reverie. "Only three sisters."

"A pity," she says, starting to cut the cake.

As usual, I watch her closely, but this time, it isn't fascination that holds me; it's curiosity. For as long as we've known each other, I've carried this fear that our friendship was fragile, temporary. Something that could vanish without warning. So I've savored every moment with her almost greedily, like someone crossing a desert unsure when they'll find water again, afraid Birdie might wake up one day and see me differently.

But lately, something has changed between us—especially since Gabrielle's been out of the picture. Being around Birdie feels easier now. Natural, even. Maybe this is what real friendship is supposed to feel like.

"What?" she asks, catching me staring.

Just then, my phone buzzes, rescuing me from having to respond. I glance down and can't help but smile.

"Jess is inviting us to a party," I say, reading the message aloud.

Since we started hanging out, she's added me to a WhatsApp group with PM and a few of her other friends—an honorary member of her little circle.

Birdie barely looks up from her slice of cake, unimpressed. "Sorry, can't."

I take a piece of cake for myself and settle cross-legged by her coffee table, hesitating for a beat before speaking again. I'm not sure asking this is a good idea—but I do it anyway.

"Why do you dislike Jess so much?"

"I don't," she answers quickly. Too quickly.

I eyeball her, and she shrugs. Seems to hesitate. "You don't just grow on social media out of nowhere today."

"What do you mean?"

"I mean, I heard about her before we met. People talk and what's being said..." She exhales through her nose. "Jess started posting what, a few months ago to be where she is right now? I'd be surprised if her 'self-made' backstory was as cute and flowery as she makes it out to be."

I blink, pondering the implications of Birdie's words. Does she know something I don't? Perhaps a deeper dive into this topic over a bottle of wine is warranted; it might loosen her tongue. But then, is whatever story she might have on Jess worth the risk of losing her as a friend?

"I didn't say when the party was," I counter, deciding there's no need to press the issue just yet.

Birdie looks at me, all innocent. "When is it?"

"Tonight."

"Sorry, still can't," Birdie repeats, licking the knife.

I HAVEN'T POSTED ON @FauxEver in days. I could blame it on the time I've been pouring into my personal account, but the truth is, the tips trickling into my DMs lately have been dull—nothing worth chasing. And maybe, just maybe, I've been toying with the idea of letting it go altogether.

So what happens next catches me off guard. I'm getting dressed for Jess's party, half-distracted, scrolling through @FauxEver's comments and deleting a few critiques, when an unfamiliar account starts mass-commenting on all my posts:

More Hot Takes On Parisian Influencers On Our Page

I click the profile. It's a knockoff version of my own—six posts in, already trying too hard. A few blurry photos, some limp gossip, nothing remotely original. It lacks what @FauxEver has: a sense of high-stakes purpose and genuinely juicy takes. No wonder they've only scraped together two hundred followers and feel the need to advertise under mine.

I sigh, staring at the screen. What should I do with this copycat? Calling them out feels beneath me—but letting them ride the wave I created doesn't sit right either.

"Are you going out again?"

My head jerks up. Daniel's standing in the doorframe of our room, frowning.

"Jess' party. Remember I told you about it?"

"Right," he says, taking a step forward. "Can I come?"

I absentmindedly twirl the star-shaped earrings Birdie gave me from her upcoming collection. "Do you want to come?"

Knowing Daniel, who's usually in bed by ten, I hadn't even considered inviting him. But Jess likes him (she says he's a nerdy Harry Potter type), so maybe I could text her, ask if she can add him to the list…

Daniel shakes his head. "No, I was just testing the waters. I've got papers to grade. But actually, there's something I wanted to talk to you about."

"Yeah?"

"My director's updating the school website," he says, flashing me a small, hopeful smile. "He's looking for a photographer to take some pictures of the classrooms. I told him about you—he'd like to meet and discuss the details."

School pictures? I bite my lip, a flicker of irritation rising. "Uh… well." I graduated from UAL; doesn't he see how much of a downplay that is? It's almost insulting. "I don't really do that kind of photography, Daniel."

His smile fades. He studies me for a long moment. "You don't actually do *any* kind of photography lately."

I let out a quiet scoff, thrown by the edge in his voice. But he stays perfectly calm.

"Not true," I counter, forcing a faint smile. "You'd know that if you actually downloaded Instagram—and followed me."

"That's not…" He blinks a few times. "Ugh, you never even applied for that contest you were so excited about."

"There will be other contests," I say, growing increasingly frustrated with the conversation. "I've been caught up with everything, and—"

"Chloé," Daniel cuts in. "You do realize that whatever you're doing doesn't count as a real job, right?"

"It *is* a real job for Birdie—"

"You're not Birdie!" he snaps.

I stare over at him, hoping my face doesn't betray how much of a slap that actually was. He's been like this for weeks now, acting all weird. I get that social media isn't his thing, but I would have expected him to be more supportive.

"I know," I say quietly. I get up and face the mirror. My reflection stares back: the short cottage-core House of CB dress I scored on sale, cowboy boots, the Jacquemus bag Jess insisted I *needed* (she usually turns out to be right). It took me an hour to nail the makeup—YouTube tutorial and all—and I'm actually proud of how I look.

"You look like you're about to perform in a circus," Daniel says.

Our eyes meet in the mirror. My brows knit. "That's not a compliment."

"I didn't mean it as one."

I turn, anger flaring. "Is there a problem?"

"I don't know, Chloé, you tell me," he fires back. "I offer you a real, decent way to earn money, and you turn it down because you think you're too good for it?"

"Yes!" The word bursts out louder than I mean it to. "I *do* think taking school pictures is below my qualifications. I'm following another path—but I guess you haven't noticed."

Daniel's gaze hardens. "Oh, I did notice."

I think he's angry. I've never seen him that way before; the way he's looking at me makes me instantly regret losing my cool.

"Listen," I say finally, grabbing my bag. "I can't do this right now. The Uber's downstairs and he's already called twice."

In the car, I grit my teeth. *Not a real job,* my ass.

If only Daniel knew the kind of battle I'm fighting here. But of course he doesn't—he has no idea I'm @FauxEver, that I'm on a mission, that it's me against *the lie.* All he sees is me waking up late, scrolling on my phone for hours, and walking out the door dressed in clothes I wouldn't have been caught dead in a few months ago.

I sigh and make a mental note to pretend I'm working on something he might consider "more real"—just to keep the peace.

In the meantime, I open the app and finally post a new @FauxEver update, using one of the tip-offs I got in my DMs last week: a quick video of a micro-fitness influencer arriving at the gym, snapping a few mirror selfies, and leaving without so much as breaking a sweat. It's not groundbreaking, but it's enough.

A reminder to everyone watching: I'm still here. And no copycat is going to take my place.

14

I get to the address Jess sent me a bit late, thanks to Daniel, but luckily, she's still waiting out front, framed by the pulsing neon spilling from the club's entrance. When she spots me, her eyes brighten and she waves both hands in the air, the fringe on her crop top flickering like silver sparks in the light. She looks incredible.

"So sorry for being late, I had... a thing at home."

"We just got here, love, no worries." Jess gestures to the pretty brunette beside her in a red nylon trench. "Meet my girlfriend, Louise."

We exchange greetings and quick cheek kisses before following them inside.

The entrance opens into a long corridor drenched in neon, the bass thumping softly beneath our feet. As we move closer to the main room, the sound swells—an electronic heartbeat that pulls us in. My eyes take a moment to adjust to the low light and shifting colors. Futuristic art lines the walls; bodies move in sync with the rhythm; laughter and cheers rise and fall like waves.

This isn't usually my scene. I've never really been a party girl, but lately, I've been saying yes to more things. So far, it hasn't disappointed.

At the center of the venue, I spot the source of the energy: a DJ on an elevated platform, commanding the decks like a conductor. He must be someone big—the crowd around him is euphoric.

"Wow, the vibe is so good," I shout to Jess.

"What?" she yells back, grinning.

"The vibe—it's so good!"

Jess laughs. "It's just a Thursday night! Come on, it's calmer in our corner."

Jess leads me to the roped-off VIP area, where Louise immediately drops onto a couch and starts chatting with a small group. I spot PM among them and flash him an excited smile. He waves back, mouthing *later,* before turning back to his conversation.

"What are you drinking?" Jess asks. "We've got vodka, gin, champagne..."

Grateful to finally be able to talk without shouting, I glance nervously at the table. "Hmm... what's the average price of a cocktail here?"

Daniel was right about one thing: as much as my Instagram was growing, it still wasn't paying the bills. And since I'd been turning down Fiverr jobs to keep up with my posting schedule, I needed to be extra cautious about spending. Tonight's budget allowed for one, maybe two cocktails—if I made them last.

"Oh, it's fine," Jess says breezily. "We can have whatever we want. The management just asks us to post a couple of stories tagging the club." She takes my hand and pulls me toward the couches. "But you're our guest—you don't have to post if you don't want to."

"No, I will," I say quickly, crossing my legs to hide my nerves. "I just hit ten thousand followers... I know it's not much yet, but—"

Jess claps her hands together. "I saw that this morning and *screamed*, didn't I, babe?"

Louise leans in, smiling. "It was quite the scene."

"That's actually what I wanted to talk to you about," Jess says, dropping onto the couch beside me. "Louise and I are represented by this agency that's *huge* in Paris right now, and they're always scouting for new faces, so..." She pauses dramatically, grinning like a cat with a secret. "I sent them your profile earlier—and they want to meet you."

I blink, searching her face for any hint of a joke, but she isn't kidding. "Wait. Are you *serious*?"

An agency. A *real* one. That meant jobs. That meant money. That was something I could rub in Daniel's face later.

"Yeah, girl, of course," Jess says, beaming. "You've been growing so fast. They'd be stupid to miss out on Birdie Bay's new bestie."

I cringe a little at her choice of words and turn to Louise for a distraction, needing a moment to gather myself. "So, you're an influencer too?"

She shakes her head. "I'm a DJ, babe. I'll be mixing here in about an hour."

Jess jumps in before I can respond. "They don't just represent influencers anymore—that's kind of passé. They work with all sorts of talents now: artists, actors, models... anyone who's more than just a pretty face."

Louise plants a quick kiss on Jess's cheek and winks at

me. "I'm gonna check on the sound team real quick." Then she slips off the platform and vanishes into the crowd below.

My heart beats a little faster, and I take a long sip to moisten my suddenly dry mouth.

"It's just..." I glance toward PM, but he's deep in conversation with a group nearby. "I don't know if I'm really cut out for this," I admit to Jess, relieved that the neon glow masks the warmth rising in my cheeks. "You, Birdie... you all seem born for it. You know how to pose, how to network. And me—who am I in comparison?"

I hadn't meant it as a plea for reassurance, but the words spill out before I can stop them, and I instantly regret it. What if it makes Jess reconsider her offer?

But she looks at me with an intensity that catches me off guard, batting her long lashes.

"Listen," she says, leaning closer. "I'm not going to feed you that *'there's a place for everyone'* bullshit. Instead, let me tell you a story about how I got started."

I already know the basics of Jess's rise to influence—thanks to a few late-night deep dives into her old interviews. Supposedly, she was discovered by a so-called fairy godmother while performing in a school play in the Parisian suburbs. She dabbled in modeling at sixteen, then pivoted to posting daily "get ready with me" videos.

Still, I'm sitting at her table, sipping her gin, so it feels only polite to let her have her *me, myself, and I* moment.

"There's the story I tell the press, you've probably heard it, the one where I was scouted?" She doesn't wait for me to nod. "Well, there was no fairy godmother. Just an older guy with a thing for younger women. He was my classmate's uncle and worked for a small modeling agency in Paris."

I shift uneasily, palms growing damp. Suddenly, I don't

want her to keep talking. I like Jess, and I'm not sure I can be trusted with this kind of personal information about her.

But she keeps going. "He said he had connections—and he did, a few. Not as many as he claimed, but enough to land me a couple of small campaigns. He swore he'd make me a star." Her tone hardens slightly. "But I didn't need him to *make* me. I was born for this. So I dumped him the moment PM got me into *Vogue*."

Her gaze locks with mine. She isn't looking for pity; she wants it to land as a lesson. "It's not the proudest chapter of my life, but the point is: most of us don't get fairytale beginnings. We have to build our own. You have to be willing to grab every opportunity if you want to climb higher."

I feel the shift happen between Jess and me, almost as if she's peering straight through me, silently saying that everything I've done to get here is *okay*. It's the first time I feel like I've met someone who might understand why I created @FauxEver, and it's on the tip of my tongue to tell her everything when PM works his way over to our side of the table and slides his arm around my shoulders.

"Chloé, darling, it's been a minute. Loving those boots."

Jess uses the moment to lean in and whisper, "This stays between us girls, okay?"

I lock my mouth up and throw the key over my shoulder.

She grins. "Good. Now, let's do shots."

Partying with Jess and her friends is unlike any night I've ever known—and, honestly, I'm glad Birdie didn't come.

There's a striking contrast between Jess and Birdie. For Birdie, the rare moments of solitude are her only escape from the endless grind of fame. Every public appearance is work; every smile, a performance. She's traded the quiet joy of curling up alone with a book for a life lived entirely under scrutiny.

Jess, on the other hand, revels in it all. She wears her privilege like a glittering crown, thriving in the chaos—dancing, laughing, fully alive.

And then there's me, freshly initiated into this glittering world. Between the endless drinks and the glow of attention that comes with being young, pretty, and seated in a VIP booth, it feels like I've finally unlocked the pulse of the life I've always dreamed of.

Near closing time, a young waitress approaches and asks how Jess would like to pay—cash or card. Jess bursts out laughing, tossing her hair back in mock disbelief.

"Darling," she says, "we don't *pay*. The club pays *us*."

15

It's about time I pulled a move I should've made ages ago—a @FauxEver post, all about yours truly.

Why bother, you ask? Because the grander the hustle, the harder it is to spot.

So I settle in and let the idea of crafting my own exposé simmer. It's a delicate balance to strike—biting enough to feel authentic but not so harsh that it chips away at my carefully constructed image.

And then, suddenly, I know where to begin.

I navigate to my old primary school's website, heading straight to the "Achievements" section. There it is, tucked away in the archives of 2012—the year I won my first photography prize. Once upon a time, that photo of me clutching a cheap little trophy, smiling shyly at the camera, would have been my worst nightmare. But now? Now, I screenshot it myself and unleash it on @FauxEver with a sly caption. One click and it's out there for the world to see.

A message from Jess comes first, as I had expected.

> Girl! I just saw the post about you!! How are you feeling?

I reply quickly.

> Shocked

> I always hoped no one would find that awful photo of me...

Jess doesn't miss a beat.

> You looked fantastic even then. Don't let anyone tell you otherwise.

I send a few heart emojis. She "likes" them immediately.

You know, there's something I hadn't noticed before my @FauxEver era—one of the most insidious toxins of social media: *toxic positivity*. The "good vibes only" disease. I'm tempted to call it a trend, but who even knows which direction the world's spinning anymore?

It's saying "*look on the bright side*" when someone loses their job.

It's saying "*happiness is a choice*" when someone's heart is breaking.

It's saying "*everything happens for a reason*" when someone's lifelong dream falls apart.

It's Jess, looking at that photo of me and saying, "*No, you looked great.*"

There's a fine line between positivity and optimism, and it's the same line that separates listening from merely hearing.

Back in high school, when that picture was taken, I didn't feel good in my body. I was overweight, and people at school called me *Pumbaa.* I'm not saying curvy isn't beautiful—I'm saying *I* didn't feel beautiful. Ignoring that truth, smothering it in forced positivity, that's the real insult. I didn't post that photo for strangers to gush that "all bodies are beautiful," because why state the obvious? What I wish is that people could stop numbing real feelings with sugar-coated lies.

Anyway, thanks for coming to my TED Talk.

Then Birdie calls. And that's the thing about her—she *calls,* never texts. She says it's faster, but I suspect it's because calls don't leave evidence.

"Wow, you were huge," she says by way of greeting. "How much did you weigh back then?"

See what I mean about evidence? Ignoring the sudden dryness in my throat, I sigh and give her the number.

"Shit. I didn't notice any stretch marks when we went swimming."

"Good genes and oils, I guess," I reply, fingers brushing the faint lines etched into my skin. No amount of oil ever really erased them.

"I would never have pictured you *chubby* before. That's wild."

"Well, it's not exactly something I advertise..." I say, steadying myself for the tightrope act ahead, a delicate dance between acknowledging the past and sculpting the present. "I've struggled with my weight ever since I was six."

"Shit, sorry, babe. Is that why you're so weird around food?"

She noticed? My lips twitch into a half-smile.

"Yeah. It's worse under pressure, but honestly, it's always there."

She pauses. "For what it's worth, you're a damn warrior for looking like the snack you are today."

I'm surprised—and somehow, it's the perfect thing to say.

"Thanks, Birdie," I answer softly.

"Wanna hang later?"

"Can't. I'm meeting with RevCom, remember?"

Birdie lets out a hum. "Right. Guess I'll binge the new *Bridgerton* alone then."

"Cool. Don't spoil it for me."

She hangs up without answering.

I'M MEETING PERRINE, one of the agents from RevCom, at Hôtel Costes.

The dress I'm wearing is one of my prettiest—a PR gift from Maje (still pinching myself that this is my life now). It's pink with a delicate floral print and enough frills to make me feel perfectly at home in a place like this—a five-star hotel perpetually humming with celebrity energy.

Today, it more than lives up to its reputation. White cloths drape every table, champagne bottles glint in defiance of the 2 p.m. hour, and as I weave between guests, I spot more designer bags than at a Christie's preview.

And there she is, Perrine, tucked away at one of the back tables.

A little pre-meeting research told me plenty. On LinkedIn, she's the picture of early-millennial professionalism: crisp white shirt, minimal makeup, arms folded just so—like *The Devil Wears Prada's* Andrea Sachs on her first day at *Runway*. But her Instagram tells another story: strobe lights, late nights, and more club selfies than you'd expect from someone who lists "brand strategist" in her bio.

Our eyes meet. She takes in my outfit with a practiced once-over, then smiles—a mirror-perfect gesture.

"Chloé!"

"You must be Perrine," I say, my voice a little too bright as nerves kick in.

She laughs lightly, gesturing to the seat across from her. "Sit, sit. I was just about to order. What will you have?"

I take a seat opposite her, and a statuesque waitress, all legs and poise, arrives to take the order without even glancing at us. Perrine, unfazed, carries on, so I try to relax my face, too.

"I love this place," Perrine remarks. "RevCom's office is not far, so we often have appointments here."

"Yes," I reply, aiming for a grown-up and confident tone, though I suspect I come off more as dazed. "I heard their French fries are very good."

Birdie told me. I don't even eat anything fried.

"They are! Shall I order you some?"

She waves at the waitress, but the legs-for-days server somehow develops selective blindness. Perrine follows her with a frown, and I quickly glue my attention back to her. Out of the corner of my eye, I'm ninety percent sure that's Timothée Chalamet at a nearby table, but I refuse to check. I'd rather die than let myself appear star-struck.

I clear my throat. "So... you guys specialize in micro-influencers?" I ask, parroting something Birdie told me.

She hadn't exactly shared my enthusiasm when I mentioned the agency's interest. "I don't get why small accounts like yours would need management," she'd said—her tone casual, but the words landing like a slap. "What do they even do? Open two or three emails for you and accept a couple of unpaid collabs?"

"The agency can help me grow, maybe offer some new opportunities." I'd replied, sounding far more defensive than I wanted to.

But Birdie never liked anything that had Jess's name attached to it, so I hadn't expected her to be thrilled. Still, the eye roll seemed kind of excessive.

Perrine sighs and abandons the attempt to flag down the waitress. "Micro, macro—numbers aren't what we care about. We're building a community of *individuals*, of *talents*," she says, stressing the word the same way Jess had, "who bring something unique to the table."

I nod slowly, pretending to think about how I'd fit into that world. The only truly remarkable thing about me is @FauxEver—but that's not exactly a card I can play here.

"My specialty is photography, actually," I say, my voice flatter than I intend. "I have a degree from UAL, graduated with honors. I've done several photography internships here in Paris too. I can provide references if you'd like..."

Perrine gives me an amused look. "That's nice, really nice, but I don't think that'll be necessary. We've reviewed your profile, and the team's impressed! You've got great, relatable content and solid engagement. I always tell my clients—replying to comments isn't cringe, it's life! And of course, that million-dollar friendship of yours doesn't hurt."

I frown slightly, my fingers worrying the edge of the tablecloth. "I don't understand..."

"Birdie Bay," she says, with a knowing little wink. "You two seem pretty close."

"Uh, yes, we've been spending some time together..."

"Would you say you're best friends?" Perrine presses, eyes locked on mine.

I shift in my seat. "I—I don't know," I manage, though the

truth is obvious. We're not best friends. Not really. But I can tell that's not the answer she wants.

Just then, the waitress appears with our order—two cappuccinos, even though we both asked for iced coffees. Perrine doesn't bat an eye, just lifts hers and takes a sip as if that's exactly what she meant to order all along.

"Ever hear of Jordyn Woods?" she asks.

"Kylie Jenner's best friend?"

"*Ex*-best friend," she corrects smoothly. "But you're making my point: she started as a nobody from who-cares-where, and by orbiting the Kardashians, she built her own brand. And even after the scandal..." Perrine's grin widens, clearly pleased with her own example. "...she only went up. If anything, the drama boosted her."

I blink, unsure whether to be flattered or insulted. Perrine tilts her head, reading the hesitation on my face.

"I'm not calling you a nobody, of course," she adds, lowering her voice. "But you have an opportunity. Not many young women get that early in their careers, and it would be foolish not to capitalize on it."

The coffee's scalding, and there is no AC here, and I feel like I'm maybe about to faint. I breathe in deep. I'm not fainting in front of Timothée Chalamet today.

"I see," I manage, though what I'm really seeing is that RevCom isn't the clean slate I imagined—it's just another game to play.

"It's just that," Perrine continues, "ten thousand followers isn't much in a market like France. At RevCom, we typically don't consider talent until they hit six figures—unless they're actors, of course." She gives me a pointed look, as if willing me to read between the lines, then drains the last sip of her coffee. "So, if RevCom were to take a chance on you, we'd need to make sure it won't be a waste of time and resources for us."

So much for not caring about numbers.

"Well, I certainly wouldn't want to waste anyone's time," I reply, struggling to conceal the hint of sarcasm in my voice. Perrine either doesn't notice, or simply doesn't care.

"We also saw the post about you on that account... *Faux* something?"

"@FauxEver," I correct, forcing a small laugh. "Oh—yeah, that." I even throw in a modest downward glance for effect.

"It's good that you're generating buzz," she says, her tone bright again. "We like that at RevCom."

"Oh?" I repeat like an imbecile.

"It was great talking to you, Chloé. I'll run this by the team and we'll be in touch, all right?" She signals for the check with a casual flick of her wrist.

"Cool, yeah. But just to be sure I understand well: you don't think I should keep on posting about my photography?"

Perrine makes a *hmm* sound before flashing me what appears to be her saleswoman smile. "Let's not close any doors, shall we? If photography is what you want to do, we could find a way of integrating it into your social media strategy in the future."

Roses are red, skies are so blue, and with every step, all my dreams are about to come true.

By the time I make it back home, the bitter taste I had after the meeting is nearly gone. After all, it doesn't matter *why* the agency wants me as long as they do want *me*. Jess was right: not everyone gets a fairytale origin story. And mine isn't half as tragic as hers (well, if you set @FauxEver aside). In a few years, when I have millions of followers of my own, no one will care that I began as Birdie Bay's best-whatever. They'll only care about the content I create. Until then, *fake it till you make it* feels like as good a strategy as any.

I text Jess.

> Meeting with Perrine went well, she said she'd stay in touch! Do you have an idea of when it might be? I'm kind of excited now lol

I see that Jess opens my message but doesn't type anything back. Weird.

Daniel isn't home yet, and I'm grateful for the quiet. When he's around, I make a conscious effort to seem less glued to my phone, just to avoid his disapproving looks and thinly veiled remarks. It's not entirely his fault—he simply doesn't understand the gravity, the pull, the *necessity* of social media.

With him still at work, I shed my elegant dress for my softest Skims loungewear and sink into the couch, indulging in some guilt-free screen time.

I scroll through my Instagram feed, trying to see it with new eyes. People are tired of the same recycled faces—the ones who gush about a "holy grail" serum one month and push a competitor's the next. I think of Birdie, how I once saw her as untouchably cool. Until I met her, and the illusion shattered. It's only a matter of time before others wake up too. When they do, I'll be here, ready. I'll do whatever RevCom needs me to do to rise. A new face, untainted by scandal.

I can already picture it: my headshot on glossy campaigns, the bright laughter, the glow. The travel, the invitations, the money.

I won't be greedy like the Anias of this world. A few indulgences—a couple of designer bags, a Cartier Love bracelet, maybe—but beyond that, I'll stay grounded. I'll give back. Charities, photography workshops for expats in Paris. I'll connect with my audience, host monthly giveaways, share promo codes. Never will I turn down a fan asking for a photo.

I'll be a different kind of influencer. I *swear it.*

And suddenly, it all feels worth it: going after Birdie, going after all these people, if, in the end, I can make myself a better version of what they were.

Have you ever heard that theory claiming the reason you want something so intensely, whether it's a dream job or a pair of shoes, is because, somewhere in the future, you already *have* it? The universe is just pulling you toward what's meant to be yours. I've always liked that idea. It makes every questionable choice feel like destiny—a necessary step toward the life that's waiting for me.

I refresh my page for the umpteenth time, relishing the steady climb of likes and followers. But this time, it's the comments that grab my attention. The number looks... off. Higher than usual.

Did I just go viral? Did my last post—

I freeze.

#JusticeForBirdieBay

I can't believe you.

She's the fakest of them all.

My pulse spikes as the words blur together—twenty, maybe thirty variations of the same outrage flooding my notifications. Most of them tag another account: @theRealFauxEver.

I click the handle.

And just like that, I know I'm completely, utterly screwed

16

There's a single post on @theRealFauxEver's account.

And it's a picture of me, smiling, a cappuccino cup pressed against my lips.

I don't immediately open it to read the caption; I just stare at the thumbnail, unblinking. Jess took that portrait about a week ago. She had asked me to join her at Carette, a.k.a. the most Instagrammable café in Paris. We ordered cute coffees, strawberries with chantilly créme, and various sorts of pastries—too many treats for two. My stomach had churned at the sight of all this food.

But Jess just laughed. "It's for the aesthetic."

We spent the next half hour snapping photos and filming short clips of each other, adjusting angles and pretending to be effortless. By the time we each had a hundred options to choose from, the coffees were stone-cold and the strawberries had shriveled into props.

A pit begins to grow in my stomach. I don't want to open the post, but I open it anyway because I need to read the caption. To understand where the blow is coming from.

It's short and simple and feels like a double-decker slamming into me.

@ChloeLeWarner is behind @FauxEver, proof will follow

My hands are shaking. Who posted it? What proof do they have? When will they share them?

I know I shouldn't, but I still open the comments section.

She's a rat

Wow, poor @BirdieBay

@JessDreams you should be careful girl

My cheeks burn, heat flooding my face as I scroll, hands trembling. I can't stop, even as each new comment hits harder than the one before.

Jess texts me back, and it's not about my meeting with Perrine.

OMG have you seen this?

Following with a link to @theRealFauxEver.

I close my eyes, wishing I could wake up from this nightmare. In my mind, I can almost see myself laughing it off, stepping outside, and embracing the promise of my future. But when I open my eyes, the illusion shatters, and a raw, dry sob catches in my throat. I'm still clutching my phone, perched on the edge of the couch, torn between deleting every trace of myself online and crawling under the covers to disappear.

But I can't ignore Jess—not now. Silence would only make me look guiltier. With trembling hands, I force myself to start typing, fingers flying across the screen in panic.

Just did. It's crazy! What should I do? Can I report it?

There is a beat, but not a long one.

You should!!! And I'll ask my followers to report it too

Such a disgusting lie. Can't believe somebody would go after you this way. See, this is the jealousy I've been talking to you about. People are rotten

I bite my lip, feeling a small wave of relief wash over me at her support. If she believes me, maybe it's not all lost yet. I hadn't realized until this moment just how much I needed her to believe me.

I wonder what "proof" this person has on me. It's all fake of course, so why promise proof?

Dots, dots, dots. Jess doesn't answer straight away.

For the buzz, babe

They are bluffing, pretty sure it will be their only post

I swallow hard; she's right. There can't be any proof, right? It's not like Instagram's going to spill my location or anything; this isn't a James Bond movie. The only real link between me and @FauxEver is my phone and the login access on it. As long as nobody gets their hands on it, and I keep denying everything, it's all just speculation.

However, casting a quick glance at the window, my confidence wavers. What on earth am I going to tell Birdie? There's no way she hasn't seen that account yet. If I've been tagged on it countless times, her followers would surely have sent her the page too. My legs feel like lead as I shuffle towards the window and push the curtain aside. Birdie's lights are on, but her living room appears empty. In an ideal world, I'd go over there and explain myself, but in this world, I just bury my face in my hands and emit a deep, guttural sigh.

A sudden knock echoes through the apartment. I freeze. Surely…?

"Chloé, I know you're here," Birdie calls out.

In a desperate move, I shove my phone under the cushions and go to open the door.

Birdie's standing there in her Ralph Lauren pajamas, the ones with the little bears on them that we bought together. My eyes drift down to her feet—she's wearing slippers, as if she'd come here in a hurry. She holds out her phone, and I see @theRealFauxEver's profile glaring back from the screen.

"Tell me it's bullshit," she says, almost pleading with her eyes. It's all over her face how hurt she is, how afraid.

I don't take the phone; I don't need to see that post again.

"It's bullshit," I mutter, my voice emerging low and raspy. I clear my throat and repeat, louder this time, "Of course it is; I mean, earlier today, @FauxEver basically fat-shamed me!"

She blinks a few times, eyes shiny. "It did," she concedes in a small voice.

Her answer emboldens me, so I decide to double down. "Besides, you know me. I wouldn't do something like this!"

She meets my eyes, and I can tell she wants to believe me more than anything. But she hesitates, lingering on the threshold, not coming in.

The silence between us stretches for the longest of seconds and I feel like I lost her. The same pit that opened when I first saw the account grumbles inside of me now. It's all over.

"Birdie," I begin, my voice shaky as I try to find the right words, the right way to explain, to apologize, anything to make her stay and hear me out.

But then, to my utter astonishment, she bursts into laughter.

I freeze, my eyes widening as her laughter swells from a faint chuckle into something wild and uncontrollable. She doubles over, clutching her stomach, gasping for breath, her face contorted into something almost manic.

"Ah, Chloé..." she manages between shuddering breaths. "I'm sorry. I know it's fake, of course. But when I got the screenshot from Gabrielle, I freaked out for a second."

My mind goes blank. "Gabrielle sent you this?"

Before Birdie can respond, Daniel emerges from the staircase, puffing and sweating.

"I'm cursing the day I was born for thinking that the fourth floor without an elevator was a good idea, really," he grumbles through clenched teeth before halting abruptly in front of us.

"Hey, you two," he says, his brow furrowed. "Everything's alright?"

"All good, professor," Birdie says, wiping away the tear that fell out of her eye.

But it's me Daniel is looking at, and I see him go from my pale face to the side of my loungewear top I'm clenching in my hand with all my strength. Realizing this, I relax my hand and pinch my lips ever so slightly. "Yes, fantastic."

We stand there, the three of us, caught in a strange,

awkward silence. The tension hangs heavy in the air until Daniel breaks it with a breezy laugh that doesn't quite reach his eyes. "Well, then... Will you stay for dinner, Birdie? We can order something and—"

"Nope!" she interrupts, gesturing to her pajamas with a quick flick of her hand. "I need to get back home. I think I need to smoke some pot or something. I've been pretty tense these days."

I nod, trying to keep my tone light. "Call me if you need to talk," I offer as she turns and starts running down the stairs.

"See you around!" she shouts over her shoulder, her voice echoing back up the stairwell as she disappears from view.

So, the cat is out of the bag: Gabrielle must be behind @theRealFauxEver.

When you think about it, the whole thing reeks of Gabrielle's *Carnal Flower* by Frédéric Malle fragrance. It can only be her. She knows I've been following her; she has already voiced her concerns about me to Birdie the other day in the kitchen, and really, who else would hate me enough to go so far as to create an entire account just to sabotage me? I haven't even gathered enough influence yet to have earned any other enemies.

Daniel walks past me into the apartment, frown still in place.

"What's the deal this time? Did you notice she was in slippers?" he says, kicking off his shoes—a pair of dark green imitation Loro Pianas I can't stand. You either get the real thing or skip the trend altogether.

I shut the door behind him and exhale. "I don't know. Maybe she's still reeling from that drug scandal."

His head snaps toward me. "You think that's what this is about?"

I study him for a moment. "Maybe. Honestly, Daniel, I don't know. Birdie is... Birdie."

"What's that supposed to mean?"

"She's breezy," I say with a shrug, looking away from him. "I love her, but let's not forget—she's doing drugs, not just buying them. For all we know, she might be high right now."

He doesn't respond, and I'm grateful he doesn't press the matter further. I've had my fill of lies for the day.

Teeth gritted, I attempt to compartmentalize my emotions and fish my phone from behind the pillows. I open Instagram again. The comments are harsh, flooding both of my accounts. I'm labeled as Judah, an opportunist, a leech. There are calls for Instagram to deactivate @FauxEver (as if!). My DMs are even worse, filled with death threats and more. It's ironic, really. When @FauxEver was anonymous, it was hailed as a good Samaritan, the face of truth. But slap an actual face on it, and suddenly the narrative shifts.

You should rebrand yourself as @ForNever, somebody writes under my personal account.

I exhale through my nose and continue scrolling.

Some comments defend the micro-influencers I had previously posted about. Some even support Ania, which is unheard of. However, the majority are here for Birdie Bay.

Betrayed by a friend, so sad

Birdie deserves better!!!

I want to roll my eyes, but it would be tasteless. These

are the same people who were throwing rocks at her a week ago. How am I the double-faced bitch in the story?

I text Jess.

Do you think I should get off socials for a while?

Why?

It's all so absurd, it'll blow over by tomorrow

When I wake the next day, it hasn't blown over—it's only blown up.

More death threats in my DMs.

Reposts on every major gossip channel.

Even my copycat accounts have posted about it. *Kill me now*.

Luckily, I haven't lost too many followers. A few smaller creators have unfollowed, but overall, the numbers are inching up.

Thinking strategically, I text PM, suggesting lunch. It takes him a while to reply, and when he does, it's the gentlest brush-off imaginable:

Hey beauty, would love to but it's busy at the office right now. Maybe next month?

It only confirms what I already feel—there's a growing wave of vitriol against me. It doesn't matter that most of it's just talk; as long as this cloud of doubt lingers, no one will want to be seen with me. I can feel everything slipping away before it's even truly begun.

Somewhere, Daniel gets up and takes his shower. I hear him say something, but it's distant, muffled. I keep scrolling, unable to tear my eyes from the screen. The door clicks shut —he must have left. I know I should get up, go for a run, clear my head. But my body feels like lead, and my willpower's made of air. Without a plan, I can't move.

But isn't it the hardest to come up with a plan when your head is swimming?

I lean back, staring at the ceiling, weighing my next move. Birdie doesn't believe the accusations; she's on my side. I should show that—make it public. But how?

Posting an old selfie would reek of desperation.

Reposting @FauxEver's first post—the one with Birdie buying drugs—would look like damage control, not solidarity. No, I need a new approach, something fresh to stand by and repost to show my support against all this "slander."

I close Instagram, eyes fluttering shut. The decision forms quietly, solidly. I know exactly what I have to do, even if I won't enjoy it.

A new @FauxEver post about Birdie Bay is the only way.

Maybe I'll take that run after all.

In hindsight, I recognize the fragility of my plan. But desperate times call for desperate measures, and I'm as desperate as it gets.

I check the time: nine twenty. Ten minutes later, I'm out the door, cap pulled low, waiting for Birdie to appear. She didn't call this morning. I tell myself not to read into it—we don't run together *every* day—but still, it's strange.

Then she steps out of her building, glowing in a bright yellow Lululemon set, white Adidas runners from her latest collab, and a pair of new AirPods Max framing her face like a halo. I glance down at myself—black, camouflage-style set, the same outfit I wore on our first coffee date. The symmetry isn't lost on me. It feels like coming full circle.

Adapting my running rhythm to match hers, I follow her as I did in those early days. The sky is overcast, and the air feels heavy. A bit of rain would be a welcome break from the stifling heat.

Jess was wrong (again!). @theRealFauxEver had posted a second update, and it had taken my breath away for all the wrong reasons as I was heading down the stairs.

The post's photo was that first shot of Birdie and me at the Dyson event—a shame that such a good memory was nowtainted. I steeled myself and clicked to read the caption.

@ChloéLeWarner has always been obsessed with @BirdieBay, so when Birdie moved into the apartment facing Chloé's, she began following her every day in the hope that she would slip. And when Birdie did slip, Chloé was quick to shoot those incriminating pictures you've all seen.

Fucking Gabrielle. The accusation hit painfully close to home, although I didn't follow her because I wanted to sabotage her—at least not initially. I just happened to be at the right place at the right time.

Yet even incomplete, this second post made me dizzy, and I considered going back home and burying myself under my blankets—until I realized it lacked the promised evidence. If this was the worst @theRealFauxEver could publish, maybe I could get through this after all. I had half-expected Gabrielle to use her de Terron money to hire an IT expert to hack @FauxEver and deliver screenshots.

It's not a James Bond movie, I remind myself once again. It's just gossip. No pictures, no screenshots, no video or audio recordings mean I'm still safe.

I can stick to my rehabilitation plan.

All I need is that croissant shot of Birdie Bay. I weave between two abandoned e-scooters and keep my eyes fixed on Birdie's fuchsia-clad figure, determined not to lose sight of her. One shot—it's innocent enough. It might cost her a few vegan followers, perhaps stir up a minor controversy about her honesty again, but it won't inflict significant damage. Similar to that picture of myself I posted on @FauxEver, it's just a means to an end.

I'll repost it to my stories with a heartfelt message about cyberbullying and the importance of standing by your friends. Classy as ever, I won't even acknowledge the rumor about me being @FauxEver. As if it's too ridiculous for me to even comment on. Birdie will like the story, and everyone will be reminded that it's us against the slander. It's a solid plan.

A few minutes into the jog, Birdie surprises me by taking a different route—turning left instead of our usual right by the park. Fortunately, ever since we started running together, I've actually gotten better at this. Faster. More alert. So I pivot left too, into unfamiliar territory, a part of the city I've never seen before.

The street is quieter than our usual route, with fewer delivery vans and shops—fewer places to disappear if she suddenly stops or changes direction. I ease my pace, keeping just enough distance. Birdie runs on, never once looking back, and though I hate to admit it, a small, twisted thrill runs through me. She's heading somewhere new. Maybe she'll do something reckless again. She did mention wanting to smoke some pot.

My camera is ready whenever you are, Birdie.

Without breaking stride, she turns into a narrow alley, and I can't help but smile at my luck. I hadn't planned on catching her doing anything noteworthy today, but at this point, the content is creating itself. I'm already counting the likes under this new post of her.

Moth to a flame, I follow, positioning myself at the corner and pulling out my phone. There is no way this works, but also, *please work*. Trying to remain discreet, I set up my camera, only to realize it isn't an alley but a narrow passage leading to a larger parallel street, now deserted.

Grinding my teeth in frustration, I drop my phone and take a step into the passage.

"Chloé?"

I pivot and come face to face with Birdie.

17

It's the way Birdie says my name that throws me off more than the simple fact that she's caught me red-handed.

Usually, she tosses my name around casually, almost blending it into her sentences without much emphasis. Her usual repertoire includes "babe," "bitch," or "girl," and never before has my name carried any weight in her speech.

Once, she called me "bestie," and it felt like the best day of my life—until I realized it was just another playful nickname to her.

But this time is different. She utters my name like a whisper, as if it slips out before she can catch it.

"Hey, Birdie!" I blurt out, my mind scrambling for a plausible explanation for my presence here and now, but nothing comes to me.

I search her face, waiting for the blow to come from the hurt in her expression, but she's not looking at me anymore. Her eyes are on the phone in my hands.

A peculiar shift occurs; it's as if I've detached from my body and am observing the scene through Birdie's eyes. I see myself standing there in my old black leggings and hoodie despite the stifling heat. My face is ghostly pale, eyes wide with guilt, and I'm clutching my smartphone, which is displaying pictures of an empty street. I look exactly what I am—caught in the act of creeping on her.

"Okay, I can explain..." I stammer, taking a hesitant step toward her.

Birdie recoils. The hurt in her face curdles into disgust. "It's true, then."

They say you discover whether you're a fighter or a flighter in moments of crisis. Well, confrontation has never been my strong suit, and an instinctual urge to throw my phone away and run in the opposite direction washes over me.

"Birdie," I plead, eyes searching hers.

"How could you? How..." She blinks rapidly, no doubt grasping the implications of this revelation. "All this time, while we were hanging out—and when I complained about those goddamn pictures... Were you gloating?"

"No..." I search for the right words. Is there a right way out of a path paved with wrongdoings? "I wanted to stop. After that first post about you, I didn't mention you at all. I shifted the focus to the bigger picture and..."

She interrupts me, her chest heaving. "I trusted you! I trusted you, and you're behind the worst moment of my life."

"I know." And I want to add that I'm sorry, that I wish things had unfolded differently, that it wasn't worth it. But I don't say these things. I let silence hover between us, and somehow the words I don't say become unspoken truths. Deep down, I understand that if given the chance, I would make the same choices again without hesitation. And now Birdie knows it too.

Around us, people start to turn their heads and watch.

Birdie throws a glance over her shoulder, takes a shallow breath, and her expression shifts. She seems to regain her composure within seconds, transforming her face into a mask I've never seen before. Although yes, I have. She looks like Birdie Bay from her Instagram account.

"Fuck you," she spits, pointing a finger at me. "Don't you ever speak to me again."

And she sprints past me in a flash of yellow and blonde, not sparing me another glance. It feels as though the sun is leaving with her, leaving me in the shadows all alone.

I'M no stranger to loneliness. I remember it clearly, as if it happened yesterday—the day my mother left.

I always told my dad I didn't remember, because it would have made him sad. But I did. What six-year-old recalls the color of her mother's trench coat—electric blue, with a small stain near the hem—or the exact shade of lipstick she wore before deliberately stepping out of her daughter's life? She kissed me goodbye, leaving a burgundy print on my cheek. She didn't say *see you soon*. She didn't cry. She just pinched my nose, the way she always did, and whispered, "I hope you take after your father." Then she left.

When my father came home from work, he found me sitting alone in the dark.

"Where's Mom, Chloékins?" he asked.

I told him what she'd told me—that she went to the hairdresser.

Dad looked toward the window, confused. "Was it a long time ago?"

"She made me lunch," I said, "then she left."

It was already supper time. He ran to the phone. The hairdresser was closed, so he called hospitals, the police, even the morgue. No one had seen her. He was up all night, pacing our tiny Notting Hill apartment. In the morning, he finally reached Fabio, my mother's hairdresser.

"Elizabeth?" Fabio said. "I haven't seen her in weeks."

Dad hung up and turned away from me. His shoulders slumped, and when he finally spoke, his voice sounded heavy, hollow.

"She didn't go to the hairdresser," he said.

I went to him and hugged him. I was sad too, though not surprised. I'd known she was lying—who spends an hour styling their hair before going to the hairdresser?

As I grew older, I started telling people my mother had died. It was simpler. People respond to death with pity, even tenderness. Death is an acceptable kind of absence. But when you tell them your mother left and never came back, there's a pause, and often a flicker of doubt that crosses their face.

Because when men abandon their families, they definitely suck. But when women do, people start searching for reasons—postpartum depression, a breakdown, something, *someone*, that must have driven them away.

And when they looked at me, I could tell they were wondering if that someone was me.

It's all over, then.

Birdie knows, which means I've lost her. And losing her means losing everything I've been working toward. All it would take is one post from her—a single story, one line of text—and it would all collapse.

I don't remember getting home, showering, or changing into a dress, but I must have, because now I'm walking beside Daniel through the Marché des Enfants Rouges.

It's a Saturday ritual of ours. We grab our string bags and head to the covered market in the Marais. We blend in with the locals, nibble on food stall snacks, pick up fresh flowers for the apartment. I usually love it. It makes me feel like the lead in a French film, the kind where the plot quietly unfolds around her. *Oui, oui.*

But today, I feel like an extra—silent, background, irrelevant.

"...since she's vegetarian?" Daniel says, and it takes me a second to realize he's been talking to me. I blink, trying to catch up.

"Sorry, what?"

"Birdie," he says, frowning. "I know she's vegetarian, but does she eat eggs?"

"Oh." I pause. "Why do you ask?"

He looks at me, unblinking—slightly irritated. "Maybe because she's dining with us tonight?"

Right. I'd forgotten she was supposed to.

"She canceled," I say quickly. "Sorry, I forgot to tell you."

He gives me a look I can't quite read. "Why? Did something happen?"

"She must have her reasons," I mumble, turning toward the flower stall before he can notice the heat rising in my cheeks.

Then the rain starts, and thunder follows close behind. Daniel and I rush back to the apartment, groceries clutched to our chests, trying not to let anything slip.

When we get home, I tell Daniel I need to catch up on some Fiverr orders—another lie to add to the pile. I haven't taken a single job in a month.

Instead, I sit at our desk and refresh my Instagram feed, bracing for the storm. I expect a tidal wave of vitriol, worse than anything before. But there's nothing—just the occasional comment mentioning @theRealFauxEver, which I delete and block. They keep coming anyway, multiplying like mushrooms after rain.

When a new post from @theRealFauxEver pops up, I'm not even surprised. Another selfie of me with Birdie—this time pulled straight from my own account. I frown and open it.

@ChloéLeWarner befriended @BirdieBay while actively continuing to post on @FauxEver

So, nothing new. I suppose that's good news. Still infuriating—Gabrielle's clearly set on destroying me—but without fresh evidence, the outrage might fizzle out sooner than I thought.

The comments beneath the post are already piling up. They all say the same thing.

Proof?

These influencers would do anything for clout

It's starting to sound made up

It does, right?

Feeling slightly vindicated, I sink into my seat and try to focus.

What would I do if it all fell apart—if Birdie posted the truth, or if @theRealFauxEver finally delivered the proof everyone's waiting for? What would be left of me then?

Sometimes I wish I'd never tasted any of it—the followers, the attention, the opportunities. Because once you've had them, there's no going back. The thought of returning to invisibility feels unbearable. I've made ordinary life impossible for myself.

The pit inside me is so deep that only one thing can fill it.

I walk into the kitchen, where Daniel's cooking with his back turned.

Most girls I know swoon when I tell them my boyfriend cooks most nights. *You're so lucky*, they say—and I am. But it's also what I'm used to. My dad cooked every day for me. He used to say cooking was how he expressed himself, the way I do with photography.

My heart sinks beneath the weight of everything I'm trying not to feel.

I open the fridge, find a block of cheese, and cut off a piece. Without thinking too much, I put it in my mouth. Daniel hums a Francis Cabrel song, oblivious. The cheese sits heavy in my stomach. I take another piece, this time with bread.

It feels good—immediately, soothingly good. I knew this was what I needed. The relief floods in, sharp and temporary, and suddenly that's all I want. I pull out the rest of the cheese, the bread, the ham—everything—and pile it on a board.

"I'm gonna take it to the living room," I say, though my voice barely sounds like mine. Daniel doesn't answer.

I eat as I walk—ham, bread, anything I can grab. I don't even chew. I just shove it all in until my throat tightens and I start to cough. I can't stop. The hole inside me demands more, more, until I'm full to the point of pain.

And then it's too much.

I rush to the bathroom and turn on the tap to mask the sound. The motion is so familiar it hurts. Tears come before I even touch my throat. I'm crying, retching, and the relief that had seemed so close a minute ago is gone, leaving only raw pain. It always ends this way.

Daniel knocks on the door.

"Chloé? Are you sick?"

His voice folds into another—my father's. I hear him as if he's here again, from all those nights he found me like this, holding my hair, whispering, *It's alright, Chloékins. It's alright.*

I knew I was breaking his heart, and I despised the part of me that mirrored hers.

Because it started right after she left.

At first, I stopped eating—really stopped. Not on purpose, not out of some unconscious wish to punish her for abandoning us. Food just became... repulsive. Even imagining it touching me, entering my body, made me sick. I grew thin, ribs showing and everything. When Dad noticed how my clothes hung off me like empty sleeves, he drove me to the hospital. They tube-fed me for days before sending me to a pediatric psychologist.

Then I started eating again—but not like normal people do. I binged. I tried to bury the ache under piles of food, to quiet it by swallowing everything I could find. I think Dad was so relieved to see me eating that he didn't stop me, not until someone at a school recital called me fat.

More therapy followed.

Over the years, Dad became meticulous about my meals, turning nutrition into our daily ritual. He tried to shield me from every possible trigger, and for a while, it worked. I stopped overeating, started losing weight—almost melting away. I felt good, lighter, almost proud.

But a few years ago, just before my final year of college, it came back. That sharp, hollow pain in my chest. And I slipped into the only coping mechanism I knew. This time, terrified of gaining weight, I started purging.

It's been four years now.

"Yeah," I say over the toilet, feeling like the biggest failure alive. "My stomach's just a bit upset, that's all."

"Do you want me to come in?" Daniel asks.

"No, I'm fine," I reply, forcing a brightness I don't feel.

When I step out, Daniel's waiting by the door, worry creasing his forehead. I wish I could fall into his arms, let him hold me like he used to. But we still haven't talked about our recent fights; truth is, we don't talk much anymore, and it scares me. We used to be so much more to each other.

"You look pale," he says. "Are you sure you're okay?"

I lean against the doorframe and rub my face. "Better now. Don't fret."

He nods, grabs his keys, and starts putting on his awful shoes.

"Where are you going?" I ask.

Avoiding my eyes, he mutters, "To the store. You ate everything I'd bought for starters." His tone isn't accusing, but my cheeks still burn.

"Sorry," I murmur.

"It's fine." He pauses by the door. "Must've been bad stuff anyway if it made you sick."

"Right," I say quietly.

"Right," he echoes, meeting my gaze. "Need anything from the store?"

I shake my head. "No, I'll skip dinner. Let my stomach rest."

"Okay."

The door clicks shut, and the apartment feels impossibly

still. I walk to the drawer and take out the binoculars, hesitating. It's been weeks since I last used them, and part of me hates that I'm doing this again.

But when I reach the window, I see I won't need them anymore.

Birdie has installed thick cream curtains.

18

"Are you absolutely certain my presence is mandatory?" I whine for the fourth time during the drive.

Daniel doesn't answer. His eyes stay fixed on the road, jaw tight. He's clearly had enough of my attempts to weasel out of his cousin's wedding—and I'm equally exhausted from pretending I'm not obsessively refreshing Birdie's Instagram page.

Two days have passed since she caught me in the act, and she still hasn't posted a thing—not even a story. It's like being suspended in limbo, Anne Boleyn waiting for her fate, unsure whether I'll be spared or lose my head.

At least @theRealFauxEver has gone quiet, too. Maybe after that second post with zero proof, Gabrielle finally realized she wasn't doing the damage she thought she was and decided to quit. A girl can dream.

We've been driving for over two hours now, heading to a small coastal village in northern France called Étretat. I've never been, but I've heard it's charming—seafood, cider, striped sweaters, all of that. And the air is supposed to be fresh, which feels like a luxury after a month of Paris's suffocating heat. Unfortunately, the farther we go, the darker the sky gets. I glance nervously down at my new Jacquemus sandals. Surely the wedding isn't outdoors?

"What did we get them again?" Daniel asks, breaking the silence.

It's my turn to be annoyed. Is it some unwritten rule that men immediately forget whatever their partner bought with the joint budget?

"It's a Laurastar steamer," I say flatly.

He frowns. "Right. I still don't get why Flore and Mark need a five hundred-euro steamer."

"Yeah, you wouldn't," I mutter, rolling my eyes. (He also doesn't know I got it half off using Jess's promo code.)

Daniel's cousin Flore is what I'd call an *improvised housewife*. Only two years older than me, but she behaves like the matriarch of a suburban family of four—with a golden retriever and a matching set of Le Creuset pots. She spends her days cooking, cleaning, and daydreaming about the moment Mark finally knocks her up. Once, she told me she dedicates her Sunday mornings to ironing. *Ironing*. Do people still do that? Hence, the steamer.

Flore isn't mean, exactly; just unbearably dull—which, in some ways, is worse. I can tolerate someone cruel if they're at least entertaining. But when a person's personality has the texture of a frying pan, what can you possibly work with?

Her fiancé, Mark, is fun enough once he's had a few drinks.

Normally, I'd be thrilled at the excuse to dress up and party, but with everything going on around @FauxEver, I can't shake the feeling I should've stayed in Paris. I know it's irrational—if Birdie decides to destroy me, being a block away won't save me. Still. When I tried to skip the wedding, Daniel hit me with the whole *"This is my family"* and *"You never make an effort"* speech, so I caved. I'd rather not give him any reason to start asking questions I can't answer.

So the plan is simple: show up, smile, endure the ceremony, and drive back tonight. We're skipping the hungover brunch tomorrow. Thank God for small mercies.

By the time we reach Étretat, the wind has picked up considerably, and I can see black, menacing clouds moving our way over the sea.

All of Daniel's family is already there, gathered between the tiny casino and the restaurant they booked for the occasion. It's all cheek kisses and hugs, and there are way too many of them.

I'm not used to big family reunions; for years, it's only ever been my dad and me. Sometimes, my aunt Zelda would visit, but here, I see uncles, grandparents, dozens of cousins I don't even recognize, and... Julienne.

"Finally! I was so scared you'd arrive late for the ceremony!" Daniel's mother cries, cutting through the crowd to reach us.

I brace myself and plaster on a smile, but of course, Julienne only has eyes for her son. She throws her arms around him, dramatic as ever, as though she hasn't seen him since the war—when in reality, it's been six days since brunch.

"Chloé, we're so glad you could make it," she says at last, and her smile is as rehearsed as mine. I catch a whiff of

Chanel *Chance* on her vintage black tweed jacket as we exchange an obligatory hug.

"It's good to see you, Julienne," I lie smoothly, then glance at Daniel. *See? This is me making an effort.*

His eyebrows flatten, but by the way his mouth corners tug up, I know he's pleased.

Julienne pinches an invisible piece of lint from her son's blazer before turning back to me. "So, Daniel told me you're not staying overnight because you have a work thing?"

There we go.

I look at Daniel for support, but before he can respond, Diane emerges from behind their mother.

"Mom, let Chloé have a glass of wine before you start throwing accusations," she says.

Relieved, I flash her a grateful smile and make a mental note to stay glued to her side for the rest of the day.

"All I'm saying is that it is a long road, and I don't want my boy to drive at night," Julienne retorts, swiping her hands through the air. "I'm sure we could have arranged for Uncle Kevin to take her to the train station..."

"Mom..." Daniel finally interjects while pressing his cheek affectionately into his sister's. "Flore and Mark did say that tomorrow's brunch was optional. Anyway, where is the happy couple? And where can we drop this," he says, gesturing to the large wrapped box at his feet.

As Daniel and his mother navigate through the maze of relatives to reach the present table, I'm left alone with Diane.

"I'll be frank with you," she says, removing her glasses to wipe them. "I'm actively avoiding Mark's younger brother. He seems to think our being here together constitutes a date —and I squarely blame my mother for that. She's convinced the next wedding will be mine. Ugh. How about we make a strategic retreat and pretend we're checking out the flowers by the ceremonial arch?"

I follow her gesture toward the arch, perched uphill and fully exposed to the wind. I grimace. Diane's eyes flick down to my shoes, and she sighs.

"Didn't you know heels are a no-go around here?"

A gust blows through, undoing the curls I spent an hour perfecting with my Dyson Airwrap.

"Apparently, I also missed the memo about mandatory head coverings," I say, eyeing her flawlessly tight updo.

She laughs. "Welcome to the charms of Normandy. I might have a pair of sneakers in the car—what's your size?"

Is she joking? My face must give me away because Diane rolls her eyes, amused.

"I get it," she says. "But don't say I didn't warn you when your heels are in shambles later."

She glances over her shoulder at a small man in a gray suit grinning at her and winces. Mark's brother, I assume.

"Listen," Diane says, "if you come with me, I'll let you hold on to me. It's that or endure the elders grilling you about marriage plans. I'm telling you, this family lives for weddings."

Fair point. "Lead the way," I sigh.

As we make our way toward the arch, I tread carefully over the gravel path, slick and unguarded at the edges. This place is a lawsuit waiting to happen. Whose idea was it to host a wedding here?

"So," I start, breaking the silence that makes clinging to Diane even more awkward, "what's wrong with Mark's brother?"

Diane snorts. "Let's just say wisdom's been chasing him his whole life, but he's always been faster."

"*Chic*," I say in French.

"*Merci*," she answers, lolling her head to the side and revealing a flicker of Daniel in her expression.

We finally reach the top, and I can't fathom how the arch and the chairs are still standing in this wind. Diane seems to have the same thought; her brow furrows as she crouches to gather a few fallen bouquets.

Not knowing what else to do, I follow her. "How's the new job?"

She puffs out her cheeks. "Fine. Lots of old dudes, daily mansplaining—mostly the same crap I was already doing in Versailles."

"But it pays better," I remind her, trying to sound encouraging.

"It does," she concedes, sinking into a chair and tugging me down beside her.

"Hey, want to hear something fun?" Diane says after a short pause. She doesn't wait for my reply. "The other day, I was having lunch with this colleague—guy's old enough to be my dad—and he asks if I'm on Instagram. I think he's hitting on me, so I say no. And he goes, 'Well, you should join, there's some fun drama over there.' I'm like, 'Oh?'"

She gives me a strange look, and my stomach knots.

"He says, 'Apparently, some big blogger just got outed for doing drugs by her own best friend.' I say, 'Wow, wild world,' and he loves that—launches into this whole speech about how our generation is doomed because of social media. You know, the usual boomer talk. I tuned out halfway through."

I blink, working hard to control my expression. If the story's already reached random middle-aged men, how long before everyone knows? It's a miracle Daniel doesn't. What would I even tell him?

If he believed me, he'd want to talk to Birdie.

But if he didn't...

Neither option sits well.

I clear my throat, forcing a casual tone. "It's crazy what people will make up for a few views."

"Yeah. Crazy," she echoes. For a second, I think she's going to let it go—but I forget she's a lawyer.

"It must be tough for you, though."

I freeze, and not because of the wind.

"I've seen you post tons of pictures with that girl, Birdie Bay. It's cool. Especially since you've said you want to grow your socials; it's obviously a great connection." She pauses. "But forgive me if I'm overanalyzing. Occupational hazard, you know? I remembered something else you said that day we were having drinks."

I don't remember. And a part of me hopes I'm misreading her tone, that this isn't going where I think it is.

"You whispered, 'Maybe the grass seems greener because it's fake.' I remember it because it was such a funny line. So... accurate."

Did I actually say that? The memory's a blur, probably drowned in too many glasses of rosé.

Diane glances around, quick and discreet. We're still alone on the hill. No one to interrupt what's coming.

Her gaze finds mine again. "Chloé, are you..."

I inhale, bracing.

"...@FauxEver?"

19

Diane's crimson lips stay pressed together, her expression impossible to read. I can't help but feel that if she knew I was @FauxEver, she'd be more entertained than shocked.

"Are you?"

I could tell her. It wouldn't even take words; just a nod. And lawyers have to keep secrets, right?

But then I think of Daniel.

He can't know. He's not like Diane; he'd *care*. Care in the kind of way that would break us.

"What?" I mumble, feigning confusion. "No."

She studies me for a moment. I can't tell what she sees, but her mouth curves into a small, knowing smile.

"Oh, my mistake then."

There's a flicker in her eyes, something between amusement and complicity, and it makes my stomach tighten.

"Still," she says lightly, "it must be hard dealing with all these rumors."

I lift my chin, forcing calm, pushing away the image of Birdie's face when she found out. "It was unexpected, yeah. Especially the hate. People are nastier online. It's like the screen turns them into something else. I try not to let it get to me."

"You're right," Diane says, her tone soft, maybe even kind.

"But the hardest part," I add, meeting her gaze, "is not knowing who's really on my side anymore."

Are you on my side here, Diane? The silent question hangs between us.

She shifts in her chair, watching me. "Okay, I'm not saying this because we're by the sea—it's from a book I read recently." A small smile returns. "Ships don't sink because of the water around them. They sink because of the water that gets in. So don't let what's around you weigh you down."

I smirk despite myself. "Deep."

"I know," she says with a small shrug. "So, what are you doing about that account? The one claiming you're behind @FauxEver?"

"I..." A gust of wind sweeps my hair across my face, and I try to flatten it. "Well, nothing. There's nothing to address because it isn't true. I don't want to give it oxygen," I say casually, like we're chatting about the latest episode of *Selling Sunset*.

"So you haven't tried to reach out? To figure out why they're targeting you?"

Her tone is calm, but it lands like a challenge. I blink, caught off guard.

"Because *if* it's really baseless," she goes on, "wouldn't you want to know why they chose you?"

I bite the inside of my cheek, unwilling to admit she has a point. *Is this how someone innocent would act?*

Guests start arriving, their voices rising in a chorus of Ohs and Ahs as they crowd around the floral arch.

"Is that legal advice?" I ask, half-joking as I stand to look for Daniel.

"Hmm, yes, my secretary will bill you," she jokes but quickly gets her face straight again. "Let's say it's more like strategic advice. Although, I would recommend taking screenshots, just in case."

She gives my hand a reassuring squeeze, and I try not to dwell on the glint I catch in her eyes again.

I CAN COMPLAIN about the location all I want, but I can't deny it's breathtaking. The cliffs rise like sentinels against the horizon, and the rhythmic crash of waves against the pebbled shore carries a strange kind of calm. Honestly, this is probably the kind of place I'd choose for my own wedding—if Daniel and I ever got that far.

Flore makes her entrance, then joins Mark beneath the arch. They stand there smiling at each other, utterly oblivious to the wind and the storm gathering above. Their happiness is so seamless, so complete, that I have to look away.

My gaze drifts toward the sea instead. Somewhere beyond that gray stretch of water lies England, and the thought hits me with an unexpected ache. A rush of homesickness swells inside me, soft and smothering, drowning out every other worry. I picture my dad in his little countryside home, pretending he's fine—talking about his dance classes with the neighbors, feeding the stray cat that never lets him pet it. But I know it's just a façade. He's been lonely ever since I left.

And suddenly, I can't help wondering what I'm doing here, faking smiles and living a life that doesn't feel real, when I should be with him. The one person who never turned his back on me.

A pang of sadness hits me, and I close my eyes, and it's a good thing that most people around me have glassy eyes from Mark's speech because a tear slides down my cheek.

Daniel takes my hand in comfort, but I keep my eyes shut, afraid that if I let go, the floodgates will open, and I won't be able to hold back the sobs. The weight of it all is too much—the fear of exposure from @FauxEver, navigating the actual exposure by @theRealFauxEver, and Birdie now knowing the truth.

Flore says, "I do," and the groom kisses the bride. My phone buzzes, and I open my eyes at last, heart hammering as I read the notification. The crowd erupts in applause—everyone except me.

Because Birdie has finally posted something.

Time seems to stop. The sounds around me fade as my fingers move on their own, unlocking my phone and opening @BirdieBay's profile. I brace for the worst: a photo of us with *liar* in the caption, maybe a screenshot of @FauxEver's page with a long, damning explanation. Something that screams declaration of war.

Instead, it's just a selfie. Birdie, sitting on her Bubble sofa, holding a glass of homemade lemonade. She's makeup-free, no doubt going for that effortless, relatable vibe, and she's smiling her usual camera-perfect smile. The caption reads:

still haven't found a single place in Paris that does it better than I do. Recommendations?

It's not about @FauxEver. It's not about me.

I start clapping, a beat too late, earning a few puzzled glances from Daniel and his family—but I couldn't care less. The relief that floods me is dizzying, almost euphoric. I feel like I should have a drink. Or two. Or twenty.

My luck comes to a screeching halt right after the ceremony. Just as everyone is offering congratulations to the happy couple, the heavens open up—not with a mere drizzle, but with torrents of rain typical of seaside coasts.

Chivalrously, Daniel unbuttons his blazer and drapes it over my shoulders as we begin the trek down the cliff to the restaurant.

Once we're finally inside, everybody's dripping and shivering. I overhear a woman, who I think is Daniel's great aunt, exclaim, "A rainy wedding is a happy wedding!" I applaud her enthusiasm, but whoever first came up with that saying mustn't have seen the sorry state of my Jacquemus sandals, now completely ruined.

Flore comes over, her simple white long-sleeved dress soaked and splattered with mud, though she doesn't seem to care. I wish I weren't the kind of person who frets over things like that, but I am. Still, I give her a bright smile—partly because Daniel mentioned she follows me on Instagram now and thinks I'm "gorgeous."

And partly because, well, she's the bride.

"Chloé, can you take some pictures of the guests? The

photographer had some kind of emergency and had to leave," she asks, putting her hand on my arm.

I blink, caught off guard. "Oh, I didn't bring my camera," I say, and for some reason, a flush of embarrassment rises in my cheeks.

Flore's smile falters. "But aren't you a photographer?"

"I am," I say slowly. "But I wasn't planning on working today, so I came without my equipment..."

"*Attends,*" she blurts in French, turning to Daniel. "*Elle n'a pas pris sa caméra?*" Her tone is suddenly accusatory.

I glance between them, my head bouncing like a ping-pong ball. It's clear there's been some conversation I wasn't aware of.

Daniel looks uncomfortable, torn between frustration and guilt. "*Merde, j'ai oublié...*" he mutters, rubbing the back of his neck. And that's when it clicks—he told her I'd handle the photos if needed. He just forgot to mention it to me.

I make a mental note to have a serious talk with my boyfriend later. But since the unspoken rule is that the bride always gets what she wants, I put on my sweetest smile and say, "I can take some shots on my phone, if that helps?"

Flore shoots me a look that makes me instantly regret buying her that fancy steamer.

"*Oublié?*" she snaps, completely ignoring my offer. "*C'est littéralement la seule raison pour laquelle on a accepté que tu viennes avec!*"

"*Flore, calme toi, Chloé est ma petite amie!*" Daniel retorts, eyes wide.

Flore opens her mouth to answer but is interrupted by Julienne. "Come on, come on. Let's not spoil this wonderful day by fighting." She leads the bride away but not before giving me a disappointed look, no doubt docking points on the invisible scorecard she keeps in her head. "Ah, you two, even when you were children..."

Guess I was wrong about one more thing: Flore.

Daniel and I stay facing each other.

"Can you believe her?" he says, shaking his head in disbelief.

I grimace. "Yeah, I actually can."

"What?" he asks, having the audacity to look surprised.

"Daniel, tell me you didn't bribe my way in by promising I'd help around."

The guilty look on his face is answer enough.

"Holy..." I mutter, lowering my voice as I notice a few family members starting to give us curious looks. "I told you nobody here likes me. I shouldn't have come."

"Don't be ridiculous," he says, pulling a face, trying to brush off the tension.

Oil to the fire, that's what it is. "Ugh, give me a little credit for fuck's sake. Don't you think I understand a tiny bit of French by now? *Why else would we have invited her?*" (That's what she said, by the way.)

"Forget it; she didn't mean that. It's just the wedding stress talking," he says dismissively. "I'm gonna get us drinks."

I wish he'd stand by me, but that's not the hill I'll die on. "Fine," I say. "Then bring me a glass of something strong."

As he navigates through the crowd toward the bar, I discreetly pull out my phone, open Birdie's page, and refresh the comments section. It's her first publication in days, and after such a break, in light of the recent developments, her followers must be throwing her a party.

I blink and re-read some of the comments that are now

getting hundreds of likes under the post. Not sure it's the welcome-back party Birdie had imagined for herself.

What's in the glass Birdie lol, now we just wouldn't know

Nobody believes your act anymore

Trying too hard!!!

These are mean but not surprising, considering her drug scandal is still pretty fresh, but the comment that is really going viral right now is a different kind.

I'm sure she's behind @FauxEver. Hear me out: she knew she was becoming irrelevant, especially since she moved to Paris, so she needed a scoop about herself to start trending again. Creating @FauxEver to give herself some clout is brilliant. She's in her Bad Girl era and I'm here for it

That's ... new. If @FauxEver weren't mine, I could have almost believed such a conspiracy theory myself. I check out what's being said under that comment, and a lot of people validate the idea.

I wouldn't put that past any influencer

Sickening if true

I refrain from whistling. Past the initial annoyance of @FauxEver being attributed to someone else, there's a silver lining in this mix-up. The swirling rumors linking Birdie to @FauxEver could surprisingly work in my favor—they make the whole story muddy and sloppy. It blurs the lines linking me to the account. Because why would it be more me than Birdie or Ania, Jess, or even Melinda?

I scan the crowd for Daniel's silhouette and spot him engrossed in conversation with Julienne, my drink all but forgotten in his hand.

With a sigh, I reluctantly make my way toward them.

"...at the end of the day, it's her decision," Daniel says, his switch to English indicating he's acknowledged my presence.

"*Je sais, chéri*," Julienne purrs before turning her attention to me, eyeing me up and down. "Chloé, my dear, have you eaten anything today? You look so thin!"

"I had a sandwich on the road earlier," I lie. Daniel had a sandwich; I just pretended to eat mine.

"Good, we wouldn't want you to faint or something..."

"Mom," Daniel interjects.

"All I'm saying is that she's getting thinner and thinner; it's not healthy for a girl..."

"Mom," Daniel repeats, his tone a touch sharper.

"*Oh là là, on ne peut plus rien dire!*" She rolls her eyes but appears pleased with herself. "Speaking of food, *chéri*, I've made some of those *financiers* you love so much."

Daniel's face lights up. "With chocolate?"

Julienne laughs, patting her son's arm. "Of course. They're by the entrance. Chloé, be a sweetheart and pack them with your things so you don't forget. They might be the only decent thing you'll eat on your way home."

I accept the jab with a tight smile and turn toward the entrance, where the pastries are indeed waiting.

Without looking back, I make my way to the wardrobe, stealthily swallowing one pastry and taking a second for later. Every bite feels like a tiny act of retribution. If I didn't get my drink, Daniel can survive without a few financiers.

The wardrobe is mercifully empty, and aside from the faint hum of laughter drifting in from the next room, it's perfectly quiet. Exactly what I need. I half sit on the windowsill and pull Daniel's blazer around me. His scent envelops me. He never wears perfume, so it's all him, and it's incredibly soothing.

Outside, the storm rages, and Diane's words replay in my mind. Maybe she's right. Maybe I *should* reach out to

@theRealFauxEver. Not because I need to understand why they're doing this—if it's really Gabrielle, the motive's obvious. I took Birdie from her, and now she's trying to take her back. But if I'm going to keep playing the innocent card, I need to look the part.

So I start drafting messages. Different openings, different tones. Trying to find the version of myself that sounds most convincingly blameless.

I know it's you so cut the crap

You're such a fucking psycho

GABRIELLE could you have been any more obvious?

I delete every draft. This message isn't for Gabrielle—it would mean nothing to her. This is for me—for my future defense, for the record that I was ignorant, innocent in all of this.

So I write:

Hi, it's Chloé. Listen I don't know why you're doing this, sharing these lies, but I hope you get the help you need.

Satisfied, I press send. Then the weirdest thing happens: something vibrates.

I look down at my phone—it's not it.

The coincidence prickles at me. I send another message, a single sad emoji, just to check.

The vibration comes again, faint but unmistakable.

Heart quickening, I reach into the pocket of the blazer around my shoulders and pull out Daniel's phone.

My two unopened Instagram messages light up the screen.

20

I could have fallen in love with Daniel a hundred times over.

When the morning after we first slept together, I woke to find him in the kitchen making breakfast. "I didn't know what you liked, so I probably went a bit overboard," he said, flashing that disarming smile of his. He looked so handsome then, curls a mess, sunlight on his bare shoulders.

Or when it turned out I had a rat in my apartment—not the cute kind from *Ratatouille*, but a large, filthy thing that probably carried diseases—and he spent two days setting traps. When he finally caught it, he didn't kill it. "Poor thing must be terrified," he said softly, before releasing it in a park.

Or that time he surprised me with a trip to England to see my dad. "Pack your bags, *ma belle*. It's time I met your father," he teased. I remember watching the two of them together, the most important men in my life, and feeling something inside me go still. Peaceful.

But none of those moments compared to the day I finally

told him the truth about my mother. He listened quietly, his eyes widening as I spoke, and when I finished, there was no judgment, no pity. Only compassion. He held me for a long time before saying, "You know, I've always hated that saying, *we don't choose family*. Maybe we don't choose the one we're born into, but we do choose the one we build. We choose our people. We create our homes." Then, after a pause: "What your mother did was unforgivable. But know that I'll always be there. With you."

And I believed him. That was the moment I truly fell in love with Daniel.

He had always seemed incapable of cruelty: someone steady, good, safe.

Which is why what's happening now feels so impossible.

"What the actual fuck?" I mutter, rereading my messages on Daniel's phone.

I tap the notifications. Of course he doesn't have a passcode. It's all there—black on white. @theRealFauxEver is logged in. The three posts with me. My messages sitting in his DMs among dozens asking if it's true and who he is.

Daniel is @theRealFauxEver.

"Here you are. I think they're about to cut the cake, so—" he says as he slips into the wardrobe.

I spin around, eyes wide and glassy. Daniel's phone is in my hand, and the moment he sees it, a flash of realization crosses his face, then vanishes as he schools his features into calm.

"Ah," he says. "I guess we should talk."

"You... guess?" I snap, my brain scrambling. "What the fuck, Daniel?"

He inhales as if steadying himself, hands raised slightly. "I know what you think, but I did it for you."

"For me?" I stare, incredulous.

He nods slowly. "I thought it would show you how wrong this is. That you'd learn your lesson and stop."

My breathing accelerates. I have the sudden urge to fling his phone at his self-satisfied face. "I'm not one of your students, Daniel. You had no right."

He steps closer, jaw tight, pushing his glasses up the bridge of his nose. "You are not the one to decide what's right and wrong," he says, voice low and steady.

It knocks the air out of me. My mind spins, replaying everything he must've done—the creation of @theRealFauxEver, the posts, the accusations, all this hatred... None of it fits with the man who woke up beside me every morning, who cooked for me, who took me on dates and made me laugh.

"How did you..." My hand drifts to my throat, as if to steady myself. "How did you even know?"

Daniel meets my gaze, unblinking. "That first evening when Birdie stayed over. She mentioned having a stalker, and I looked at you—I don't even know why. You do this thing with your lips when you lie, or when you're caught. You pinch them slightly. You did it then."

I can't answer. Words don't come.

"You're not as good a liar as you think you are," he adds quietly. "At least not to people who actually know you."

So in the days that followed, I started paying closer attention. You were always on your phone, always getting notifications. It didn't take long to put two and two together.

The thought of him studying me like that, tracking my tells, watching me unravel, makes my stomach turn. All this time, I was terrified he'd find out online, forgetting the truth was written all over my face.

"You could have come to me directly," I say, hating how small my voice sounds. How broken.

"Could I have, though?" Daniel cuts in, louder now. "I tried, Chloé. I've been trying to talk to you for weeks, but you wouldn't listen." He shakes his head, gaze dropping. "I've watched you change right in front of me, becoming someone I barely recognize." He gestures toward me, a bitter laugh escaping him. "This isn't you. You haven't picked up a camera in months. It's all parties, new faces, pictures, likes, comments. You never cared about that stuff before."

"But I *did*," I say, my voice cracking like glass. "This is what I always wanted. Don't you see? I'm living my dream."

"Your dream?" he echoes, half-whisper, half-scoff. He rubs the back of his neck, as if trying to steady himself. "What about Birdie's dream? Or all the other girls you've stepped on to get here?" He doesn't wait for an answer. "God, Chloé, what you did to Birdie—exposing her like that, pretending to be her friend while using her to climb—it's disgusting."

"That's not..." I swallow hard. "It's more complicated than you think."

He meets my eyes, arms crossing over his chest. "Then uncomplicate it for me."

"They're liars," I whisper. "All of them."

Something in his face softens—no, collapses. And what replaces it isn't anger but pity.

"And you're not a liar, Chloé? Really?"

Silence stretches between us, heavy and sharp, neither of us willing to look away.

Funny how I used to admire this about him—his unshakable conviction, the way he stood by what he believed in no matter what. Others called it stubbornness, but I saw it as strength. Now, that same strength is my undoing, because he genuinely believes he's right.

In a flash, my urge to make him understand gives way to something colder, sharper—a realization. He's not going to back down.

Something deep in my gut tells me this moment matters. I'm standing at the edge of that invisible line I swore I'd never cross. But that's the thing about survival—it drags you toward your own darkness, to places you once promised yourself you'd never go.

I don't want to hurt Daniel. But he hurt me first. So fuck it—the line is crossed.

I lift my chin and meet his gaze, defiance hardening every word. "You're not going to reveal anything else," I say, my voice cold, unfamiliar—like it belongs to someone else entirely.

He shakes his head, still unaware of the shift between us. "Chloé, this is up to you. You stop, and I stop."

For a split second, I almost feel sorry for him. Almost.

"No, Daniel," I say evenly. "You're going to delete your pathetic little account. Right now. Or tomorrow morning, I'll be calling your school to let them know about you and that girl. What was her name again? Estelle?"

Color drains from his face, the impact hitting fast and hard. For once, I don't look away.

It happened a few months after Daniel and I moved in together. He'd taken on a handful of students over the summer break so we could save for a trip to New York. The group was small—five or six teenagers who'd failed their English exams and needed to prepare for the August retake. One of them, Estelle, stood out. She was far more invested than the others, always staying late after class and throwing herself into Shakespeare, clearly hoping to impress Daniel. She even baked him cookies for his birthday. I never met her, but he mentioned her in passing a few times. She was sixteen.

I joked she probably had a crush. We laughed it off—who hadn't once fallen for a teacher? I couldn't really blame her. If any of my teachers had looked like Daniel back then, I'd have been a model student too.

Two weeks before the end of summer classes, Daniel came home white as a sheet. At first, he wouldn't say a word, and from the look on his face, I thought something terrible had happened to his family. But when he finally spoke, he told me Estelle had stayed late again to discuss the play they were studying. They talked, laughed more than they should have—and then she kissed him. He said he'd pulled away immediately, told her she was mistaken, that she was just a child. The next day, he called the school and withdrew from teaching for "personal reasons."

"I can't risk it, you understand?" he said. And even though I was disappointed about canceling New York, I supported his decision. I remembered how shaken he'd been when one of his colleagues was falsely accused online by a student. That scandal haunted him. Nothing that happened with Estelle had been his fault, not really—but he knew how dangerous rumors could be. In the wrong hands, even the truth could destroy a career.

Now, facing him, I can see the memory flicker behind his

eyes. He blinks quickly, color creeping up his neck. The silence between us thickens.

"You wouldn't," he says at last, his eyes darting over my face like he's trying to convince himself.

"I stop if you stop," I reply, meeting his gaze, my eyes steadier than my heart feels.

He takes a step closer, palms raised. "Chloé..."

"No." I pull back, pointing a finger at him. "You went public behind my back, trying to destroy everything I worked for. So tell me—how would it be any different from me reporting you to your school?"

"Reporting?" he repeats quietly, scanning my face. "I didn't do anything wrong."

"I know," I say, voice sharp. "It feels unfair to be exposed like that, doesn't it?"

He stares at me as if he's seeing me for the first time. "It's not the same. Don't you see that?"

I clench my jaw, refusing to answer.

"All I wanted was to protect you from yourself," he whispers. His body seems to cave in on itself, shoulders slumping, arms hanging limp, before his expression empties completely. "Fine. I'll delete the account."

A wave of dizziness hits me, like I've just been struck. "Thank you," I murmur, unable to hide the relief in my voice.

Daniel closes his eyes for a beat, his jaw tightening. "We're done, you and I," he says. I nod, even as something inside me splinters at the sound of it. I knew the moment I dropped the Estelle bomb we were finished, but hearing him say it out loud makes it so real that it starts to hurt.

Outside, the party carries on, laughter and off-key singing bleeding through the walls to the rhythm of a Stromae cover.

Daniel glances toward the door. "You should go. I'll tell everyone you felt unwell and went home. That I decided to stay for brunch after all."

I part my lips to remind him it's a three-hour drive back to Paris and I don't even have a car, but he's already turned away, the door clicking shut behind him.

21

I wake the next morning with my head pounding and reach instinctively for my water bottle—only to find an empty bottle of Bourgogne on the bedside table instead.

"Mmmh," I groan, long and dramatic, because I can. There's no one here but me.

When Daniel's uncle Kevin dropped me at the train station after our fight, I'd felt hollow and sad. Then, during the three-hour trip back to Paris—two transfers in the middle of nowhere, people staring at me in my wrinkled floral dress—I'd felt nauseous. But by the time I finally made it home, darkness settling outside the windows, sadness had curdled into rage. Rage at Daniel for betraying me so completely, and rage at myself for being too blind to see it. Other girls check their boyfriends' phones, but I never did. I never worried about Daniel. How stupid of me.

The second I stepped into the empty apartment, I went straight for his precious wine fridge and grabbed a bottle from the top drawer—the expensive ones he always saved for "special occasions." If he couldn't repay me for the blow to my reputation, then this would do for now.

A few glasses in, drinking alone started to feel pathetic, so I texted Jess:

Hey, want to hang out?

She replied almost instantly:

Can't, babe! Louise and I are having a date night. But wait, aren't you in Normandy?

I hadn't answered. Now, blinking through the dull ache behind my eyes, I see she's texted again. Two missed calls.

Is everything alright? I'm here if you need to talk xx

I pull the blanket over my face. Daniel's side of the bed is still perfectly made, and the sight hits me like a punch. Even drunk as I was, I'd somehow crawled into my side only, leaving his untouched.

He hasn't texted to check if I got home safe. Hasn't called. Not even a single "are you okay?" Did I expect remorse? I suppose I did—hoped for it, at least.

I try to rekindle the anger I felt last night, anything to fill the hollow ache spreading in my chest, but it's gone—flushed away with my post-wine vomiting fit.

Groaning into the pillow, I ask myself, *what now?* I've never lived with a guy before, so I have no idea how breakups work when leases are involved. Who keeps the apartment? I *could* handle the entire rent myself with a few extra Fiverr gigs, but do I even want to stay here anymore? I hate the floors and the bathtub and the stairs, and Birdie has curtains now, so it wouldn't be that big of a loss to move out.

Only I shouldn't be the one to move out. Daniel started this whole mess—he threw the first punch. So even if I hate this place, I'll stay. Out of sheer spite, if nothing else.

Feeling oddly justified, I roll out of bed and stumble into the kitchen to make coffee (though what I *really* need is 400 milligrams of ibuprofen).

My eyes catch on the open wine fridge, then on Daniel's beloved espresso machine, and finally on the stack of pretentious literary magazines he likes to skim over breakfast.

Will he come back for his things?

The thought makes me hopeful and also a tiny bit happy, and as the happiness comes, it just highlights the dark pit of sadness I'm in right now. You know, like when something stupid makes you laugh, and you realize you haven't laughed in months, and it makes you sad. I feel that now, and suddenly it's like a physical pain, and I'm bent in two, and everything hurts because Daniel knows who I am now. He has seen the bad, he has seen the ugliness in me, and nothing can bring back that image he had of me before. I remember how he looked at me on that first rendezvous of ours, like I was the brightest star in the sky, and I kept reaching for those looks ever since, slowly kind of starting to believe he was right about me, that I was shining.

So there I am, sitting on the kitchen floor, crying in the most Hollywood-pathetic way imaginable, when the doorbell rings. I freeze. Daniel? No—he has a key. Birdie? My heart lurches. I scramble to my feet, don't even bother wiping my tears, and lunge for the door to unbolt it.

It's Jess. I blink at her, surprised.

"Thank God you're alive!" she says, leaning on the doorframe. "You didn't answer my calls. I was worried."

"Sorry," I mutter. "Rough night."

Jess glances past me, and I'm pretty sure an empty wine bottle chooses that exact moment to roll into the middle of the hallway.

"I see. Can I come in...?"

"Yes, yes, of course," I say, although I don't really want her to.

She steps inside, takes in the mess with one swift glance, then turns back to me, eyebrows raised in a silent question.

"So, what happened?"

Where to start? I could go back to the day I first saw Birdie Bay through her window, or when I snapped those goddamn pictures of her buying drugs. I could come clean, I'm sure it'd feel good. Tell her that it's all true, that I am @FauxEver.

But that's not what I say. "Daniel and I, we... broke up."

Jess presses her lips together and tilts her head to the side. "Shit, sorry, babe. That sucks."

I nod because I don't want to talk about it. "I was about to make coffee, want some?"

"Sure," she says in a small voice and follows me into the kitchen. Today, she's wearing a long black low-rise skirt and a red crochet halter top. I make a mental note to look for the same top later as I pour the coffee.

"Did you hear back from Perrine?" she asks when I hand her a steaming Harry Potter mug (Daniel's).

I shake my head.

"You will, I'm sure of it," she says, rubbing my arm.

"I'm afraid," I sigh, eyes lifting to the ceiling, "that after the whole @FauxEver thing, no one's going to take a chance on me anymore."

Saying it out loud feels oddly cathartic. Like naming the fear makes it real, but also lighter. What really terrifies me is the thought that Daniel might have tanked every opportunity I had ahead of me, and that I, in trying to hold everything together, ended up ruining us.

"Don't be ridiculous—anyone with half a brain could tell it was just a stupid joke," Jess says, wincing as her coffee burns her lip. She sets the cup down and folds her arms. "Besides, Louise told me the account's gone."

I snap my head up. "It is?"

So Daniel actually did it. Of course he did. As self-righteous as he is, even he wouldn't risk his job over this.

I wait for the pit in my stomach to ease, but it doesn't.

"Yeah, and Birdie and you, you're good, right?" Jess searches my face.

Birdie hasn't posted anything. She hasn't even unfollowed me, which would've only thrown more fuel on the fire, so it doesn't seem like she plans to expose me.

"Of course," I answer. "She doesn't believe in that story."

The more I think about it, the more my worry starts to feel childish. I know Birdie—she's not one for scandal. If anything, exposing me would mean admitting she actually did buy drugs in an alley, and that's not something she'd ever do.

I let out a long breath through my nose and drop onto a kitchen chair.

"You see? All good and settled. They'll call soon," Jess says, taking the seat next to me. Her golden bangles clink together softly. "Look, I get it. Right now it feels like the world's crashing down on you, but trust me, that's how social media works. Give it a week, and some new scandal will steal the spotlight. Yours will be ancient history."

I scoff, but she leans closer, wrapping me in a cloud of English Pear & Freesia by Jo Malone. "I mean it. Just wait it out."

I study her face. Could she be right? Will this actually fade on its own? Would the storm really pass if I just stay quiet? She's been in this game for years—and Birdie even longer. And now that I think of it, isn't that exactly what Birdie's been doing all along? Waiting for her own scandal to lose heat?

But I'm not a Birdie and not even a Jess. I don't have their background, their history, or their contacts. All I had was a castle made out of cards, and it took just one blow from Daniel to topple it. On the bright side, it seems like two of my biggest problems—my only problems?—have suddenly vanished. Daniel has deleted @theRealFauxEver; it's gone as if it had never existed. And Birdie isn't going to expose me. So maybe, eventually, I *can* just wait it out.

"Thank you, Jess," I say. She squeezes my hand tighter, and I look down at her hands when the thought crosses my mind.

Jess's secret.

Of course, the answer has been right in front of me all along. She was underage when it happened; he was married and much older. The implosion of her origin story and reputation—it would make one hell of a headline. Big enough, even, to pull the spotlight off me and back onto her.

I could wait for the storm to pass... or I could keep being the storm.

My thoughts start to clear, a dangerous kind of focus setting in. Logistically, I can't be the only one who knows about Jess's affair, right? So if @FauxEver posted it, no one would immediately point fingers at me. Sure, there'd be gossip, but Jess stood by me through the Birdie mess; maybe she'd back me again.

But then the cracks start showing. What proof do I even have besides her drunken confession? I didn't record anything. I don't even know the guy's name, or what agency he works for.

Nothing. I have nothing.

"Always," Jess says, flashing a reassuring smile, and guilt twists in my stomach for even letting the thought cross my mind.

22

"Dad?"

I blink in disbelief at the middle-aged man of medium build standing in front of my building, holding a bouquet of flowers in one hand and a battered travel bag in the other. Even from behind, I'd know him anywhere: my father, in his favorite flannel shirt that's seen better days (years ago, in fact) and his trusty cargo trousers (he wouldn't be caught dead in shorts, even during a heatwave).

He turns, and his face breaks into a grin so wide it could light up the street.

"Chloékins!"

In an instant, I'm wrapped in a bear hug that smells faintly of pine aftershave. I blink away the sudden sting in my eyes.

"What are you doing here?" I manage to say.

"Daniel texted me to say he'd moved out." He rubs his ear, that telltale sign he's embarrassed. "So, I take it you two are...?"

I drop my gaze and nod twice.

"Right," he says, clearing his throat before repeating, "Right."

And just like that, I know that's all we're ever going to say about it.

So Daniel kept in touch with my dad? I try not to let that thought bother me—but it does. It's been five days since we broke up, and I haven't heard a single word from him, yet he apparently had no trouble texting my father. Totally fine. Completely fine.

"You'll be staying for a bit, then?" I ask.

"Just a couple of nights," he says. "Miss Tania wouldn't be too chuffed if I left Sir Paws with her much longer. Not exactly an animal lover, that one."

"Miss Tania?"

He chuckles. "We met at dance classes. You know, the ones I told you about? She started coming along a few months back. Lovely woman. My Foxtrot's been improving ever since."

I raise an eyebrow. "You two seem close."

He gives a small, bashful laugh. "We're... something. I suppose you'd call it flirting. But truth be told, it's just nice to have someone about. Didn't think I'd meet someone like her at my age, but there you go. You'd like her, I reckon."

I want to be happy for him, really, I do, but there's a small, petty part of me that bristles at the idea of him having a new little family. It's something I'll need to work on.

"Alright," I say lightly, "I'll set up the sofa for you, then."

"No need, love. Miss Tania's daughter sorted me out with an Airbnb. And you'll never believe it—it's in your building! Was just waiting for the landlady to pop by."

The satisfaction of having been right about the old neighbor fades almost instantly, replaced by a sharp pang of jealousy. The idea of my dad building a little life of his own, with someone else, stings more than I'd like to admit.

"I thought we could have a bit of a wander today," he suggests. "Unless you've got other plans, of course. I know I've turned up out of the blue..."

My plans? Let's see. The past few days have consisted of crying over my phone, scrolling through hate comments on both my accounts, re-reading old notes from Daniel, and sleeping at odd hours between emergency junk-food runs.

So, yes—very busy schedule.

But I smile, take the flowers he's still holding out, and straighten up. "Are you kidding? Of course we're spending the day together."

He smiles, visibly relieved, and something in my chest eases. My dad's so easy to please that it's almost impossible not to catch a bit of his warmth myself.

Over the past few years, my dad has visited me in Paris plenty of times. Every birthday, without fail. It's our little tradition: stick a candle into a pain au chocolat and wish for "the sweetest year ahead." One Christmas, two years back, we spent the whole day hopping between five different markets—a day forever remembered as *Merry Sore-feetmas*.

Sometimes, he'd come for no particular reason at all, just to be with me (and, back then, with Daniel). We'd wander through art galleries, linger over lazy brunches at quaint cafés, or stroll along the Seine. He'd always walk a few steps behind, giving us space while quietly smiling at our joined hands. I know he loved seeing us happy together.

But today, I want to keep his mind far from Daniel, far

from any talk of heartbreak. My goal is simple: keep him busy, fill the day with enough small joys that he won't have a chance to notice what's changed.

I take him to Montmartre, where the once-starving artists now sell their work for five hundred euros apiece—maybe I should start selling my photos here too. We wander through the cobbled streets until we reach the Sacré-Cœur Basilica.

"Magnificent! You ought to take a picture of this!" my dad says with genuine excitement. I smile, a little embarrassed.

I hadn't even thought to bring my Leica, something that would've been second nature a few months ago. Instead, I snap a quick photo of the dome with my phone and post it to my stories. Hashtag *family day*.

He doesn't seem to notice the difference. Or maybe he just decides not to say anything.

After a wrong turn or two, we end up at *Le Mur des Je T'aime,* the wall covered with "I love you" written in over 250 languages. Couples crowd around it, taking the same picture a thousand others have before them. There's even a wedding shoot in progress. The bride, not much older than me, beams in her white dress, radiant beside her shy groom.

I wait for that familiar flicker of sadness to cross my dad's face—the one that always appears when something reminds him of Mum. But it doesn't come. Instead, he smiles softly.

"Ah, the French do know how to celebrate love. It's inspiring," he says.

And this time, I'm the one who chooses not to comment.

The day drifts by, and come evening my dad and I are still wandering through the city. Normally, I'm not one for long walks, but with him, it feels different. He keeps me entertained with stories about Miss Tania—stories that somehow make me warm to her despite my earlier doubts. Between tales of dance classes and his cheeky "Foxtrot mishaps," he slips in gentle questions about my life here, the kind that make me feel like I actually know what I'm doing.

It hits me, with a rush of relief, that I haven't looked at my phone in hours. No Instagram, no hate-fueled scrolling, no obsessive thoughts about Daniel, Birdie, Gabrielle, or Jess. Just silence. Just me and my dad. And for the first time in weeks, the world feels... light.

Before I know it, we're crossing the bridge to Île Saint-Louis, and my dad suggests grabbing dinner at one of the touristy brasseries there.

Usually, I'd say absolutely not. The place doesn't have a view worth posting, the plates aren't particularly pretty, and it's certainly not the kind of spot that ends up tagged by influencers. Not Instagrammable enough.

But then I think, what the hell? My dad couldn't care less about that stuff, and I don't have any content to create today. So we weave through the crowded terrace, murmuring a series of polite *"excuse me"s* until we finally find an open table.

"What do you fancy, love?" he asks, peering over the menu.

I catch the careful way his eyes flick to me—how he'd watched me polish off a cheese crêpe at lunch but skip the ice cream after. To put him at ease, I pick something hearty, something that says *see, I'm fine* without having to say it out loud.

I've become something of an expert at performing normal. That's what this feels like—sitting in a brasserie with my dad, pretending my world isn't still smouldering online. I laugh at his jokes, sip my wine, play the part of an ordinary twenty-something who doesn't spend her nights doom-scrolling through hate comments. I push past the heaviness in my stomach and the fleeting thought that I might slip away to the bathroom later.

I also push aside the stranger's glance that makes me wonder if she recognizes me, the fact that I still haven't found a way out of the digital wreckage surrounding Birdie, and swallow the creeping dread that it might already be too late. That maybe I've already ruined everything.

"A penny for your thoughts?"

"What?" I blink, dragged back to the present. The sense of freedom I'd felt earlier now feels like a trap. What on earth was I thinking, stepping away from social media for an entire day? What if something important happened while I was here, oblivious? What if Daniel reactivated @theRealFauxEver while I sat here, completely unaware?

"You seem a bit agitated, baby girl. Everything all right?"

"Of course." I force a bright smile, the kind that usually does the trick, but today, it doesn't quite land. My dad sets down his fork and leans in, elbows on the table, fingers laced together in that gentle way of his.

"There's something I've been meaning to talk to you about," he says.

Ah. There it is. Can't say I didn't see it coming. The only real surprise is that it's taken him this long. I shift in my seat, trying to brace myself. What will it be this time—a word about my eating, a nudge toward therapy, or something work-related? Pre-emptively, almost defensively, I take a bite of bread and swallow it too quickly.

But that's not where he goes.

"I think it's time you came home," he says, his voice kind but steady, his eyes searching mine.

I frown. "Dad, if this is about Daniel—"

"It's not just about him," he cuts in gently. "Yes, there's the breakup, but it's more than that, love. Your work—it's not quite going the way you'd hoped, is it? I can tell. You've sent me photos of these girls you call friends, but you've not mentioned a single one of them today. And then, of course, there's your health..."

"Ah, Chloékins," he sighs, and I wish he wouldn't—not like that, not because of me. That sound alone splinters something in my chest. "I'm worried about you."

He presses on, eyes twinkling with concern. "I know how much you wanted to be in Paris, love, but I just don't think it's making you happy."

I fall silent, unsure what to say. What could I possibly say to that?

I know what this is: a lifeline. A chance to walk away from the chaos, to start over. And maybe I should take it. Lately, Daniel's last words have been echoing in my head: *"All I wanted was to protect you from yourself."* As much as I hate to admit it, there was truth in that. Maybe I do need protecting—from myself, from my own patterns, from the shadows I keep tripping over.

Because I did use Birdie. I used her to climb, to chase something that wasn't mine to begin with. I betrayed her trust, just as I did with Daniel, twisting his concern into control, his love into leverage. And now, here I am, on the verge of doing the same to Jess—the one person who's been nothing but good to me—for a shot at reclaiming a world that's already burned me once.

I made @FauxEver.

There's a darkness in me that frightens me, and I'm afraid of what I might do next.

But not too afraid to run away.

I reach across the table and take my dad's hand, pressing gently against the vein that runs along his wrist, the way I used to when I was small.

"I'm sorry, Dad," I say quietly. "But I don't want to go. Not yet. I promise I'll visit soon. But if I leave now, I'll never know if I could have made it."

I mean it. Every word.

And beneath it all, there's the truth I can't say aloud: *I still believe I can.*

I just need to find the way back.

23

My dad always told me never to make an important decision while feeling emotional.

"It's the easiest way to screw up. Impulsivity only leads to disaster, believe me."

He's right; he's always right. So after he leaves, I give myself one more day to cry, to mope, to gather Daniel's things (who still hasn't reached out, by the way) and to delete our pictures from my phone. The usual breakup housekeeping.

Daniel never realized how lucky he was. I'm pretty *and* ambitious: not exactly the type he'll find at that little school of his. Maybe he's too angry right now to see it, but he will. Especially once he catches sight of my post-breakup glow-up.

So I book a facial and a manicure, and order a new Lululemon running set.

Only when my mind feels as uncluttered as my apartment do I let myself start planning ahead.

If I want people to look away from my drama and onto someone else's, I need to post something big. A revelation that eclipses my story and makes me seem like yesterday's news. But what could possibly do that? None of the tidbits sliding into my @FauxEver DMs have the potential, and I know I only have Daniel to blame.

Now that @FauxEver has a quasi-official face, people are less inclined to share juicy details from their personal profiles. Maybe they worry I'll expose them too. It wouldn't be very professional, in my opinion, but to be honest, I'm so deep in this mess that I can't completely rule it out anymore.

For what feels like the hundredth time today, I find myself drawn to the window, staring at the curtains in Birdie's apartment. If anyone holds the key to getting me out of this, it's her. Birdie always had the sharpest read on everyone. All that time on social media turned her into an encyclopedia of influencers, PRs, and brands. I tear my gaze away as a memory surfaces.

Birdie and I were lounging at her place, and as usual, after a few drinks, her tongue started to loosen. She began scrolling through Instagram, dishing gossip about other influencers.

"That Martina girl bought followers. Everybody knows it, and nobody gives a fuck..."

Normally, I would've hung on her every word. Anything she said could turn into gold for @FauxEver. But that day, my attention was split by something Daniel had mentioned. Lately, he'd shown this sudden curiosity about Instagram and how it all worked, asking endless "explain this" and "show me that" questions. Naive me thought he was just trying to take an interest in my new project. Looking back, maybe I should've paid closer attention to him too.

"...nobody's worse than her. Can you believe they actually call the girl the French Birdie Bay? Hello, guys, I *am* French."

That snapped me out of my thoughts. "Sorry, who are you talking about?"

Birdie huffed, clearly annoyed. "Henriette Geoff. Haven't you been listening?"

"Who's that? Never heard of her."

"Oh, but you must've seen her. She's France's sweetheart." Birdie typed her name into Instagram and shoved her phone toward me.

I did know her. Henriette was L'Oréal's ambassador; she'd graced the covers of *Vogue*, *Elle*, *Harper's Bazaar*, and had even starred in a recent Netflix period drama.

"She looks... cool," I said, trying to sound unimpressed. But honestly, she was phenomenal. Not just conventionally beautiful like most models—there was something softer about her face, a warmth that made her seem effortlessly kind. I couldn't wait to stalk her profile later, properly.

Birdie gave me a look. "She's a joke. Everyone compares our stories, saying we both rose from nothing—rags to riches and all that. Only I actually did. Henriette's been crafting that narrative from scratch. Excellent PR, I'll give her that. But I know for a fact she comes from a wealthy, well-connected family. Henriette is the definition of a nepo baby."

She threw back the rest of her wine, reached for more, and realized the bottle was empty. Now she was irritated—and an irritated Birdie never needed much prompting to start trashing someone.

"Her real name isn't Geoff. It's Gernault. Ring a bell?"

It didn't at first. But when it did, Birdie caught my expression and smiled, vindicated.

"The Gernault family?" I blinked.

There'd been a recent *Business of Fashion* piece on them —shady labor practices, sexual misconduct, money laundering. They were the fashion world's Trumps: despised, feared, and impossible to ignore. Their influence ran so deep that the scandal had been contained, but everyone knew it was a ticking time bomb. No wonder Henriette hid behind a new name.

"How do you think she landed ambassadorships even stars like Angelina Jolie can't get? She's clever enough to hide behind a false identity to dodge her family's reputation, but she still uses Daddy's connections. Nepotism at its finest," Birdie scoffed. "Bet she wouldn't want that little detail to leak."

———

YES, Birdie, I bet she wouldn't indeed. But wouldn't it be a win to be the one to leak it?

I'm completely absorbed now, scrolling through Henriette's profile. I don't know her well—I only started following her recently and never took the time to really look. But now I see what Birdie meant. Henriette leans hard into her rags-to-riches narrative.

All of her most liked publications are about how grateful she is, how she would have never dreamed something like this would happen to her, and how her teenage self would die if she saw her on the cover of a magazine. Maybe you'd say that these words can all be twisted, that anyone coming from any background has the right to feel grateful about an accomplishment, and you'd be right.

But the Gernault family isn't your typical lineage, and when your rise to success can be attributed to funding from one of France's most notorious dark webs, it's hard to see Henriette's outward displays of gratitude as anything more than a smokescreen. In any case, Henriette's connection to the Gernaults remains a gray area she has no intention of exposing.

And as it turns out, it's exactly the kind of gray area that could work in my favor right now. I sit cross-legged in front of my computer.

Instagram allows a maximum of 2,200 characters for a caption, so it needs to be catchy and straight to the point. I begin typing the post while it's fresh on my mind. A Gernault baby! I spill the beans, urging people to read BOF's article on the Gernaults, and of course, I add @HenrietteGeoff's tag (five million followers!).

I lean back and look down at my screen. It's good; probably my best caption so far.

Now that I have the story, all I need is something visually captivating. With Birdie's revelation, the focus was on the pictures—they spoke for themselves. But with Henriette, it's all about the message. Still, Instagram thrives on visuals, so I need something fresh to pull people in.

I could recycle an old photo from her page, but that feels too lazy for the effect I'm aiming for. So I start digging—Googling her name, scrolling through Instagram, then TikTok. It's on her BeReal that I finally find what I need.

She's just posted a picture of herself at the gym. What gym, exactly? I take a screenshot, open my gallery, and zoom in until I spot a red flame logo reflected in the mirror behind her. *Form Room.* A Google search confirms to me that there is only one in Paris—and call it lucky girl syndrome, but it's just two metro stations away from my place. I don't hesitate. I slip into some biker shorts, grab a beige hoodie, and run out of the apartment.

I know what you're thinking. That I've completely lost it.

That I didn't learn my lesson with Birdie. But hear me out. I'm just someone who wants the truth to come out. If it happens to get me out of the mess I'm in, I call that a bonus.

And really, what's the worst that could happen to Henriette? She might lose a few followers, maybe a brand or two. Though, with her family's influence, I doubt even that.

That's where my mind is as I make my way toward Henriette's gym, phone in hand. I scan the area, searching for a discreet but well-positioned spot. Options are limited—until my eyes land on the Starbucks across the street. A smile creeps in.

Since moving to Paris, I haven't set foot in a Starbucks. But this one, with its wide glass windows, feels made for the job.

Inside, the coffee shop is buzzing with life, which feels strange for 3 p.m. Don't these people have better places to be? Thankfully, the window bar seats are free, and I claim one after ordering a Frosted-Caramel-something. From here, I have a perfect view of the entrance to Form Room.

Five minutes pass. Then ten. My drink melts into a small puddle on the table. Maybe I missed her? No. A BeReal post can't lie, and hers went up less than thirty minutes ago. She must still be inside.

A burst of laughter from a group of girls a few tables away pulls my attention. Three friends meeting for coffee. They look so carefree, so happy. I feel a sharp pang of jealousy at their easy closeness. What is Birdie doing right now? Did she find herself a new friend? Crawl back to Gabrielle? One of the girls catches me looking, and I quickly turn away—just in time to see Henriette leaving the gym.

I wouldn't have recognized her if I hadn't seen those turquoise leggings in her BeReal, but it's definitely her: sandy blonde hair, a heavy upper lip, and a runway model's walk. She's with a girlfriend, deep in conversation. I start snapping photos, but Henriette keeps turning her head toward the other girl, and when she doesn't, her oversized Celine sunglasses and long hair hide her face. My pulse quickens. They're almost out of view, and I still don't have the shot.

Then the friend stops, says something to Henriette, and gestures in the opposite direction. Henriette shakes her head, clearly refusing. The friend steps closer, lifts Henriette's sunglasses, tilts her chin with one finger, and kisses her. It lasts barely a second. Most people would have missed it—but my camera didn't.

I look down at the photo and grin. It's sharp, perfectly timed, and without her sunglasses, Henriette is clearly recognizable.

I didn't know Henriette was gay. But then again, celebrities often prefer to keep their dating lives private.

"It's bad for business," Birdie told me once. "People want to see us as desirable and free. Post a relationship and suddenly you're not selling the fantasy anymore."

I stare at the picture. Did I just hit the likes jackpot? I quickly shake the thought away. I'm not here for petty gossip this time. I'm doing investigative work.

Still, revealing the new crush of France's sweetheart? That's just the cherry on top.

There's a bounce in my step as I walk home.

It's such a peculiar feeling, knowing you hold in your hands the power to end all your problems.

I upload two pictures. The first is the kiss, for the *wow*

effect. The second is a shot of Henriette glancing over her shoulder—I found it poetic, given the theme of my post, and it's also the only other photo where her face isn't hidden by her hair.

I paste my caption onto @FauxEver and sit back, waiting for the post to explode.

Unfortunately, that's when everything starts to go downhill.

24

Thinking back to the day I posted Birdie's pictures, what stands out most vividly is the rush I felt when the post went viral. It was like a surge of adrenaline flooding my veins as I watched the numbers climb—an attention bath so wide I could swim in it. I wouldn't go so far as to call it the best day of my life (that would be awful to admit), but it definitely ranks among my most unforgettable moments. Like my graduation, or the first time Daniel and I kissed.

And I think I've been chasing that feeling ever since.

But when I refresh Henriette's post, the expected euphoria twists into something else. The numbers are good, rising fast, but it's the comments that make my stomach drop. They come in waves, sharper and louder than anything I've seen before.

Damn, Henriette is gay?

Is FauxEver outing people now? Disgusting.

Unfollowing! You should be ashamed of yourself

I press my hands to my face, massaging my brow, trying to think. Wait. It's one thing if she hadn't made her relationship public—fair game, in a way—but if she never came out... Shit.

A cold wave hits me. I feel sick. I fling my phone away and rock myself for what feels like forever, trying to process it. I outed her. Like that *Variety* journalist who outed Billie Eilish on a red carpet but worse because Henriette was actually *concealing her sexuality,* and now she will have to relive it over and over again. Have I really become that kind of person? No. I go to Pride marches. I have gay friends. I'm an ally.

Panicking, I grab my phone and delete the post. It's only been what—ten, maybe fifteen minutes? Surely it hasn't spread too far yet.

But it's true what they say: you can never fully erase something once it's online. I watch in horror as screenshots of the kiss start circulating on gossip pages. I silently beg them to stop tagging @FauxEver, but it's useless. The situation escalates with terrifying speed and spirals beyond my grasp, mutating into a disaster entirely of my own making.

Surprisingly, amid all the chaos, Henriette's connection to the Garnaults fades into the background. A few people mention it, but they're in the minority. It feels trivial compared to the bombshell of her coming out.

Jess posts a story in support of Henriette without directly tagging her.

Gentle reminder that it's never ok to out someone!

I came out to my family when I was sixteen. It was one of the hardest things I ever had to do, and I was lucky to have been met with support and understanding, but I acknowledge it for what it is: luck. And unfortunately, we live in a world where not everybody has that. So don't deny someone their choice, their moment, and their power.

I reply to her story immediately, pretending not to be aware of the beef. She replies with the link to one of the accounts that has reposted @FauxEver's post.

Wow, it's so shitty, I write back, shoulders tense.

Yeah, it is. I'll tell you that: I didn't think much of that FauxEver thing before, but now it's getting on my nerves.

Phone still clutched in my hand, I rummage through the pantry and grab the first thing I find: biscuits. I bite into one; it tastes like ash. Then, like an addict disgusted with herself but desperate for another hit, I keep scrolling, driven by a morbid need to see the full extent of the damage.

I read every comment, mentally drafting the responses I'll never post. My follower count keeps dropping on both @FauxEver and my personal account. I scroll, refresh, scroll again, shoveling food into my mouth as I go. The more I see, the more I eat, and when my stomach starts to turn, I think, *good.* I deserve it.

Then Henriette posts a white square on her profile with this caption:

Feeling shocked and distraught right now. Going off socials for some time. Thank you to all for your love and support.

I swallow hard. This is bad, and I wish I could cycle back and never post what I had posted. I want to find Henriette and tell her I'm sorry. But no amount of words can repair what I did.

All I wanted was a scandal big enough to eclipse mine. I never meant to become the scandal again. Still, I tell myself, as long as it stays contained to @FauxEver, I can keep pretending it has nothing to do with me.

Spoiler alert: it doesn't stay contained.

Less than two hours after I post Henriette's pictures, the hate starts pouring into my personal account. Comments, threats, insults. I'm called a homophobe, a creep, a monster. People tell me to die.

At first, I can't make sense of it. Maybe it's old gossip resurfacing from Daniel's posts? But as the minutes tick by, the storm keeps growing. This isn't old news.

Then I notice the mentions—everyone's talking about a TikTok video.

I'm not even on TikTok, so I download the app, create a fake account, and immediately feel about a thousand years old. My For You page is full of people dancing, and I have no idea how to find what I'm looking for. After wasting several minutes figuring it out, I finally type *FAUXEVER* into the search bar.

And there it is—the video that makes my stomach drop.

It's me. Beige hoodie, green biker shorts, messy bun. No doubt about it. I'm sitting at the Starbucks window bar, pointing my phone outside, taking pictures. *It's not good, but I can find a way around it.*

The video zooms in on the street outside. You can't see faces, but it's clearly two people, and one of them is wearing a turquoise gym set—the pop of color makes it unmistakably Henriette. *Shit.*

Then the camera pulls back, showing me at the window, scrolling through my photos, grinning. *Shit. Shit. Shit.*

I sink to the floor. The room tilts and spins, and I feel trapped on a rollercoaster I can't get off. I watch the video again and again. I try to stop, but I can't look away. I'm the car crash.

And somehow, seeing myself taking the pictures is the

worst part. In my head, I'd been discreet, clever, invisible. I didn't think I looked that... small. That pathetic.

Daniel once read me a philosophical paper about how shame only exists under someone else's gaze.

"Imagine," he said, "you're peeking through a keyhole, spying on someone."

"Mmmh," I replied, only half-listening, though the topic suited me.

"You wouldn't feel ashamed by the act itself," he continued. "The shame would come only if you were caught —because you'd see yourself through their eyes."

No need for eyes when you can film, right? The girl who posted the video is the one I'd exchanged glances with at Starbucks. Her caption reads: Wasn't going to post this, but after seeing Henriette's story, it felt like the right thing to do.

The clip racks up nearly a million views and hundreds of comments in just a few hours. I click on her profile—no other videos, barely three hundred followers. She didn't even post it to go viral.

I can't blame her; she thought she was doing the right thing.

I blame myself for being careless. When I filmed Birdie, I was a nobody. There was no image to ruin. Now people know my face; I can't run @FauxEver's business and expect to stay invisible.

With trembling hands, I text Jess again:

> So crazy—looks like someone's still trying to pin that @FauxEver thing on me

She'll be on my side. She always is.

Jess opens the message but doesn't reply, and my heart drops.

I keep typing:

Do you think I should post something about it?

Nothing.

Jess?

I know I sound guilty, but panic keeps my fingers moving.

Can I call you?

Two minutes later, she blocks my number.

GETTING into the club is more complicated without Jess.

"You're not on the list," the bouncer repeats for the tenth time.

"I know—" I groan for the eleventh time. "But my friend is inside, and I really need to speak with her."

The bouncer, a burly guy who seems built for the job, shakes his head while checking other names, waving people through as if I'm invisible.

"Jess and... Louise. Louise actually performs here. She's the DJ! Although I don't know if she's performing today, but—"

He gives me a slow once-over, a smirk tugging at his mouth. "Last names?"

"Uhm, I don't know their last names," I admit. "But I can show you their Instagram accounts?"

"You're on Instagram?" he asks.

"Me?" I blink, caught off guard. "Yeah, I'm on Instagram."

"Show me."

I hesitate—partly because I don't want him finding me later—but realize this is my only way in. I hand him my phone, my profile open.

He lets out a low whistle. "Twenty-one thousand followers? Not bad."

"Thanks," I say, unsure whether to sound proud or apologetic. I haven't posted much lately, but ever since the @FauxEver disaster, the numbers keep climbing anyway. These people aren't there for my outfits or pictures, but beggars can't be choosers.

"You should've mentioned you were an influencer," he says, almost accusingly.

"Um... sorry?" I mutter, because I'm in no position to tell him to shove it.

He sighs, glances at the queue, and finally unhooks the rope.

"You can go in."

INSIDE, it doesn't take me long to spot Jess.

She's perched at the bar, cross-legged and laughing. Our eyes meet across the dancefloor, and she doesn't smile back. A lump rises in my throat as I push through the crowd toward her.

"Hey..." I start, but she cuts me off.

"What are you doing here?"

Her tone throws me. She's never spoken to me like this before, never failed to smile. Louise steps closer, giving me a cold, assessing look over Jess's shoulder, and beside her stands PM. Heat rushes to my cheeks—I knew exactly where Jess was because he'd tagged the club in his story.

"Can we talk? Somewhere private?" My voice trembles.

"No," she snaps. "Go away."

"Please, Jess." I didn't mean to plead, but here I am, watching my last friendship crumble right in front of me.

She rises from her stool, arms crossed over her chest, standing toe to toe with me.

"Did you create that fucking account?"

I inhale sharply, catching myself just in time before I press my lips together. The words don't leave my mouth, but the mere hesitation is enough for Jess to shake her head at me in disgust.

"Did you out Henriette?"

"I didn't know it was a secret! I swear."

She blinks a few times. Behind her, Louise shakes her head.

"That's your excuse?"

"I wanted to share the story about her family," I say desperately. "Jess, if you knew the things people send me about content creators, I don't even post half of it. Let me show you." I fumble for my phone, hands trembling.

Jess stops me, her voice rising. "No, Chloé, no! I don't want to see anything. I don't want to hear any more excuses." She presses a hand to her mouth, looking away. "I've always had your back. When the whole Birdie thing blew up and people started throwing shade at me because of you, I defended you. Because you were my friend." Her voice cracks. "But all this time, it was you. You were the one posting all that crap about everyone. You can justify it all you want, but you're the one who *chose* to expose people's worst secrets. To hurt them."

There's a brief pause, and I already know I'm going to regret what I'm about to say. But it's sitting on the tip of my tongue, so I say it anyway.

"I never revealed your secret," I blurt, even though I almost did. But almost isn't the same as actually doing it, so I lift my chin and meet Jess's eyes because I didn't. *I didn't.*

"You..." She blinks a few times, then exhales sharply, like she's blowing out a dozen candles. "Do you expect *gratitude*, Chloé? For not exposing something I told you in confidence?"

My chest tightens. "I..."

I reach for her.

"No." She raises a finger, and I fall silent. Her voice shakes. "Do you want a fucking award for being a decent human being for once?"

"Jess," I say, taking a small step toward her. "I'm so sorry. If you could just listen to my reasons, I know you'd understand why I did it."

It's all rehearsed in my head—my talk about holding influencers accountable, about truth coming to light. Jess believes in that too; I know she does. She practically said it herself that day after the museum.

But she just shakes her head, her big hoops swaying. "Chloé, get the hell out of this club before I throw you out myself," she shouts. Her voice cuts through the music, and people start to turn their heads. I stay rooted to the spot, not sure why. Maybe it's delusion; the faint hope that Jess might see the truth in my eyes.

In my peripheral vision, a bouncer starts toward us, and

someone raises a phone to film. I can already imagine tomorrow's TikToks: Stalker girl has a meltdown in a club.

PM steps between us, his gaze heavy. "You know the way," he says.

I nod to no one in particular and start to back away. I haven't had a single drink, yet the world tilts around me in a dizzy blur. The neon lights, the staring faces, the raised phones—it's all too much. I'm certain that if I were to collapse right now, no one would help; they'd just keep filming, hoping for the most views tomorrow.

The crowd parts around me as if my cancellation were contagious, and I stumble out of the club through the back door. The air outside bites colder, and the pounding music fades into a heavy silence.

Behind me, the door closes and opens again. PM steps out.

"Did you really think it was a good idea to come here tonight?" he asks, lighting his IQOS.

I turn my eyes away. "If she had let me explain..."

"Truth be told, we all saw the video, and forgive me, but it speaks louder than words."

Anger rises in my chest. Am I a screw-up for what happened with Henriette? Of course I am. But I did nothing to Jess except be a good friend. And how is she treating me in return? She won't even hear me out after I came all the way here in the middle of the night, after I begged her to listen.

Then a cold realization settles in. Maybe this isn't just about Jess or Henriette, or even Birdie. Maybe it's something deeper—something I've been avoiding. Hurting people doesn't just break them; it ripples outward, touching everyone nearby. Even those you never meant to hurt. Jess might not be angry because of what I did to her directly, but because she can see what I'm capable of—the damage I've already done.

It feels like a stain on my character, one that seeps into every relationship, every exchange. I let Birdie down, badly. And even though that's a separate story, the way I failed her still hangs between Jess and me. Maybe Jess sees that version of me now and can't unsee it. Maybe she's afraid I'll expose her the way I exposed Birdie. Or maybe she just can't separate who I was with Birdie from who I am with her.

The anger inside me fades, leaving a bitter taste. I thought coming here would prove something—that I was still the friend she could count on. But trust is fragile. Once you break it with one person, everyone else starts waiting for their turn.

I wish I could tell her I'm not that person, not with her. But maybe my actions have already spoken too loudly.

All I can do now is deny everything. I shake my head and meet PM's gaze. "I'm not @FauxEver."

For some reason, I'm daring him to call me out. Maybe I'm all fight after all? But he doesn't. He just watches me quietly, studying my face. Then he takes one last puff before slipping his device into his pocket.

"One piece of advice," he says. "Stop everything now. Go away and start over. Do something you actually love. You don't strike me as stupid, so you certainly see that you're ruining yourself and other people's lives, and for what? A few freebies? It's not worth it. I thought you'd have figured that out by now."

I wipe my face, trying to hide how much his words sting. When I look up again, he's gone, the club door closing behind him.

I'm alone. Again.

25

Add this to the list of things I never told my dad: I actually saw my mother again a few years ago.

It was just before my final year at UAL. I was shopping for supplies somewhere in London when, in the middle of a Waterstones, I thought I recognized a voice. It's a strange feeling, when every cell in your body insists you know a voice but your mind can't quite place it. I followed it through the aisles, and there she was. My mother.

She didn't look much older than in my memories, but she dressed more maturely now. A light camel cashmere jacket, beige trousers, a big Chanel bag slung over her arm. I stared, frozen, as she reached for a book, the diamond pavé wedding band catching the light.

For some reason, whenever I thought about my mother, I never pictured her in London. Because she left us, you know? So surely she'd gone somewhere far—another country, another continent. Far enough that we'd never cross paths by accident. Maybe, over time, I even believed my own lie and thought of her as dead.

But I guess she was always here.

"Excuse me, am I in your way?" she asked when she caught me staring. She shifted politely, still holding her book. Not a flicker of recognition. You'd think a mother would instantly know her own child, but her eyes held nothing but the kind of politeness you offer a stranger.

I opened my mouth to speak, but the words caught when a little girl appeared beside her.

"Mom, can we go?"

She looked older than I was when my mother left—maybe seven or eight. Dressed in a private school uniform, freckles scattered across her face, the same full upper lip as mine.

"Give me another minute, baby, I just requested a book," my mother said, leaning down to pinch her nose lightly. I inhaled sharply.

The girl pulled back, frowning. "Oh, stop doing that." She caught me watching and straightened. "Can Fernando drive me home?"

"In a couple of minutes," my mother said calmly. "I'll pay, then we'll head home together."

"Fine," the girl sighed, rolling her eyes.

That day shattered one of my longest-held illusions—that my mother had left because she felt unworthy of my dad and me. Silly, I know. I used to cling to that idea, reading her parting words—*I hope you take after your father*—as an admission of her own shortcomings, maybe even guilt.

But the truth was simpler, colder. She hadn't left out of shame. She left to start over—to build a new family, as if we were nothing more than a trial run, an imperfect draft she needed to refine into a more polished version elsewhere.

FOLLOWING THE FIGHT WITH JESS, I seriously consider taking my dad up on his offer to fly back to the UK. The thought of escaping the scandals and noise of Paris suddenly feels like a lifeline. I think of the quiet of his countryside home, where you can go days without seeing or hearing anyone. That's what he'd wanted after my mom left: peace. So when he retired, he sold our place in Notting Hill and moved us to a small village in the south of Kent.

I remember hating it at first—thirteen-year-old me thought it was an unfair downgrade from London life. But looking back, I understand why he couldn't leave the city fast enough. He bought an old cottage—a small farm, really—and spent over a year fixing it up, turning it into the home it is today.

I'm on Skyscanner, hunting for cheap flights, when a text from Daniel appears.

Hey

My heart skips.

I quickly type back, trying to pour warmth into words that feel empty now.

Hey

He starts typing. The dots blink, blink, blink. It's a long message, and I can't look away, afraid that if I do, they'll vanish, and he'll vanish with them.

> So I was wondering if I could come by to pick up my things tomorrow afternoon? I'd prefer if you weren't there. I hope you understand. I'll leave my set of keys in the mailbox afterward.

Every word cuts deep, sharp against my fast-beating heart. I take a steadying breath and keep reading through the blur of tears.

> I talked to Diane, and she'll help sort out the rent papers. Starting next month, the contract will be in your name only. I'm leaving you my part of the deposit.

Ignoring the ache blooming in my stomach and the tremor in my lip, I type OK and head to the kitchen, where an unopened bag of Cheetos feels like the only comfort left.

I KEEP READING my emails because I'm a masochist. But also because, deep down, I know that once you've hit rock bottom, there's only one way to go—up. Am I there yet?

To my surprise, I'm getting a lot of partnership requests.

A cheap lingerie brand wants me to be the face of their new "Liars" campaign, which—mind-blowingly—features sheer underwear embroidered with the word *liar*. I pass.

A cannabis energy drink company offers to release a limited-edition can with the slogan *FauxEver is high on truth*. Catchy, but I pass.

Then a well-known smartphone brand slides into my inbox. They want me to promote their latest device, and for a brief, shining moment, I'm thrilled. I spend an entire day putting together a detailed proposal and portfolio, pouring myself into it. Immersed in concepts and visuals, I remember why I fell in love with photography in the first place—the creativity, the freedom to build something from nothing.

By the end, I'm proud.

But when they follow up, it turns out they weren't interested in any of that. They don't want *me*; they want @FauxEver. They want me to keep doing what I was doing—exposing people, tearing down influencers—just this time using their phone's Ultra HD camera.

The final blow lands when a prominent anti-LGBTQ+ political group emails me. They've seen my Henriette post and—kill me now—say it "aligns with their beliefs." They want to meet to "discuss ideas."

I don't even bother to pass. I delete it immediately. It's a new low.

My fingers hover over the DELETE button on @FauxEver more than once. There's no reason to keep the account now that everyone knows. Nothing left to hope for, either. Jess was right—no one reputable will ever want to work with me again. And yet, each time, I hesitate, coming up with excuses. I can't bring myself to pull the plug.

I keep crossing my own moral line, always finding new *yes buts*. First, it was *yes but* @theRealFauxEver has no proof. Then, *yes but* there's no video of me actually being @FauxEver. And now it's *yes but* I haven't confessed to anything.

If I were a better person, I wouldn't hesitate. I'd delete

@FauxEver and move on. Each time I back out, I know deep down I'm not the person I wish I were.

The next day arrives. I don't really have anywhere to be lately, but I choose to honor Daniel's request and give him space to collect his things without me there. As much as I want to see him, to talk to him, maybe make him laugh one last time, I take my bag and head to the neighborhood movie theater. With no particular film in mind, I pick the first available show—a French romance without subtitles. Surprisingly, I don't mind the language barrier; the darkness of the theater offers a rare refuge where I can disappear, safe from being recognized.

When I return home, Daniel's keys are waiting in the mailbox. Standing in the doorway, I take a moment to look around our apartment—my apartment now. To a stranger, everything might look the same: his family's rug still spreads across the floor, the lamps sit where they always did. Yet it's the small absences that hit the hardest. His black jacket and ugly shoes are gone, along with the tiny Lego figurine that used to sit on the coin tray.

I take a deep breath and step inside. Against my will, my eyes keep seeking the things that aren't there.

Daniel's clothes in the closet.

Daniel's diploma above his desk.

Daniel's ridiculous photo where he pretends to hold up the Leaning Tower of Pisa.

All of Daniel's books. The only one left on the shelf is Peter Lindbergh's, the one he gave me on our first date.

It hits me then that this might really be over. It's strange—how, in the heat of it all, I told myself it was just another fight when I was ready to kick him out myself. But I would've preferred that. I'd rather have been the one yelling, crying, forcing him to leave, than watching him go of his own accord. It hurts more knowing he left so quickly, almost eagerly, without even bothering to take the furniture that technically belongs to him.

I try to look back at our story and make sense of it. He did go behind my back and create @theRealFauxEver. He did try to sabotage me and everything I worked for. It's a bitter truth to accept—that someone you trusted could do that to you. But maybe I wasn't the person I thought I was either.

In the hallway, I stop in front of the wall where my four printed photographs still hang. I never applied to that photography contest; the deadline has long passed. Would I have won? The prize was a mentorship with a renowned photographer and a spot in a Rive Gauche gallery. Life could have been so different if I hadn't taken those pictures of Birdie that Sunday. Now it's been two months—eight weeks spent chasing a fantasy while my real dream gathered dust.

It can't all have been for nothing.

It wasn't all for nothing.

About a week later, I'm coming back from the grocery store—cap on, sunglasses low, dressed in the blandest outfit I own to avoid being recognized or called out in the street (which almost never happens, but I'm not willing to bet on *almost*)—when an email from the RevCom agency pops into my inbox. I nearly drop my jar of Nutella.

I read it in a heartbeat, and what heartbeat am I even talking about? Because it stopped, stopped for the longest of seconds when I read the words: *we want to schedule a call with you*.

RevCom! I'd mentally crossed their name off after the Henriette scandal and never followed up with Perrine about the representation offer she'd wanted to discuss. A small part of me had been afraid to hear what everyone else already had —that I was canceled. I thought I'd burned all my bridges, but here it is—the one bridge that might just save me.

I don't lose an instant. I email back, saying that I'm available to pop in on a call whenever they are, and that same afternoon, I find myself in front of my computer, anxiously glancing at the Zoom home screen, awaiting their call.

The video call begins, and it's a young man in an Ami Paris T-shirt who stares back at me, grinning.

"Hello Chloé, it's nice to see you almost in real life."

"Oh, hi!" I respond, attempting to hide my surprise with a smile. "Sorry, I was expecting to hear from Perrine...?"

The guy chuckles as if I've made a joke. "We share most contacts at RevCom, so you might end up speaking with more than one of us at once. As for Perrine, you might not see much of her since she represents Jess and, well..." He lets the sentence trail off, and I feel the heat rise to my cheeks.

"Yeah," I mutter, wishing this wasn't how the call had started.

"Anyway, my name is Tobias. I'm pretty new to the agency but not to the influencer sphere since I used to work for Akréa. Maybe you heard about it?"

He looks like a teenager. Did RevCom really pair me with an intern? I shake my head, but he keeps going, unfazed. "No worries, Chloé. The reason I wanted to reach out is that RevCom would like to represent you, and we're ready to make an offer."

"Oh." I blink, waiting for a wave of happiness to hit me. It doesn't. "What about, um, the recent... things that have been said about me?"

He shrugs, completely unfazed. "The whole @FauxEver situation? It's genius. We love it. Of course, I wouldn't go around promoting you as its founder just yet, given the Henriette fallout, but it gives you incredible clout. Honestly, you're the most interesting figure in the influencer space right now."

I'm pretty sure my jaw drops—and my reflection in the Zoom window confirms it.

Tobias laughs. "I see it's a surprise for you, but you know what they say: any publicity is good publicity. And you might feel like it's not at the moment, but believe me, in a couple of years, once you get contacts and a name for yourself, that will all be water under the bridge."

My eyes get glassy. "You think so?"

"I know it. To prove it to you and to seal the deal between you and RevCom, we want to offer you a first digital activation."

"Really?" I manage, gawking. I know I must sound stupid, but the whole thing feels almost surreal.

"It's an influencer trip, actually, organized by Magnolia Swim. Heard of them?"

I nod frantically. I once splurged on one of their bikinis, a leopard-printed thong, and a triangle top. Not much coverage, but the amount of attention it got me at the beach made it worth every cent.

Tobias smiles, satisfied by my enthusiasm. "Good, they are quite big in the US and now want to develop in Europe too, so they are reuniting forty influencers in a huge villa in Saint Tropez for a two-day stay. All expenses covered. I believe you will be gifted a bunch of stuff to wear for their promotional video, and they also want to book a post on your profile."

"What profile?" I ask to be sure.

"Your personal one, @ChloéLeWarner."

"Right." I fight the urge to pinch my hand to see if I'm dreaming. This is something I would have committed murder to attend before. Picture me sipping free cocktails by a giant pool in a Magnolia Swim set while a photographer takes my picture. It's the dream. Getting paid for it would be beyond. But the image cracks when I remember Tobias mentioned forty influencers. As much as I want to grow on social media, I'm not walking into a gilded trap.

"Earth to Chloé, are you still here? Is it a connection problem?" Tobias moves his computer closer to a window.

"Sorry," I mumble. "It sounds fantastic, but... I have to admit that, with everything going on, I don't know how comfortable I will feel sleeping under the same roof as other content creators..."

Tobias sighs. "I understand, of course. But from experience, I'd say that these girls are *mostly* harmless. What's the worst that could happen anyway? That they gossip about you afterward? They will do that whether you're there or not. And if you go, you might actually make a friend or two. All these girls want is to get more followers; I'm sure some of them will see any association with you as a boost."

I hadn't thought of that, and although I'm dubious about this being an opportunity to make friends, I do remember that nobody bothered Birdie at the Dyson event, her first public appearance since the drug scandal.

"Will Jess be there?"

"No, she refused the partnership," Tobias says, offering no further detail.

I don't have the heart to ask if her refusal had anything to do with me.

"And... Birdie?"

"We don't represent Birdie, so I can't say for sure, but I believe they're only bringing European influencers this time since it's their target audience."

"Oh, okay," I mumble.

Sensing my hesitation, Tobias clasps his hands together. "Listen, I probably shouldn't say this before you've signed anything, but we managed to negotiate a solid fee for you. Actually, thanks to your recent clout, the brand's willing to pay more than they usually do for someone with your following."

He says the number, and I let out a single dry laugh. That's all it takes for me to start packing my bags.

26

My bag is heavier than it should be because I impulsively decided to pack two of my cameras and an extra lens.

And why not? The trip was supposed to be Pinterest-level beautiful, and what better chance to get back into photography than under the golden light of the Côte d'Azur? Time to remind RevCom—and my followers—that I'm more than a gossipmonger. I'm a photographer. A good one.

I take a direct flight from Paris to Nice, where a chauffeur from Magnolia Swim is waiting at arrivals, holding a sign with my name on it. My name! On an airport sign! I nearly lose it and end up snapping a dozen photos like a total maniac. The driver probably thinks I'm nuts.

It's only the first of many surprises. As we pass through the gates of the three-story cream-colored mansion—aptly renamed Villa Magnolia—I step into my room (or rather, my suite), I'm greeted by an explosion of luxury: five bikinis, two swimsuits, three cover-ups, two dresses, two straw hats, two pairs of sandals, and one straw bag embroidered with my name. Nestled among them is a small envelope with a note wishing me a wonderful stay and assuring me that I won't have to worry about hauling everything home, that Magnolia Swim's team will handle shipping them to my apartment after the event.

"This is insane," I whisper to no one before letting out a full-on shriek and throwing myself onto the massive bed, surrounded by my new treasures.

I lie there for what feels like forever, soaking in the moment. Who would've thought that barely three months after spotting Birdie Bay in the apartment across from mine, I'd be living her life? This was it—the gifts, the travel, the money. I still couldn't believe I was getting paid to vacation.

Caught up in that thought, I quickly get up from the bed and rearrange the gifts back into their original shape. Then I take a few videos and photos of the setup for my stories. I post them right away, tagging the brand and adding big, bright smileys.

Tobias texts me the program for the day.

1pm: welcome drink in the lobby

2pm: glam

3-6:30pm: photoshoot on Villa Magnolia's property

7pm: cocktail in the garden followed by a dinner curated by a local Michelin-starred chef

What's glam?

My question is fair, but I'm hoping he's not rolling his eyes at my ignorance. (He probably is.)

He answers within a heartbeat:

hair and makeup styling darling

they want you dazzling for the campaign

Then, a second later:

not that you're not already stunning, of course

Kiss-arsy, but I take it nonetheless.

Which of my new dresses should I wear first? Each one seems more beautiful than the last. I bite my lower lip, studying the lineup before me. They're all mine. As I run my hand over the fabrics, an uneasy feeling twists in my stomach.

Do I really deserve any of this after everything I've done? Will this sense of being a fraud ever go away? I can't stand the thought of it hanging over my happiest moments for months—maybe even years. It has to fade eventually, right?

It's been days since I was exposed as @FauxEver, and I haven't said a word about it. Instead, I've done exactly what Tobias told me to: kept posting my usual content—outfits, makeup unboxings, cute selfies. The rule is simple. Ignore the memes. Ignore the hate. Ignore, ignore, ignore.

My phone rings, and my dad's cheerful face fills the screen. We haven't spoken much since I dropped him off at the airport after his one-day visit. He hugged me goodbye, hesitated like he wanted to say something, then simply told me to keep sending pictures on WhatsApp.

"Hey, Dad," I say with a smile as I answer.

"Chloékins, can you hear me all right?"

It's so good to hear his voice. It always has this calming

effect on me. “Yes, yes, I can hear you. How was your trip back home?”

“It was fine. I slept, and when I woke up, I read a few pages of Bernard Cornwell’s latest novel... But anyway, I don’t want to bore you with that. Listen, I spoke with Daniel —he wanted to discuss transferring the apartment lease to your name.”

Just like that, the comfort I felt evaporates. Why is Daniel talking to my dad more than he’s talking to me?

“Yeah, he mentioned he’d handle it,” I say, trying to keep my tone steady.

“He also said you might be thinking about moving somewhere else...”

What? Since when does Daniel get to decide where I live?

A knock at my door saves me from having to answer.

“Just a sec,” I tell my dad before hurrying to the door. A young waiter stands there, handsome and smiling, holding a tray with a bottle chilling in an ice bucket. *Wow*.

“What is it?” my dad asks.

“Uh, a champagne delivery to my room,” I mumble, gesturing for the waiter to set it on the coffee table.

“Champagne?” There’s a pause. “Isn’t it only one o’clock in Paris?”

“It is,” I laugh. “But, Dad, I’m not in Paris right now. I’m in the South of France for a job. My client sent the bottle.”

“A job? A job! How splendid!” His enthusiasm falters into silence. “Uh... what kind of job gets you champagne deliveries in the middle of the day?”

I juggle how much to tell him. “Well, remember when I mentioned that little side project I was working on?” Meaning @FauxEver, minus the scandal.

"The thing on the internet?"

I can almost hear him trying to connect the dots.

"Yeah, that's the one," I say, forcing a casual tone. I need him to believe staying in Paris was the right choice—that I'm not just surviving but doing well. "There've been some developments. I signed with an agency that's going to represent me. They'll get me campaigns like this one. Paid jobs."

"Oh, I see. So it's not a photography gig, then?"

There's a pause, and I catch a hint of disappointment in his voice.

"Do you want me to open it?" the waiter mouths. I nod. I'll need a few glasses for what's ahead tonight.

"Sort of," I say, "it's a new take on photography..."

The cork pops, and champagne sprays everywhere. The waiter gives me an apologetic smile and whispers that he'll return with towels.

"I brought my cameras with me," I add, sounding more like a guilty child than I intend.

"That's good, but what about—"

The yeasty scent of spilled champagne fills the room, and I rush to open the window.

Peering down from the balcony, I spot a grand French garden below, arranged in perfect symmetry. Rows of flowers burst with color, and at the center, a great white fountain gleams in the midday sun. Around it, staff bustle about, setting up what looks like tonight's dinner party. The air is thick with the scent of blossoms, carried by a soft, salty breeze from the nearby sea. I close my eyes for a moment, trying to steady my breathing.

When I open them again, I realize my dad has been talking the whole time. Guilt prickles. "Dad, I have to go now. My client's trying to reach me," I lie, something that's becoming second nature. "I'll call you in a few days, okay?"

"Go on then, love. I'm proud of you," he says, and my chest tightens.

Back inside, I pour myself a glass of champagne from what's left in the bottle. I down it quickly, then pour another. Birdie's voice echoes in my mind from the Dyson event: *"It's the only way to survive these things."* I finish the second glass and set it down.

It's time to face the other guests.

I HAVE over ninety thousand followers on my personal Instagram.

RevCom wouldn't have signed me if they didn't see potential for even more growth.

Magnolia Swim wouldn't have paid me such a generous fee if I weren't worth the hype.

I deserve to be here.

That's the pep talk I give myself as I descend the staircase into Villa Magnolia's grand entrance hall, where about thirty girls are already gathered. All heads turn in my direction—not because of my see-through red dress over a plain black bikini, but because my face has been plastered all over their For You pages for weeks. The tiny drop of confidence I arrived with drains instantly, and I feel like the bait at a bullfight.

"No way," one of the girls mutters to her group.

I recognize a few faces from the Dyson event, though thankfully none I've written about on @FauxEver. That doesn't stop them from shooting me looks sharp enough to cut glass. I force myself to smile.

A tall, tanned woman in a similar dress to mine strides over.

"Hello, Chloé, I'm Tiana from Magnolia Swim. How's your room? Is everything to your liking?" She brushes my arm lightly, her eyes on me but her focus already shifting elsewhere.

"Hi, yes, thank you so much—everything's wonderful, I..."

I hear a bit of a scuffle behind us, followed by someone exclaiming, "...the nerve to come here!" It's loud enough for everyone nearby to hear, so Tiana definitely hears, and I'm suddenly growing hot, wishing I didn't have any champagne at all because I'm starting to feel unsteady, and the last thing I want is for anyone to think I got tipsy in the middle of the afternoon before my first real influencer job.

Trying to defuse the mounting tension, Tiana claps her hands lightly.

"Lovely, we're happy to have you with us. Feel free to grab a juice or a snack. We'll wait for a few late arrivals before going over the rest of the program."

I try not to be too thrown by this lukewarm reception—I've been expecting that, after all—so I smile wider, take a glass of cucumber water from the bar, and navigate the room in search of a friendly face.

My eyes land on a redhead who I think I recognize from Instagram but can't properly place her name—Lily or Lucie, something like that. She tilts her head to the side, and I guess she's been living under a rock for the past week because she actually gives me a smile.

"I almost chose the same dress to wear today," she says. "Love this red."

"Oh, you could choose your items?" I can't help but feel a twitch of envy at the idea that even in such a tight group, there could be different levels of privilege. It's stupid, I know. With the amount of gifts I received, I shouldn't feel this way, but I would have loved to pick out my pieces.

"The bikinis they gifted me were a bit too tight, so they drove me to the pop-up boutique they have in town and told me to choose whatever I wanted. That was fun."

Relieved, I smile. "Wow, sounds nice indeed." Then, because I'm afraid she could leave to speak to somebody more interesting, I keep talking. "It's my first time being invited on such a trip," I blush as I admit it.

Her face lights up. "Wow, really? Congratulations, then. It's a milestone," she says, handing me her juice to cling to. "How many followers do you have?"

I give her the number and catch the flicker of surprise she tries to hide. Am I the smallest influencer here?

"I'm sorry—I didn't get your name?" I ask, steering the conversation elsewhere.

The redhead starts to answer, but another voice cuts in, sharp and perfumed with Gris Dior.

"Layla, believe me, you don't want to befriend that one."

I turn, startled, and find myself face to face with Melinda, Ania's friend from the Dyson event. Her raven-black hair is slicked back into a tight bun, and her pale, icy eyes fix on me like she's sizing me up. I shift my weight, silently cursing myself for not anticipating this. It makes sense she's here. I remember checking her profile when I was researching Ania—around four hundred thousand followers, not as pricey but still perfectly marketable with that polished

French aesthetic. Honestly, I'd almost forgotten about her. Next to the big names, she barely stood out.

Melinda crosses her arms over her electric-blue kimono and smirks. "Chloé is the girl behind that @FauxEver account. She outed Henriette and sabotaged Birdie Bay and Ania, among others."

Layla gives me a timid smile, as if waiting for confirmation that it's a joke. It takes me a moment to pull my features into a poker face, but it's a second too late—her jaw drops as she looks between Melinda and me.

"Well," I say with a forced smile, running a hand through my hair. "There was some sort of misunderstanding..."

Melinda lets out a sharp laugh, and the chatter in the room instantly quiets. "Yeah, bet there was one. Like your presence here today."

"I was invited by the brand." *I deserve to be here.*

That seems to silence her for a moment, but then she tilts her head, unimpressed. "I guess we should all watch our step around you, then. Who knows what kind of work you came here to do."

And just like at the club with Jess the other day, everyone edges away, leaving me alone in the corner with my untouched cucumber water.

Tiana walks over, her smile tight and a little apologetic. She lays a hand on my shoulder. "Are you okay?"

"Yes! Of course. Wonderful," I say, smiling a lot. "Just wonderful."

27

Have you ever had your hair and makeup done by a professional? If you haven't, let me tell you that the whole process is less *glam* than it might sound.

Tiana leads me and three other girls into a small room cluttered with makeup palettes and hairstyling tools. A bearded man in his thirties greets me at the door.

"My name is Frédérique, and you must be Chloé?"

"Yes, nice to meet you," I say with a smile, feeling a bit intimidated. He gestures for me to sit by the window. The other girls settle into corners of the room, chatting animatedly in French with their own stylists.

Frédérique shows me a picture of Lily Collins. "The team wants something like this for you. Good?"

"Sure," I mumble. "But I don't have curtain bangs..."

"No worries, I'll cut it real quick," he says, already reaching for his scissors. "It'll look nice enough for the photos."

I don't even have time to ask if it'll also look nice enough for real life before a girl with pink hair spins my chair around to face her.

"*Salut*, I'm Mona, your makeup artist. How are you?"

"Hi! A bit overwhelmed, I admit..." I say, distracted by Frédérique tugging at my hair.

Mona lets out a small laugh. "Don't worry, we're used to working together. The brand wants a natural look—gold-to-brown tones on the eyes, full fluffy brows, and glossy lips."

"Oh, nice. Could you maybe go easy on the brows? I did a strong brow look once, and it looked kind of weird on me."

Understatement. I looked like someone who'd just survived a lightning strike.

Mona purses her lips and studies my face. "*Non*. Trust me, you'll like it."

The session starts, and between Frédérique burning my neck, chopping off my hair like it's nothing, while Mona experiments with brow gel on my face, I don't really feel extra.

"Move her head to the left," Mona tells him, and I'm just like a rag doll in their hands. I wish there were a mirror around to reassure me I don't look like a clown, but all I get is Rowan, the photographer who's been assigned to me, shooting pictures and videos while mumbling a series of *pas mal* (not bad) under his breath.

"*Et voilà!*" Mona sings as she dusts the last bit of blush on my cheeks.

"*Magnifique,*" Frédérique adds with a satisfied nod.

I offer them a small smile. "Thank you. Do you guys have a mirror...?"

"I'm sure there's one in the bathroom," Mona says, already turning to greet the next girl.

I stand, determined to see what they've done to me, but before I can make it far, Rowan appears in the hallway.

"The first part of the photoshoot is this way," he says, gesturing toward the gardens.

"I know," I mumble. "I just wanted to—"

He cuts me off with a shake of his head. "We don't have much time. Please, follow me."

When I finally return to my room, I'm sore, exhausted, and starting to wonder if I'm really being paid enough for whatever this job has turned into.

In the program Tobias sent me, the mention of a three-and-a-half-hour photoshoot hadn't seemed like a big deal. What's that compared to a normal nine-to-five? But I hadn't imagined I'd be posing in three different rooms of the villa, climbing in and out of the pool, and even up a tree—a small one, but still. I lost track of how many bikinis and cover-ups I'd worn; by the end, I was fairly sure I'd modeled every piece in the collection.

"Hmm, do you think I could have a glass of water?" I'd asked Rowan at some point. Tiana was nowhere to be found, and for hours I hadn't seen anyone except other influencers shooting content.

"Sure," he said, though he made no move to get it, and so we just kept going.

About an hour later, I caught my reflection in the pool's water and felt a flicker of relief. My hair and makeup had held up. I actually looked good. But that small spark of confidence dimmed when I noticed a group of girls being photographed together. They looked like they were having the time of their lives—laughing, hugging, all in matching Magnolia Swim sets. Their shots would be stunning.

"When do we shoot the group pictures?" I asked, trying not to sound too envious.

Rowan shook his head. "Ehm, we won't."

"Why?" I looked at him, daring him to say what I already suspected.

He rubbed the back of his neck. "The other girls, they didn't want to shoot with you. I don't know why."

My cheeks burned as I nodded silently and repositioned myself for the next shot.

After we wrapped up the photos, I was on my way back to my room when a videographer stopped me and said it was time for the video content, and could I change into that zebra suit I wore earlier and climb back on the tree?

I did what I was told, even though, out of the corner of my eye, I could see the whole group of influencers already sipping Aperol Spritzes on a side terrace. Layla caught me looking her way and quickly turned her head.

Why did they finish before me? Was something wrong with my content? Was it because of my stretch marks? I'd done my best to hide them, but there's only so much you can cover in a bikini shoot. Maybe the Magnolia Swim team wasn't happy—maybe they'd looked at the photos, rolled their eyes, and wondered why they'd chosen that Brit instead of a "real" influencer. Maybe that's why it was taking so long.

I swallowed the lump in my throat and smiled wider for the camera. *I deserve to be here.*

When I finally make it back to my room, I check the time and groan. "You've got to be shitting me."

I have less than thirty minutes to touch up my makeup, fix my hair (my new curtain bangs looked bouncy and sophisticated during the shoot, but now they cling flat against my face), and get dressed for the party. My whole body aches as if I've just run a marathon. When I glance at the coffee table, the champagne bottle is gone, replaced by a small bouquet of peonies. A shame—I could really use a drink right now.

By the time I stumble into the garden in my Jimmy Choo heels and pink mini dress, I'm late, but at least I look *pas mal*. My bangs are still a little limp, but I managed to coax a curl or two into them, so they might just pass.

I hadn't had time to peek down from my balcony to see how the decorations were coming along, so when I step onto the terrace, I'm met with a sight so breathtaking it momentarily makes me forget the dozens of eyes on me. Twinkling lights and oversized pink magnolias adorn the trees, and around the great white fountain, tables are dressed in soft pink linens, candles, and lush matching bouquets. The whole scene looks like something straight out of a movie.

"What do you think?" Tiana appears at my side. For a second, the beauty of the setting almost makes me forgive her for disappearing during the shoot.

"It's magical," I say, then turn toward her. "Um, Tiana, I've been wondering... The photographer said the other girls refused to shoot with me. I hope it didn't cause too much trouble?"

She suddenly avoids my eyes. "Yeah, well, don't worry about it. We got more than enough content to promote the collection."

I nod, still searching her face. "Have you seen my pictures yet?"

"Your pictures? No, I haven't."

I can tell she's lying.

Tiana gives my arm a light, distracted touch. "Enjoy your evening, Chloé. And try the Porn Star martinis at the bar. They've renamed them Magnolia Stars, and they're delicious."

She walks off, leaving me standing awkwardly in the middle of the terrace. Layla passes by without a glance, and other girls openly stare. I thought I looked good until I saw them—intricate hairstyles, fresh makeup. How do they all look so fantastic after the long afternoon we've had?

Clenching my teeth, I head down to the garden and make a beeline for the bar. I grab a cocktail, and Birdie's advice echoes in my mind like a quiet mantra. She was right —it really is the only way to survive these things. I finish the first glass quickly and order another.

About twenty minutes later, the bartender finally breaks the silence. She glances at my fourth Magnolia Star and asks if I'd like some appetizers. I decline, feeling light and fizzy, finally tipsy enough to stop caring about the whispers drifting around me.

A little floaty now, I melt into the crowd and begin scanning the tables for my name, dreading the moment I find it because it'll mean I'll be left purposeless. I'm brushing past the second table when a girl with duck lips and a Gucci bag bumps into me, shoving me just enough to make it feel intentional.

I squint at her, though she's barely an arm's length away.

"Victoria Thoumieux?" I ask, amused by the coincidence. I didn't spot her at the welcome drink earlier, but I would have recognized her—after all, I paid good money for her Instagram success course a few months ago.

She turns, momentarily startled, hovering between

pretending she doesn't know me and deciding whether to respond.

I don't give her the chance.

"I know you!" I say brightly. "I took your masterclass on social media strategy a while back."

The memory almost makes me laugh—maybe I even do.

Victoria glances around, clearly uneasy. "Right, yes, probably..."

"*The key is confidence*," I say, imitating her with both hands raised near my face. "That was some serious bullshit."

"Excuse me?" she says, staring at me in disbelief.

"Your class," I add with a smirk. "It's such a ripoff."

Someone beside her lets out a low chuckle. "Oh God, Vicky's gonna draw blood tonight."

Victoria steps closer, towering over me. "You've got some nerve, FauxEver girl. Now that everyone knows it's been you all along, I thought you'd die of shame or something."

My heart pounds, but I don't let it show. Instead, I lean in, close enough that only she can hear. "Oh, Vicky—can I call you Vicky too? If you knew what I have on you, you'd be humbler."

She swallows and lowers her voice. "You have nothing on me."

"Hah!" I frown up at her, my tone sharp but playful. "Don't you ask your students to pay in cash so you don't have to declare the income from your little masterclasses? Not very patriotic of you. Though I guess that leaves more money for Gucci."

Her jaw drops. "That's—"

I cut her off, pressing a hand to my chest. "Before you try to lie your way out of this, *your honor, I have screenshots*."

Victoria jerks back as if I'd slapped her.

I know I should stop here, have something to eat, and go slower on the Magnolia Stars, but I feel exhilarated. Powerful for the first time in weeks.

"In fact," I say loudly, social filters all gone. "I have so many screenshots that would make you all look like the fucking clowns that you are..."

Now it's not just Victoria's group—there are twenty, maybe thirty girls surrounding me. I eye each of them, but my vision blurs, and I do feel a bit drunker than I want to be.

"You're the only clown here," someone says. My head spins toward the voice—and lands on Melinda. *Fuck.*

My shoulders drop as I try to summon a clever comeback, but nothing comes.

"If you had an ounce of pride, you'd already be on a plane back to Paris," she says, her tone sharp and confident. A ripple of approval moves through the crowd, though no one else dares speak. Maybe they're afraid of ending up in my little Burn Book.

"I was invited by the brand," I repeat, but my voice lacks the bite it had earlier.

Melinda shakes her head, her jet-black hair swaying. "*Oui*, that much we got."

Chin high, I move to walk past her, but she stops me with a hand.

"Look around you. Nobody wants you here," she says coldly. "You might get invited to other events like this one, but that's just because the brand wants to parade you like the circus freak you are. It doesn't mean you're one of us. You'll never be."

I look around, a bit self-conscious now, and all I see is contempt. I bite back my rising tears. *Do I really deserve to be here?*

"I don't want to be one of you." The words slip out, barely audible over the murmur of the fountain.

"What?" Melinda's brows knit together. Her smirk returns, crueler this time. "Is that another one of your delusions? You're just a wannabe, always chasing, never the main act."

"Oh, shut the fuck up," I snap, anger flaring. "You make it seem like you've got the perfect life, like you're above everyone. But not everyone wants to be like you."

Layla gasps, Victoria's eyes widen, but Melinda doesn't flinch.

"Maybe not everyone," she says coolly, "but you definitely do."

My mouth falls open, but before I can speak, Melinda steps closer and grips my shoulders.

"That's for Ania, you bitch."

She shoves me hard, and I topple backward into the fountain.

28

I text Tobias:

I was pushed into a fountain in front of the whole lot of influencers

wow, did somebody record it?

Memories of all the phones pointed at me flash through my mind, and I wish the bathroom floor would open up and swallow me whole.

I believe so

good

Good? I stare at my phone unblinking, but it only makes me feel sicker, so I lean over the toilets again. Vomit, again. Cry, again. Regret crashes over me in waves—for every Magnolia Star Martini I drank tonight and for everything I know I'll feel tomorrow. I roll onto my side, clutching my bathrobe like the safety blanket I should've had earlier. What was I thinking, getting drunk in a foreign city surrounded by people who despise me? People armed with cameras and massive followings.

"Nooo—" I moan to no one.

When I stumbled back into my room, soaked, makeup smudged, hair messy, all I wanted was somebody friendly to talk to. Someone who'd comfort me, take my side, and not ask questions. The fact that I went through my contacts and only found Tobias to text was a blow. But the fact that nobody from the Magnolia Swim team came to check on me? That was probably my professional burial.

Even from the bathroom floor, where I'm now curled up between a giant marble bathtub and the toilet, I can hear the party downstairs, the chatter and laughter mocking me. My disgrace, the main course of their evening. I don't need to be there to know what they're saying—how I've become a laughingstock, a spectacle.

Will it always be like this? My highest highs darkened by the few mistakes of the past? Me numbing myself with alcohol to survive moments when I feel like dying?

I'm tempted to get up and look for something to eat. Anything would do at this point. But it's pointless, I know it —the room is stocked with bikinis but devoid of any snacks. And I'd rather starve than go downstairs to beg.

I close my eyes and let my sobs lull me to sleep.

THE NEXT DAY's program is a "light" lunch on a yacht, followed by another photoshoot at sea, but I pretend to be sick and ask to fly back home in the morning. Hiding behind a pair of sunglasses, I force myself to smile one last time as I say goodbye to Tiana. Home stretch.

"Have a safe trip back," she says with a tight smile. Nobody from the Magnolia Swim or RevCom teams tries to stop me from leaving. By now, I think everyone has probably seen the videos, so I probably served my purpose anyway, stirring up buzz for the brand that goes far beyond a few bikini pictures.

I've watched the clips too. At least the first ones that were posted.

FauxEver wet

That's how we treat homophobes

The fall was a good one, from the shock on my face to the way my dress turned see-through as I struggled to climb out of the fountain (no one helped, in case you were wondering). It was pure clickbait. Once captured on video and played in an endless loop, it went viral in no time. The only small comfort was the noise around us, drowning out whatever Melinda or I said. If a fountain shove could rack up millions of views, imagine the chaos if anyone had heard a full confession.

Motion-sick and honestly just sick of it all, I delete Instagram and TikTok on the drive to the airport. Just the apps, not my accounts.

I make it through security, spend a small fortune on pastries at Paul, and eat everything I can under the disgusted stares of other passengers. Then end up rushing to the bathroom to throw up. I spend the flight shivering, my stomach in knots.

At Orly, while I'm waiting for my cab, a group of

cheerful tourists asks me to take their picture in front of the PARIS sign.

"Please," says a middle-aged woman with an Eastern European accent, handing me her Android.

I take a few full-length shots until she waves her hands, showing me she wants it horizontal. *Kill me.* I oblige; and she and her friends burst into laughter, delighted by the photos.

And I wonder what pictures are for other people. Why do they care about taking them, getting good phone cameras, trying to find good angles... whatever for if there are no likes, no followers at the end of it? Memories, sure. But let's be real, who really rewatches the fifty pictures they took of fireworks, of the tourist landmarks they got to visit? Don't these pics just end up forgotten, a waste of time and Cloud storage?

I shake my head, suddenly filled with disgust at myself. I used to like photography so much, now all I see is the gain.

"*Mademoiselle, vous montez?*" the taxi driver asks, and I jump in. We drive in silence, windows open, and for a short time I'm grateful for the impersonal hum of his broken radio.

It doesn't last.

"Where did you travel from?"

I inhale sharply, not wanting to make small talk, but what choice do I have when stuck in traffic at the entrance of Paris?

"Umm, the South of France."

"I see. It's really overrated, don't you think?" And without giving me the time to answer, he keeps on. "Now, the *Bassin d'Arcachon*...how do you call it in English, that spot by the sea next to Bordeaux?"

"The Arcachon Bay?" I offer.

"*Voilà*! That's a place you tourists should visit. It's *sans chichis*, unlike Saint Tropez."

A text saves me from answering.

Hey! Do you have time to meet tomorrow?

I frown but can't think of an excuse. Don't I have all the time in the world?

Sure

Amazing! 4pm in Palais Royal?

Just as I'm sending a thumbs up, the driver slams on the brakes and leans on the horn, shouting, "*Non mais ça va ou bien?!*" through the open window. He honks again for emphasis and lets out a frustrated snort.

"These cyclists! They've put in all these bike lanes across Paris, and for what? It's a nightmare to drive in this city now!"

I'm still recovering from the jolt when the driver suddenly swivels in his seat, eyes off the road.

"Oh, mademoiselle, look." He holds out his hand, where a tiny ladybug rests.

It's as if the altercation from two seconds ago never even happened. Bipolar much?

"Take it, *vite*! You should make a wish," he says enthusiastically while passing me the insect. Those French superstitions.

I reluctantly take it and watch it climb along my arm before flying away through the window, taking my chance at a wish with it. It's fine. I don't need a ladybug anyway. What I really need is a genie and a lamp.

The following day, I'm in the city center, praying nobody recognizes me. I check my phone and realize I'm early.

Killing time, I wander around Palais Royal Park, grab an iced coffee at Café Kitsune, and snap a picture of it on a bench with my Leica. Cliché, I know, and I don't care. It's the first time I'm actually using one of my cameras in ages, so at this point, any shot feels like a small return to myself. Coffee, however, makes me extra anxious these days, so I end up throwing it in the trash. I downloaded Instagram back last night because I'm weak. Turns out, all the drama only boosted my follower count to a staggering 500k on @FauxEver and 132k on my personal account. At this rate, I'll be catching up to Jess pretty soon.

But these new followers? They're not here for my sparkling personality. They're just waiting for the next trainwreck to happen. So, I've been avoiding the comments and DMs like the plague. My tired, bloodshot eyes are proof of how well that's been working.

I walk to the spot of rendezvous and there, by the fountain on a green lounge chair, I see somebody with Daniel's oval-shaped face, messy chestnut hair, and a pair of glasses.

I wave at Diane.

"Hey, Chloé," she says, hugging me. "Long time no see."

"Hello, how have you been?"

Somehow, I thought that by losing Daniel, I would be losing her too. Twin loyalty and all. I was surprised when she wrote me yesterday, asking to meet, until I remembered that she wanted more pictures for her LinkedIn account.

"I'm good," Diane says. And she does look good. She's wearing a simple white linen set, a large beige Polène bag, and the rosy complexion of somebody who sleeps well. "I'm not asking you about how you are, though."

I sit on a free chair next to her. "Oh—you heard."

"Yep, I heard some things, read some others online."

Feeling self-conscious, I bite my lip. "Did Daniel say...?" I struggle to form the sentence. Truth be told, all I want is for her to talk to me about Daniel. How is he? Where does he live now? Does he speak about me?

She nods. "He didn't say who ended things, though. But from his face, I guessed it was your call."

Oh. I drop my eyes, toying with the tiny emerald ring on my pinkie. My dad gifted it to me when I graduated.

"Wait, was it his?" she asks, pulling back.

I think of Daniel's look after I threatened him, and hope Diane doesn't see how my ears start to burn.

"I guess it was a mutual agreement. Things just weren't... working between us anymore."

Diane pinches her red-painted lips like someone who doesn't believe a word but is too well-raised to probe further. "Okay." She hands me a drink in a plastic cup. "Didn't know if you wanted to have a drink, so I took you lemonade; it sounded fitting."

I give her a quizzical glance.

"When life gives you lemons..." she explains with a tight smile.

"Ah, yeah," I accept the cup. "Thanks."

Some kids wildly run past us, and I follow them with my eyes. Soon the park would transform into an autumn postcard — if the weather forecast is to be believed, today is one of the last hot summer days.

"I think the best spot for the pictures would be there," I

tell Diane, nodding my chin towards the arches. "It's not really allowed to take professional pics there, but if we're quick..."

"Umm, Chloé?" she interrupts me. "That's very thoughtful of you, and we definitely need to set up a date for these pictures, but that's not the reason why I asked to see you today," she says, catching my eye.

"No?" I blink, a hint of annoyance slipping through. Why would I be hanging out with my ex's all-knowing twin if we'd broken up? Then I remember that no one really wants to hang out with me anymore, so I plaster on a polite smile.

She bats her eyelashes. "I need to talk to you about your @FauxEver."

The way she said *your* throws me a little, and I must be doing a terrible job at concealing my surprise because two lines appear between Diane's eyebrows.

"Because I guessed right the other day, didn't I?"

I bite my lower lip, thinking about lying. But it's all over the internet. Apparently, even a local TV channel covered it. And honestly, I'm tired of pretending. So I just nod.

Without meeting my eye, Diane mirrors my nod, and a million scenarios flash before me: that she will rise from her chair and throw her lemonade at me, shout that I'm despicable, record the whole thing, and *wait*, could she?

But she only lets out a huff, the kind of effortless one French women seem to master from birth. "Why did you do it?"

It's a million-dollar question, isn't it? The official version is that I wanted the world to see the dark side of influencers, yet that would be hypocritical of me to say now, wouldn't it? Because, in the process, I had turned into the dark side myself.

I search Diane's face. It would be so easy to tell her that I don't want to talk about it, or to simply rise from my chair and leave. There are always options, and I choose to stay.

"First, it was because I felt like it was the right thing to do, but then," I begin, the truth rushing out like water from an opened fountain, unstoppable. "It was because the attention I got from that first post, Birdie's post, was like a dopamine shot I didn't know I needed. And after it had worn off, I wanted more. I was hooked."

Diane gives me a faint smile, encouraging me to continue.

"Then Birdie discovered that it was me, and that was..." I shake my head, suddenly overwhelmed.

"So Birdie knows?"

"Yeah, then Daniel discovered it, and Jess. And from there it no longer felt like a dopamine shot. It was like, whatever I was trying to do was ultimately backfiring. Henriette, the Magnolia Swim trip..." I take a deep breath as everything that happened replays in my mind, and I find myself mentally drenched. You know how in those 90s Nintendo games, you have a giant bug running after you, and you spend the whole game trying to escape it? It's tiresome.

Diane watches me closely, patiently. "You lost control," she fills in.

"I guess you can say that, yes."

She blows some air through her nose, and her features change ever so subtly. I think they morph into her lawyer face.

"So listen, I think that what you have with @FauxEver is a gold mine..."

"I know, I..." I cut her off before stopping abruptly. What did she say?

Oblivious, Diane presses on. "But right now, it has a bit of a bad reputation, and the whole drama is hanging on your shoulders, which is, you'll agree, not optimal for growth. So what I would like to offer you is a partnership."

Growth? I take a sip of lemonade just to do something as my head starts swimming.

"We can create a platform or an app that would allow FauxEver to expand beyond Instagram," she says, looking ahead as if there were an invisible board with notes there. "It could be fueled in part by in-depth articles and warnings about social media, for example, and in part by user-generated content."

"What does that mean?" my voice is annoyingly childlike.

"This means people could log in, create their pseudonyms on FauxEver, and then upload their 'proof' of content creators being out of touch. I think that's what is already happening on your account, right? People are sending you intel?" She doesn't wait for my answer. "Well, it'd be the same, just not going through you directly. We'll still approve all posts, of course, but the difference is that it will feel less personal."

I search her face for any hint of irony, but Diane looks back at me through her glasses, serious as a courtroom.

"Would this be ...legal?" I blurt out.

"I can handle the legal part," she winks, then takes a sip of her lemonade. "The fact is, with @FauxEver being on Instagram, it's just a matter of time until reports pile up and the app takes the account down. But if we take it elsewhere, on a platform that we create, we can put everything in place to make our business safe."

Business. I mull this word in my head, and it has such a pleasant hum. But something stops me from really considering it.

"I don't want to expose any more people," I say, and I reckon that much is almost true.

Diane snaps her fingers. "Then it's a good thing it won't be openly posted by your hands. The public will handle the online backlash. And the core of the project will be on incentivization anyway, so that's basically charity. Think posts on educational topics like the importance of parental control and how to discuss social media's distorted reality with kids... This could possibly even lead to the development of a code of conduct for 'role models' to promote responsible online behavior."

As the idea swirls in my mind, I realize I don't hate it. "That's ... nice." It feels like circling back to the original vision I had for FauxEver, right before everything went downhill.

"Isn't it?" she beams. "A little rebranding can do wonders. And this is something you could be in charge of. That way, you won't be caught up in the drama anymore."

"What would we do about Henriette? People are saying that..."

"I know what people are saying," Diane shrugs. "We can use our first benefit to donate to a local LGBTQ+ organization. Show everyone that we're not the bad guys."

"Wow, that's..." My lemonade is melting, making my hands all sticky. "That's a lot to think about."

"It sure is, because once everything is in place, we could start with the ultimate piece of revelation: your story," she grins. "A full, in-depth confession of what you did and an exposé on why you did it. Believe me, that's the story everybody wants to read right now. Normal people don't want to be siding with the privileged Birdies of this world; they want a legitimate reason to dislike them. What you did with @FauxEver was giving them that, but by denying it was you, you're just undermining all the work you did."

I frown. I hadn't thought of that.

"But, why would you want to work with me? Daniel and I... we didn't part on the best of terms, and I'm pretty sure your whole family hates me."

Diane swats her hand dismissively, but I note that she doesn't contradict me. "There is a reason why my siblings all went to study literature, and I decided to go into law: I can sniff a good deal from afar, and in your case, you're not even that far. That little account you have is a hot topic, even people who are not in your sphere are talking about it right now..."

"You realize it doesn't make me feel any better?" I say, though I am kind of chuffed at the idea of being somebody people talk about.

She tilts her head at me. "And why not? Social media is not real life—it's for entertainment. And you have grabbed people's attention; you have *created* entertainment. Do you realize how hard it is to ask people for a few minutes of their time nowadays when so many platforms are competing against one another? Podcasts, shorts, pictures ... even books. FauxEver is fueled by the desire people have to see beyond what content creators are offering."

I understand, on a fundamental level, that Diane is right, but I find myself unable to feel good about it. Lately, everything I've been excited about has blown up in my face.

Consequently, my mind instinctively searches for flaws in her strategy.

She senses my doubt and puts a hand on my knee.

"Think it over, weigh the pros and cons, but don't take forever," she says, getting up. "I wouldn't want us to lose momentum."

29

Telling Diane the truth unlocks something in me I didn't think I still had: hope.

Her idea has its merits, I'll give her that. But doing what she suggests would mean openly admitting that I'm behind @FauxEver. Everyone already kind of knows, of course, yet making it official... I'm not sure what that would lead to. Would Henriette come after me? Birdie? Ania, or the others I exposed? Melinda already shoved me into a fountain in front of dozens of people, so what would stop someone else from doing worse?

Still, a platform like the one Diane describes could give @FauxEver—and me—some real legitimacy. Making it informative, with articles and interviews, could bring the focus back to what FauxEver was meant to be: proof that the internet is fake.

So what's stopping me?

It's 11 p.m., and I'm in bed, wrapped in the glow of my laptop as a new Netflix series plays. I can't stand the silence lately—it's too loud. I need background noise now, constantly. It's strange, really; I never thought that would happen here in Paris, a city that never stops humming. Yet even the faint sounds of traffic below don't soothe my restless mind anymore.

I should call my dad back. He's been trying all day, probably worried sick that I'm not answering. But I can't pretend with him, not right now. So instead, I type *Chloé Warner* and *FauxEver* into the search bars on X, Threads, and Reddit, scrolling through every post I can find. Reading the insults doesn't fix anything, but it's starting to feel like binge eating—if I take it all in at once, it dulls the pain for a little while. And that's something.

It's not pretty, what people are saying about me.

Imagine posting shit about influencers then having the audacity to go on an influencer trip, tweets someone. I would have hauled her into that fountain myself

Another one, a girl from Germany, writes: Can't believe she made a post ABOUT HERSELF, using her eating disorder as a means to get sympathy. So fucked up. I admit, in retrospect, that it was a tiny bit fucked up. But it's my story, so shouldn't I be allowed to use it as it pleases me?

And it escalates beyond just my activity on @FauxEver. People begin digging into my past, scouring old Facebook pictures and critiquing my photography skills. It's all incredibly nasty and heavily biased.

Some guy claims we went to high school together and posts that I used to make homophobic jokes in class. Lies! I zoom in on his profile picture, but his face doesn't ring a bell. I'm sure I would have remembered a redhead.

Some girl who hired me to edit her pictures on Fiverr a couple of months ago claims I body-shamed her by offering to "slim her waist" a bit. Which I did, but only because she'd first asked me to remove all her pimples. I figured she wanted the full Facetune package.

Some people go so deep in my history that I'm afraid they might even find my estranged mother if they keep going.

I've become a phenomenon, and my name is trending. Unfortunately, it's for all the wrong reasons.

What kills me is that I can't respond. I'm tempted to make fake accounts to push back against the hate, but I've already been burned once and won't risk adding more fuel to the fire. It feels so unfair, not being able to defend myself against the lies. All I can do is scream at my phone and cry.

I would've kept at it all night if I hadn't received that DM on Instagram.

I see you, Chloé

The account is some @Eolhc; no profile picture, no bio. It's so spammy I almost block it. But then something on the only post there catches my attention.

I squint, recognizing that bright green shirt as mine. The video zooms in, and it's me, indeed, at Jardin Royal yesterday, taking a picture of my iced coffee.

The video doesn't show much more than that—just a few clips of me walking around. I frown. There's no caption, no hashtags, and the only account tagged is mine. Why would someone go through the trouble of following me, recording that, creating a new account, and posting it? None of it makes any sense.

"Must be a joke," I try to reassure myself out loud.

It must be, right? The post has only two likes, both from

bots. Whoever posted it didn't do it for an audience. But they tagged me. They wanted me to see it.

Frustrated, I toss my phone aside and try to focus on my series. Yet something feels off, so like a yo-yo, the phone ends up back in my hand. I open the account again and blink.

Eolhc is Chloé spelled backward. What the fuck?

Without thinking twice, I slide straight into the account's DMs.

Why are you following me?

The answer is quick. *You know why*

No fucking way. Something between fear and hope grips me.

I thought we had settled that, I type slowly.

Why am I nervous? I catch myself biting my nails as I stare at the *dots, dots, dots*.

Did we?

I have a surprise for you: come by the Balenciaga store on Rue Saint Honoré in an hour

I frown. Is he for real? *No*, I type back, but don't quit the conversation.

I think you should

I place my phone face up in front of me, and the screen glows in the darkness of my room. It's nearly midnight, and although I can't be certain who's texting, I have a feeling I do, in fact, know.

It has to be Daniel, right?

Call it delusion, call it desperation, but at this point, I'm game. *I'll come*, I text as I leap off the sofa.

He must have realized his mistake by now (took him long enough!), and he's going to apologize. I'll apologize too, because I am sorry—I shouldn't have threatened him; that was a shitty thing to do. But I was angry, and anger is a terrible fuel. We have issues to work through, mostly trust and maybe a bit of resentment, but I'm confident we'll fix things. That's what people who love each other do, after all.

There is nothing like meeting with an ex to double down on appearance efforts.

I hold dresses against my body, deciding which one will make him rue the day more when he sees me: the pale pink Reformation one with the heart-shaped bodice or the simple but extra-flattering light blue linen Sézane. I go with the latter—it's older, and I don't want Daniel thinking I dressed up for him. Keeping that same logic, I do a quick no-makeup makeup look and braid my hair loosely, the way he used to like it.

Maybe later, we'll return home together.

Wrapping myself in a long cardigan, I call an Uber.

The street is deserted, typical of a shopping district at this hour, but it's well lit—City of Lights and everything. Standing in front of Balenciaga, I half expect him to pop out from the corner of a street with flowers in his hand.

A sudden movement to my left jolts me, and I swiftly pivot on my heels, heart pounding in my fingertips.

"Daniel?" I ask the empty street.

Nobody answers, but as my eyes drag further in search of him, they land on the wall by the boutique where, in big black capital letters, is written:

@ChloeLeWarner is @FAUXEVER

My legs weaken, and I'm momentarily frozen; I just stand there, staring at my downfall.

I've read these words countless times online over the past couple of days, but seeing them like this somehow makes them truer. More impactful. Tomorrow, the city will awaken to this declaration on one of the most touristy streets in the world. Pictures will be taken. Everybody will be talking about it.

Survival instinct kicks in: I can't let that happen. As I slowly approach the wall, a glimmer on the ground catches my eye.

It's spray paint.

I don't stop to question why it's there. With trembling hands, I grab the can and do the only thing that comes to mind: start covering the words. The paint is green and struggles to hide the bold black letters, but I keep going, layering it on until *@FAUXEVER* disappears, desperate to erase any trace of my connection to it.

Time slips away. My hands are sticky with paint, my breath ragged. I can't tell if I'm crying or just sweating, but my face is wet. I'm so focused on covering every inch that I don't notice the flashing red and blue lights behind me, or the officer's voice announcing my arrest.

It's only when their hands close around my arms, steering me toward the car, that I finally snap back to reality.

"You say you didn't do it?"

"I didn't."

"But you are *Chloé Le Warner*?"

"I'm Chloé Warner, but I did not tag the wall. It's a setup! If I could get my phone, I'd show you the texts..."

"You'll get your phone, *mademoiselle*. We're just asking questions. You say you didn't tag the wall, but my colleague and I witnessed you in the act."

"I was ... I was covering up what was written. I didn't want anyone to see—"

"To see that *Chloé Warner is...*" The policewoman leans over the table, scanning the photos of the wall spread out between us. "The rest of the graffiti is illegible. You did a thorough job, but unfortunately for you, it also implies guilt."

I sink deeper into my chair, feeling her sharp gaze on me. Daniel *really* screwed me over this time.

Another officer steps into the room and says something to my interrogator.

Her eyes flick from him to me. "Stay here," she says before disappearing through the door.

Left alone in the cramped room, I pull my cardigan tighter and stare at my hands. It's hard to claim innocence when I'm covered in green paint and my dress is ruined. What happens now? Should I call someone—who, though? My dad? I'd rather die.

I've never been arrested before, though I came close once.

I HAD FOLLOWED HER—MY mother—that day I saw her at the bookstore.

At first, I didn't mean to, but her car (with a chauffeur!) was parked in front of a cab station, and I thought, *what's the harm in that?* I just wanted to see where she lived, so I jumped into a taxi.

"Hi, sir. Do you see the black Mercedes there? I'm with them," I said, trying not to sound all Hollywoody.

The cabbie looked at me through the mirror, eyes narrowing. "Do you want me to follow that car?"

I guess it was unavoidable. "Yes, please."

You'll never guess where we went.

Notting Hill.

There are two sides to that neighborhood: the hipster condos, like the one my dad and I used to live in, and the rows of grand Victorian townhouses where wealthy people live.

Where my mother seemed to live.

Another blow. How many of those could a heart take before it breaks?

Not only had she not moved across the world, but she hadn't even left the neighborhood. She'd been only a few streets away all along, and yet she'd never cared to reach out.

I saw her go into the house with her little girl—my half-sister—and the big black door closed behind them.

The urge to knock, to confront her, was strong. But after I paid the driver, I just stood there in front of the house, watching.

The house didn't give much away; it looked the same as the others on the street. Pretty, big, expensive. I remember thinking: *if only I could have a peek inside.*

I don't know how long I stayed—maybe an hour, maybe two—when I saw them come out again, both in different outfits. They didn't take the car this time but walked down the street and disappeared around the corner.

I looked back at the house and, taking a deep breath for courage, crossed the street to the open black gate. I climbed the few steps to the door. Just standing there made me sweat, and I would have turned back if I hadn't noticed the slightly open window to my right.

Remember how I told you I wouldn't go all the way

when it came to breaking into Gabrielle's apartment? Well, that's because I did learn from my mistakes.

Getting to the window wasn't the hardest part—opening it from the outside was. Yet after a few pushes, I was inside. And, man, it took my breath away.

It had looked grand from the outside, but one glance around confirmed what I already knew: my mother was loaded. Polished mahogany furniture, a grand chandelier, mirrors everywhere. And above the fireplace hung something out of a movie: a large painting of my mother, a man who had to be her new husband, and their daughter.

I walked toward the staircase, lined with photos of the little girl, family vacations, and tennis and golf trophies. Up close, my sister did look a lot like me. My heart sank. How did my mother do it? See that little girl every day and never think of the other child she'd left behind?

"Just grab it quickly, and then we can go," said a voice behind me.

I spun around. She was there, standing in the doorway, eyes wide. She screamed, and for a moment I froze. It took a second to understand why she was screaming, and another to realize I had to run.

I bolted past her, past the little girl asking if she should call the police.

I ran until my lungs burned, but the pain in my chest wasn't from running. It was from what I'd seen in my mother's eyes. Beneath the shock, I could swear I saw it; recognition.

She knew who I was. And she didn't try to stop me.

The urge to cry rose up, but common sense held it back. After all this time, who were we to each other?

Not mother and daughter, not anymore.

Not strangers, either.

Just two people staring at a ghost from their past lives.

THE POLICEWOMAN COMES BACK, eyeing me warily.

"We obtained footage from a street camera near the place we found you," she says. "You told the truth. Someone tagged that wall just before you arrived."

I sit straighter, hopeful, but she cuts me off. "That doesn't change the fact that you were also caught vandalizing it. Thankfully, it was empty and not part of any shopfront, so you won't be prosecuted. You will, however, receive a fine and be asked to cover the cleaning costs."

"Thank you," I mumble, standing and wrapping my cardigan around me. Then, before I leave, I ask, "May I see the recording?"

"No."

I chew my lip, hesitate, then press on. "Please. This person tagged my name on a wall and coerced me into coming to that spot."

The policewoman studies me, and her expression softens a little. "Fine, but it won't reveal much about the vandal's identity."

The video is grainy and shot from a distance. At first it's just an empty street. Then a tall silhouette in oversized black clothes and a hood enters the frame. The officer was right: you can't tell if it's a man or a woman, guess their age, or see their face.

I don't need to see the face. I know who's behind it.

Leaving the station in the middle of the night, I text Daniel right away.

Tomorrow after your work. Our spot. Be there.

He only answers early in the morning.

I have nothing to tell you Chloé.

I text back furiously.

Well, I do

Don't make me resort to threats again

I'm not a bad person, but such a night could turn even a good one sour.

30

I'm filmed from my left. In the video, I'm completely alone by the Balenciaga store. Then I turn, and my eyes land on what I know is the tag on the wall. The quality is sharp for something filmed in such poor light; nothing escapes the lens.

It's painful to watch—my face dissolving in shock and disappointment—but you know what? Life is disappointing.

That's my takeaway from @Eolhc's second post, published this morning.

I was foolish enough to follow my heart instead of my instincts, and look where it led me. It's a relief Daniel didn't capture me actually using the spray paint—that would have made headlines for sure. But he probably had his hands full calling the cops on me.

Why would he do that?

Out of all the questions swirling in my head as I get dressed to meet him, that one refuses to make sense. Daniel already did the damage he wanted to by exposing me first.

He must know he's the one with the most to lose now... so why?

A thought crosses my mind. I'm almost certain I'm the only one who's seen the account and the videos so far. Maybe the point isn't to sabotage me, but to give me a taste of my own medicine—to follow me, to make me feel watched, small, powerless.

That would be so like him. Daniel, forever the teacher.

I shake my head. As much as I'd like to believe he still cares enough to go that far, I have to admit what happened last night feels completely out of character. Calling the police on me? The Daniel I knew would never have done that.

And yet, a small voice whispers, *he's surprised you before.*

Joke's on me, then—for falling for it again and again.

I pull on an old T-shirt and a pair of denim shorts. I'm done making an effort.

Daniel walks in, and for a few seconds, before he notices me, I take him in. A white T-shirt, a moss-green overshirt, the blue jeans I bought him last year. He's clean-shaven, with a fresh haircut. My stomach flutters in spite of myself. I've missed him, I realize. He looks good—great, even.

I frown a little. He looks too good for someone heartbroken. Could he already be seeing someone else?

Daniel scans the room, searching for me, and his brows lower when his eyes finally find me. The moment breaks, and I remember why I came.

He sits across from me. If he notices how disheveled and

tired I look, he doesn't mention it. He waves a hand carelessly, as if to say, *So?*

"I thought we had a deal," I say, trying to sound firm.

Daniel blinks twice, and I almost regret starting that way.

"As in, you blackmailing me into silence—that deal?" he says, his tone edged.

"I'm not blackmailing you." I kind of am, and I wish I weren't like that, but I am like this because when someone pushes you to the edge, you have to push back, right? "After the pretty shitty move you pulled, if I were blackmailing you, I'd already be at your school talking to your director."

"Did what? I deleted the account." He crosses his arms, and I scan his hands for black paint, but they are as clean as ever. This doesn't mean anything, though; I had rubbed mine too this morning to get rid of all the green.

"Yeah, only to create a new one."

"I don't know what you're talking about."

I open @Eolhc on my phone and slide it across the table to him.

"I know it's you, Daniel."

He frowns, opens both videos in silence. "Wait, do you think... That it's me who posted these?"

My eyes search his face, but all they find is a genuine surprise. "It's not?"

"No! *Putain*, Chloé..." He exhales sharply, trying to steady himself. I flinch—he never swears. Not even when a cabinet fell on his foot while we were moving in.

"The last time I saw you was at Flore's wedding. I'm not some creep who would—" He stops, no doubt remembering who he's talking to.

I lower my eyes and swallow hard. "Oh." The relief hits

first, but it's quickly swallowed by a wave of uncertainty. If it's not him, then who's playing with me?

I checked: Jess is on a press trip in southern Italy with Calzedonia, and Birdie's busy posting cooking videos. (They say there's no better way to fix an online reputation than banana bread recipes, so I guess she's testing that theory.) Henriette and Ania are still AWOL. To them, I add a dozen other names I've exposed over the past few weeks, and a chill runs through me as I glance around.

It could be anyone.

Daniel locks eyes with me for the first time in weeks, and I try to cling to those eyes like lifeboats. I always liked his eyes. He doesn't have eyes that get girls into trouble, nor those that Billie Eilish constantly sings about, but he has the good eyes of someone who smiles a lot. Only now, he's not smiling at me.

"I honestly would have thought you'd stop by now." His disappointment nearly knocks the air out of me.

"I stopped. Kind of." It's true—I haven't posted anything on @FauxEver since Henriette's (now deleted) post.

"Yeah, after one too many mistakes."

My fingers tighten around the untouched iced tea in front of me, but I keep my eyes on him. "How did you—"

"Learned a thing or two about social media just by being around you," he reminds me, as if I needed the reminder. It throws me off balance, and I grit my teeth.

"If that were true, you'd understand how this world works. But you don't."

Why am I being a bitch right now? It might be to fight the urge to lean across the table and kiss him.

"Oh no, I do understand. I just think it's shitty, that's all. Look at you now; you can't even sit still without looking over your shoulder." He lets out a short laugh, and it's a sad one. "I guess this shit comes with the territory. Insta-fame or whatever."

I shake my head. "It's not like this for everybody, not..."

He folds his hands on the table, his gold watch catching a glint of sunlight. "Right, not before you started posting on your little account, huh? Now nobody's safe."

"What I post on @FauxEver is different, Daniel..." I wish I could make him understand, get him on my side, but the look he gives me says it all—he despises every word coming out of my mouth.

"It's only different to you because you're the one pulling the strings. But imagine not being able to do a single thing without fearing you'll be photographed or filmed without your consent." He shakes his head, his face tightening. "Then again, I guess you don't have to imagine anymore."

"Daniel..." I plead with my eyes. "I just wanted people to know the truth."

"And yet you couldn't be honest with me—or with Birdie, who actually thought of you as a friend. What about Jess? Did you get close to her just to sabotage her too?" He shakes his head again. "You can't have it both ways, Chloé."

I bite back a reply, not wanting to turn this into a fight.

"How are you?" I ask after a beat.

His face softens for an instant before hardening again. "I'm not doing this. The only reason I came is because you're still trying to blackmail me. So if we're done here..."

He starts to rise, and I draw a sharp breath, staring into my drink before looking back up at him. "Are you, um, seeing someone?"

Daniel hesitates just a moment too long. "No."

He can't lie. He never could. I lift my head sharply and

meet his eyes. "Who's she?" I don't mean to sound salty, but the timber of my voice is the Red Sea, and bile rises in my throat.

Daniel hesitates, and for a second I hope he'll lie so I can pretend to believe him. But he just looks away. "No one you know."

Wow. Daniel isn't the only one who can see through lies. I know him too—his habits, his tells. When he lies, he does this thing with his hand, curling it into a fist. And now his hand is on the table, tightening without him even noticing.

I blink away my disappointment, trying to ignore the jealousy twisting in my stomach. I manage a small, stiff smile. "It's only been a month."

Daniel tilts his head back, exasperated. "We're not together anymore, Chloé. I can date whoever I want."

"I know. I didn't say you couldn't..."

"Then what? I don't owe you an explanation." He taps his fingers on the table, and I notice he still hasn't ordered anything.

I bite my lip, not wanting him to leave just yet. "Daniel, I'm sorry—for how it ended between us."

Something flickers across his face, and for a second I wonder if it's remorse. I take that as a sign and press on.

"Do you remember the day you told me you'd always be there for me?" I ask.

"You drove me away yourself," he says, shaking his head. "When you decided to blackmail me."

Again with that. I lean back in my chair and take a deep breath. "Would it have changed anything if I hadn't brought up that story with Estelle?"

He winces at her name, and I can't help wondering if he didn't tell me everything about what happened that day.

"Of course. It would have changed everything," he says, and blood rushes in my ears.

I tilt my head, heat rising in me. "Yeah? You honestly think you would've stayed with me after finding out what I did to Birdie? You would've just let it slide?" A bitter laugh escapes before I can stop it. "Daniel, you're the epitome of self-righteousness. Our relationship was over the moment you learned I was behind FauxEver. You can lie to yourself all you want, but you knew it was finished before you even created that account."

Daniel opens his mouth, but I don't let him. "Would you rather I were someone else?" I ask again, ignoring the sting of the memory from that night on the terrace. "I guess now you can't deny that you would."

He meets my eyes, steady and unblinking, then exhales. "The way your mind works... It's always fascinated me. This ability to pick out the truths you like and shine a light only where you want it. You see the world differently. You would've made a great photographer for that reason."

It's a knife to my heart. "I can still become that," I say with an edge in my voice that startles us both. "I can do whatever the fuck I want."

He nods coolly and, to my dismay, pushes his chair back.

"You should go to the police," he simply says, not knowing what fucking irony that is.

And then he leaves.

A new video drops later that day. It shows Daniel and me at the café. I look even worse than I imagined—dark circles under my eyes, my T-shirt marked with yellow stains under the arms. God. The person filming caught almost a full minute of conversation, and from the way my lip trembles, I know it's the moment Daniel tells me he's moved on. I look pathetic. I really do.

Unless he's working with someone, it can't be Daniel behind that account.

I slide into @eolhc's DMs again.

Who are you?

No immediate reply. Either they're busy setting up their next trap or letting it sit to get under my skin. It works. By the time the answer comes, I'm a wreck.

Your conscience, they write back.

31

My dreams are so vivid these days.

I've reached that point where I envy people who dream of monsters or kidnappings or other horrors. When they wake, it's over. They can laugh about it, tell their partner, and move on without the lingering ache that follows you through the day.

But me, I have only one dream, and it plays on a loop every night. I'm running after Birdie, my phone in hand. I lose her, look around, and then she's there, watching me. Her eyes are an ocean of hurt. She says, "How could you?" and I open my mouth to explain, but nothing comes out. There's nothing to say, is there?

With everything that's happened, I never took the time to process my short relationship with Birdie. Now that I have all the time in the world, something else has crept in—I think it's guilt.

Birdie and I lived such different lives. When we met, all I wanted to see were the similarities. We both lost our mothers young. We were both outsiders in Paris, trying to belong. We even looked alike. I admired her so much that I started mirroring her expressions, her gestures, hoping that would be enough to make us click.

But maybe that's exactly what kept me from seeing her—the real her.

Away from the screens, I found a fragile soul, one that seemed to crack a little more with every blow. It made me realize that, beneath the surface, she and I couldn't have been more different.

As hard as my childhood was, I always knew I could turn to my dad. He loved me no matter what, and that knowledge gave me strength, maybe even arrogance. But Papa Bay was someone Birdie despised, and her French family wanted nothing to do with her. In my need to isolate her, to keep her for myself, I'd pushed Gabrielle—her only true friend—away. The thought makes my chest tighten. Maybe Birdie never really had anyone who loved her unconditionally.

Maybe that's why she turned to her audience so young. The likes and comments weren't just work—they were trust. They filled the space left by everything she didn't get at home.

And now, I've shattered that trust too.

Most nights, I barely sleep. I just lie there, scrolling through old photos of Birdie, Daniel, and Jess. I never realized what it meant to be truly alone. I miss them. I miss who I was when I was with them. Sometimes, in the dark, I whisper all the things I'd say if I had the chance.

But when morning comes, I never send the messages. Doing that would mean admitting that everything I did was wrong.

So I try to go on with my life and wait for more scandals

around the world, hoping they'll bury mine in the noise. Maybe then, just maybe, I could start again.

"Hey, Tobias! Is it a good time to call?"

"As long as this couldn't have been a text, sure," he says—and isn't that the most Gen Z thing ever said? When I don't reply, he chuckles and quickly adds, "No, I mean, of course, you can always call me. What's up?"

"Hmm." I hesitate, unsure how to bring it up. "I was wondering when the payment from Magnolia Swim will come through?"

Normally, I'd be too embarrassed to call, but I'm walking out of the BnF Museum—partly because I wanted to see the Jean-Marc de Clémentin exhibition, and partly because I figured it was one of the few places where no one would recognize me. Probably not the best time to be wandering around, I know, but I refuse to let fear win (even if I kind of am scared) or give in to the @Eolhc intimidation (which, fine, is absolutely working).

Still, I'd forced myself out of the apartment, made it all the way to the museum entrance—and then my card was declined.

"Sorry, mademoiselle," the elderly woman at the front desk said. "It looks like this card has insufficient funds. Do you have another one?"

But I don't. Aside from the payment I'm waiting for, there's nothing else coming in. My dad covers my rent, but my only real income was from Fiverr gigs—and I haven't taken a single one since @FauxEver blew up.

"Hmm, let me check," Tobias says.

I'm sitting on the terrace of a café where I can't even afford an espresso, my cap pulled low in the hope that no one recognizes me.

Tobias clicks his tongue. "So, neither you nor the brand has posted the pictures yet, right? They're due in three days. Don't forget to post, by the way—the hashtags are in my last email. Once they're up, we'll send the insights report in about a week, so RevCom should get paid by the end of next month."

Shit.

A waitress stops by, iPad in hand.

"Hum, I'm waiting for someone," I lie quickly. She raises an eyebrow—which is Parisian code for *I give you two more minutes out of the kindness of my heart*—and walks off.

"Next month?" I say. "But why is RevCom getting the payment? Why not me directly?"

"Well, love, we'll deduct our fee and send you your part about a month after that."

My head starts spinning. "What fee?"

"Our thirty percent fee, as per your contract," he says, and I can practically hear the eye roll through the line.

"Right." I didn't read the contract. I was too busy packing for the South of France. "Um, Tobias? Is there any way to speed things up a bit? I'm kind of short on money."

"Ah, I feel you, girl. Acne Studios private sales yesterday *destroyed* me. I'll be eating pasta till the end of the month too."

I press my fingers to my eyes, fighting the sting there. "So there's no way I can get that money earlier than... two months?"

"Nope, but to be honest, two months is still fair. By the industry's standards, that's rather quick."

The waitress shoots me another look, tapping impatiently on her iPad.

"I see... Any chance of booking me on something else in the meantime?"

He makes a small, awkward sound. "Well, not much coming in at the moment. But you know what? Once the Magnolia Swim campaign goes live, I'm sure we'll be drowning in offers."

I wait for the waitress to head back inside before slipping away. After saying goodbye to Tobias as politely as I can, I wander aimlessly through the city center, not sure where I'm going or what I'm looking for.

People like to say Paris's charm lies in how much of its beauty is free, and I suppose that's true. Sightseeing is free. Listening to street musicians is free. But when you're a twenty-something wannabe influencer in Paris with an empty bank account, the city suddenly doesn't have much to give.

I'm about to head for the metro when a prickling sensation creeps up the back of my neck, the unmistakable feeling of being watched. Pretending to rummage through my bag, I tilt my head just enough to glance around. A boy—maybe fifteen, sixteen—stands a few meters away. He could be older, but the Pokémon T-shirt knocks at least five years off him. Our eyes meet, and I don't smile back. He's holding his phone with both hands, aimed straight at me.

My pulse jumps. I pick up my pace, slipping into the flow of people along Rue Saint-Honoré, trying to lose myself in the crowd. When the street quiets, the emptiness only makes me feel more exposed, so I turn sharply onto Rue de Rivoli, where tourists swarm the sidewalks. I duck behind a stand of magnets outside a souvenir shop. The woman with purple hair running it eyes me with suspicion as I pretend to study her display, sneaking glances past the postcards and keychains.

A minute passes—though it feels much longer when you're pretending to admire a dozen magnets of the Louvre. Pokémon-guy is nowhere to be seen, and I'm about to sigh and step out from hiding when a flash of Pikachu catches my eye. It's him, walking in my direction, scanning the crowd, still clutching his phone.

When he's close enough to reach, I step forward fast. "Hey, creep, are you following me?"

The kid has the audacity to look surprised. "What? No."

"Then why were you recording me?"

"I'm texting!" he protests, eyes wide.

I'm done playing dumb. If anyone knows this game, it's me. "Show me your phone," I say, holding out my hand.

"*Euh, je ne crois pas, non.* I'm not showing you my phone." He frowns and starts to walk off.

"Show. Me. Your. Phone."

I grab for his arm, but he's quicker. My hand knocks into the souvenir stand, sending a cascade of magnets crashing to the ground with a metallic clatter.

"Fucking crazy," the Pokémon kid mutters before vanishing into the crowd.

I WAS wrong about the magnets earlier. They don't just flaunt the Louvre—they're a miniature gallery of Parisian postcards: the Moulin Rouge, the Eiffel Tower, Montmartre...

All the places I once ached to see, to capture through my lens.

That was the story I sold my dad when I dropped the bombshell about moving abroad.

"Paris?" he repeated, his voice caught somewhere between disbelief and worry, as if I'd just announced a one-way trip to Pluto.

I gave him my brightest smile. "It's the logical move, isn't it? That city is the one place where I could really grow as an artist."

What I didn't say was that I needed to get as far away as possible from my mother.

Three months had passed since I had broken into her house and saw her again—a stranger with familiar eyes. Twelve weeks of waiting, holding on to the foolish hope that she'd reach out. Because surely, now that I had found her, she'd contact me. Wouldn't she?

But hope, like time, slips through clenched fingers, and it took me far too long to admit the truth: she wasn't coming. She would never come. It was up to me now to move on with my life.

"Perhaps," Dad said after a long pause, though his face betrayed the heartbreak every parent feels when their child leaves the nest. "I guess it'll be good for you. A change of scenery, a fresh take on your creativity..."

"Fresh, yes," I murmured.

A fresh start meant erasure—the scrubbing clean of everything that hurt. And maybe, just maybe, Paris would be the perfect canvas for that.

32

When I get home, a new video is waiting for me—me, crouched on the pavement, gathering the fallen magnets under the disapproving gaze of the purple-haired seller. I look miserable, and watching it makes me feel even worse.

Is this my new twisted reality? Being afraid to step outside because someone might be filming me? Snapping at strangers just for holding their phones?

If it were Daniel behind the videos, at least I'd have something solid to hate. But it's the not knowing that's driving me out of my mind.

I need to refocus, find a purpose again. Get my life back on track.

I open my Fiverr account and scroll through the offers waiting for me. It's surreal to think that not long ago, these small gigs used to be enough. But after attending dazzling events, shooting my first campaign, rubbing shoulders with celebrities—being one, even if only for a moment—I can't picture myself going back to that old life of minor edits and client notes.

So I close my laptop.

And then I do the one thing I should have done a long time ago: I call my dad.

He picks up almost instantly.

"Dad..." I manage, my voice cracking. I don't mean to sound so broken, but that's what his voice does to me—I hear it, and instantly, I'm his little girl again, and he can make everything right.

"Chloékins? What's wrong?"

"I... it's..." Suddenly, I can't breathe. It's like I've forgotten how. My hands clutch at my throat. Is this what a panic attack feels like?

My dad's voice sounds far away now. "You're scaring me. Are you all right?"

An image comes to my mind: my dad holding my long hair while I'm vomiting in the bathroom. *You're gonna be all right.*

I finally take a staggered breath, and then another. "Yes, no. I don't know."

"Okay," he says slowly, and I hear him rummage through some things, maybe papers. "Do you want me to come to Paris? I can be at the airport in three hours and take a night flight..."

I interrupt him. "No, Dad. No need to come again. I'm sorry if I scared you. It's just that you might have been right. I should have gone home with you."

"Babygirl, what happened?" he asks tenderly. He's not one to gloat, my dad.

"There was this... project I've been pursuing..."

"The photography on the internet?"

"Yeah, that one. I kind of put all my eggs in one basket because I really wanted it to work, but..." I trail off, searching for words that are both vague and true.

"It didn't work out?" my dad asks gently—and that's all it takes. I start crying, really crying, with shaking shoulders and hiccuping sobs. I feel myself go underwater, and the feeling swallows me whole.

"Love, talk to me," he urges; his voice is properly panicked now.

"I messed up, Dad," I choke out. "I did something... bad. To someone who trusted me. And after that, every decision I made just made things worse. Now I have nothing—no money, no job, no way out of this mess."

My father is silent in a way I don't like, and for an instant, I'm terrified he hung up.

But he would never. He clears his throat. "Darling, whatever you did, it can surely be mended with an apology."

I close my eyes and start rocking back and forth. He has that rare gift of making even my worst mistakes sound forgivable, and yet I know I can't tell him what I've done. If I did, he'd never look at me the same way again, and his love is the only thing I have left. The downside is that he can't possibly understand how deep I've sunk.

"I don't know," I whisper, sniffling. "I don't think that's enough."

"But it's a start, babygirl. That person you hurt, he's not obliged to forgive you, but telling him how sorry you are would be a first step towards opening a dialogue," he murmurs, his voice gentle. "And from there, who knows, maybe even reconciliation?"

I blink, processing his words. My dad said "he," probably

thinking I was talking about Daniel. It crushes me—how, in his mind, it's already my fault.

I hate the thought of him being ashamed of me, but what really suffocates me is knowing he wouldn't be entirely wrong.

"Dad," I say quietly. "Can I tell you something, even if it might hurt you? I just need to say it."

"You can tell me anything, you know that."

I take a sharp breath, knowing this is the point of no return. "Mom... I saw her."

And then it all spills out. The times she left me alone at home. How she'd whisper, *Don't tell your dad.* How I knew she wasn't going to the hairdresser, that she had another family, and that I followed her.

"She still lives in London. In Notting Hill," I add.

The line falls silent for a beat, leaving me to wonder if my words reached him at all. Then I hear him sigh, and it's not just a sigh; it's a symphony of a million tiny sighs cascading into one another. Instantly, tears well up anew. I hurt him.

"I know, love," he says at last.

I shake my head. Did I mishear him? "What?"

"People talk. They've seen her around town a few times," he says quietly. "I didn't want to cause you more pain by telling you. Since we don't have any photos of her at home, I thought maybe you'd forgotten how she looked."

"But... if you knew where she was, how...?"

"She did disappear that day—the day she said she was going to the hairdresser," he says, his voice soft, almost careful. "I didn't see her for a year after that. Then one morning, after I'd dropped you off at school, she appeared.

Just like that. As beautiful as ever, holding divorce papers. She didn't explain anything. She just told me to sign."

I close my eyes. I'm back in the school hallway, clutching my chemistry books. Two girls brush past me, sharp elbows catching my side. The books scatter across the floor. "That's the girl who drove her mother away," one of them whispers, and the other laughs.

Then my dad's voice cuts through the memory, and it dissolves like smoke.

"I did ask her if she wanted to see you. I told her I could bring you anywhere, that you two could spend some time together. But she said no. Said it would be too painful for the both of you. She wanted to start clean."

A fresh start.

My mouth goes dry. "She's a monster! What mother behaves like this?"

"Your mom..." he says slowly. "She always wanted more than she had—more than I could offer her. And she didn't care what, or who, she might have to sacrifice to get what she thought she deserved."

I stay still, silent. I'm not even sure I'm breathing.

"Unfortunately, it was you and I she sacrificed," Dad continues. "Had I known how much you were hurting, I would have insisted. But you seemed to have accepted her not being part of your life so well... Now I realize I only wanted to see what made things easier for me."

He exhales, and I find myself matching his breath. "I tried to make it up to you by being the perfect parent, I really did," he adds softly. "But I guess nothing replaces a mother."

And suddenly, I understand that it's not my words that made him sad, but the thought of how much I must have suffered.

"No, Dad, you've always been enough," I say quietly.

And it's true. When I look back, I see him at every milestone: in the stands at my soccer games, cheering at my dance recitals, sitting through every parent-teacher meeting, lighting candles on every birthday cake. Through every triumph and every heartbreak, he was the constant.

"More than enough," I add, because he deserves to know that her absence does not, in any way, diminish his own presence. "I couldn't have dreamt of a better childhood than the one you gave me."

"Oh, Chloékins, I love you so much, babygirl," he says, his voice choked with emotion. Then he clears his throat, because we don't usually talk about feelings like this. "And about what we talked about earlier... I still think you should come back home. Spend some time in the countryside. Reset. Clear your mind."

"I'd like that, Dad," I whisper. "I'd like that very much."

I remain curled up on the floor even after ending the call.

It's good. It's comforting. Part of me entertains the notion of staying like this for weeks, allowing my problems to fade into the background.

Perhaps, I think, people will eventually forget about me. I'd become that distant memory, the subject of a lighthearted joke shared over drinks: *hey, remember that stalker girl?* And as for my stalker, I imagine he'd grow weary over time, moving on to pursue another target.

I try to immerse myself in this alternate reality, finding solace in its simplicity. Yet, despite my efforts, thoughts of *her* intrude like unwelcome guests.

She could have been my mother all these years, but she chose otherwise. She prioritized her own happiness over mine, as if the two were mutually exclusive. The questions I will never get answers to swirl in my mind. Had she stayed, would it have changed who I am? Did I take after her more than I wished to admit?

I don't know how long I lie in my living room, but when I finally rise, there is a floor mark on my cheek, and the sun is setting. I check my phone because I'm full of shit and not going anywhere, am I? My dad had wired me some money. Hate it how it makes me feel some relief, but it does. And upon a quick check, I see that @eolhc has posted another video.

My stomach falls down a couple of stairs as I tap to watch it.

It must have been taken just minutes ago. I'm by my window, in the same clothes I'm wearing now, ugly crying into my phone. *What the—?* My gaze jerks up from the screen to the window, and realization hits like lightning.

It was filmed from across the street. From Birdie's apartment.

33

I wonder what I'll tell her.

A part of me, maybe ninety-nine percent of me, is relieved it was her. Because that makes us even. Clean slate. I hurt her, and she hurt me. And okay, there is that small percent of me that wonders: *what the fuck?* But I mute it as best as I can as I climb up the stairs to Birdie's apartment.

I knock, and she opens the door.

It's the first time I've seen her face-to-face in weeks. At first, she looks unchanged, still drop-dead gorgeous, wearing a pair of low-rise jeans and a corsage crop top. And as our eyes lock, I get a surge of adrenaline tangled with everything I feel about her—shame, love, fear. It's all combined and muddy, and I have a million things to tell her.

"Hi," is all that comes out.

"Chloé." She sounds surprised—and I'm surprised she is. Surely she knew I'd figure it out was her?

"You look great," I say, as if that's what matters.

"You got bangs," she notes, then her expression hardens

as she remembers who she's talking to. Her face tightens, and she folds her arms across her chest. "What do you want?"

It's only then, looking at her properly, that I notice something different—a glow, a light in her eyes that wasn't there before.

"I... I know it's you, Birdie." I hold back the smile I want to give her. "It's okay, you were in the right," I rush to add. "What I did to you was wrong, and that's payback, maybe..."

She blinks, glances over her shoulder, then back at me. "What payback? I don't know what you're talking about."

Is she really going to play that game? I open my mouth to answer when a voice that is both unrecognizable and familiar rings out from behind her.

"Girl, you are *so* delusional!"

My eyes pinch; this couldn't be...

Gabrielle appears in the hallway, a smirk plastered on her face.

I reel back, the realization slamming into me like a ton of bricks. "You...?" My voice cracks with disbelief. "You're the one who's been filming me all this time?"

Gabrielle's grin widens, but it's Birdie who speaks first, frowning as her eyes dart between us. "What is she talking about? What videos?"

"She—" I swallow hard. "She's been following me for days, posting videos of me..." The words trail off as the truth sinks in. It was her. All this time, it was *her*.

"Gabi, is that true?" Birdie asks, her confusion mirroring mine.

Gabrielle doesn't answer right away; her mouth curls into a sharp, satisfied smile. "Looks like the biter's been bitten. So tell me, how does it feel being the one stalked?"

"You've got to be kidding me," Birdie whispers.

Still looking down at me like I'm an insect, Gabrielle waves her hands. "She's been following me too! I saw her lurking by my place a few weeks ago; she was listening to a private conversation and..."

"This isn't true," I say, stepping into the apartment. My voice shakes, but I cling to the hope that she's bluffing, that she has no real proof.

"Oh, be my guest," Birdie mutters, shutting the door behind me.

"I fucking saw you!" Gabrielle snaps, her voice rising. "I already knew you were a snake, but that day just confirmed you were a full-on freak."

"You want to talk about freaks?" I shoot back. "You literally stalked me for days!"

Even as the words leave my mouth, doubt creeps in. I can't quite picture Gabrielle tottering around Paris in her heels, shadowing me. I'd have noticed—the sharp scent of her Carnal Flower perfume would have given her away in seconds.

"Hmm, actually," she says, a smirk tugging at her lips. "I didn't have to. But you did terrify my baby cousin earlier. He said you were completely losing it."

Of course. One of the many faceless brats of the De Terron clan. So *he* was Pokémon-boy. I bite my bottom lip while Gabrielle leans lazily against the corridor wall, arms crossed over her Celine blazer.

"Oh, and I hope that little visit to the police station didn't rough you up too much?"

"The police?" Birdie's voice is barely a whisper. Her head darts back and forth between Gabrielle and me, confusion etched on her face.

"Right," I bite out, jaw clenched. "You do realize I could

go back there right now and tell them it was you who set me up?"

Gabrielle tilts her head and flutters her lashes in exaggerated innocence. "Good luck with that, considering you don't have a shred of proof. And, well, my uncle's the Prefect of Police. Might make things a little awkward for you, don't you think?"

I meet Gabrielle's gaze and refuse to blink. Two days of spiraling, thinking I had a stalker, and it's been her all along. Why? Because I took Birdie from her? They're clearly friends again, so I can't even make sense of her twisted logic. Then Gabrielle turns toward Birdie, who stands frozen between us, and her smugness softens into something almost protective.

"Babe, do you see it now? You can't trust your instincts about people," she says, her tone scolding, almost parental. And that's when it clicks—it was never just about me. This whole thing was her way of teaching Birdie a lesson.

I let out a breath, half a laugh. "Wow. Okay. Message received. I think I'll go now," I say, heading for the door.

But Gabrielle isn't done with me.

"Admit it! Tell Birdie it was you!" she yells, stepping closer.

I turn around. "Why are you recording?"

"Not yet," she says with a nasty smile, "but now that you mention it, a full confession on camera sounds like a great idea."

"You're..." My voice falters as I glance at Birdie, who won't meet my eyes. "Oh," I whisper, letting out a small, breathless laugh before looking back at Gabrielle. "Who's the delusional one now?"

Her brows knit together. "What did you just say?"

"Birdie knows," I say quietly. "She..." I trail off, giving Birdie an apologetic look. This time, she meets my eyes. "She caught me a few weeks ago while I was following her."

Gabrielle's expression hardens. "You did?" she says to Birdie, her tone full of wounded disbelief. "So you've known I was right about her all along?"

Birdie inhales shakily, then gives a small, reluctant nod.

Gabrielle mirrors the gesture, her jaw tightening until it looks sharp enough to cut. "Then why didn't you do anything about it?"

A heavy silence hangs between us for several heartbeats before Birdie finally speaks.

"Because I didn't want my name dragged any deeper into her mess," she says, chin tilted toward Gabrielle, still refusing to look at me. "And besides, it's not my job—or yours—to teach her a lesson. Karma keeps its own score, and I knew that sooner or later, Chloé would get what she deserved."

I swallow the lump in my throat, forcing Birdie's words to roll off me like raindrops on a waterproof coat. Deep down, I know they'd burn if I let them sink in. My hand slips from the doorknob, and I take a breath, hearing my dad's voice in my head before I step closer to her.

"I never got the chance to tell you how sorry I am," I say, my voice barely more than a breath. I'm close enough to catch the faint scent of Lost Cherry on her skin. Birdie meets my eyes with an unreadable expression, still as a statue.

"When I took those pictures, I was disappointed and hurt," I continue. "You weren't the person I thought you were, and I convinced myself I was doing the right thing by showing the truth. But I know now that you don't owe me—or anyone—anything. What I did was wrong, and I'm truly sorry."

Birdie's face doesn't move. She folds her arms across her chest, holding her phone like a shield. "I..."

A sharp laugh cuts through the air, snapping both our heads toward Gabrielle.

"The right thing?" she repeats, her voice laced with mockery. "Oh, Chloey, please. Let me burst that self-righteous little bubble of yours. It was never about doing what's right. Be honest—you didn't do it for 'the truth' or 'authenticity' or whatever excuse helps you sleep at night. You did it because you're a greedy bitch. You saw a chance to claw your way into a world you'd been drooling over from the sidelines, and you took it."

I flinch. "Mind your own business. This is between Birdie and me."

She arches a brow. "Rude."

I roll my eyes, which only seems to fuel her anger.

"Do I really need to spell it out for you?" she presses, stepping closer. "The only reason Birdie ever thought she liked you is because you played the part she wanted you to play and told her what she wanted to hear. You're doing it again with this pathetic apology. She doesn't know the real you. If she did, she'd have stayed far away."

I shake my head, but Gabrielle doesn't back off, stepping closer until I can feel her breath. "Admit it."

"Fine! Yeah, that's why I created @FauxEver," I snap, meaning to sound sarcastic, but the words tear out of me, truer than anything I've said before. Out of the corner of my eye, I catch Birdie's expression shift.

"Because you liked being somebody, for once," Gabrielle goads.

I dig my nails into my palms, voice trembling. "Yes."

"And how's that working out for you now, little Chloey? Now that everyone sees you for what you are—a nobody."

I draw in a sharp breath, blinking hard to keep the tears from spilling.

Then I steady myself. "Maybe I was a nobody once," I say quietly, "but that's still better than being you, Gabrielle. Bored, bitter, and so obsessed with controlling your best friend you can't tell love from ownership."

Gabrielle lets out a sharp, disbelieving laugh. "Careful. Do you even know who my family is?"

"Oh, I'm shaking in my boots," I say, faking confidence I don't quite feel, and finally twist the doorknob.

"I'm not finished with you." Gabrielle grabs my arm, forcing me to face her. "You're going to record that confession on camera, for everyone to see."

She might not be done, but I am. I'm so sick and tired of being toyed with. "Don't fucking touch me," I snap, yanking my arm free. She stumbles back on her heels, eyes wide in disbelief.

"Did you just shove me?"

"What? No, you grabbed me and—"

Before I can finish, she uses her full height and weight to shove me hard. My back slams against the wall, my head knocking into a stack of unopened packages that topple over and burst open around my feet.

Birdie screams. "Stop it, both of you! You're insane! Get the fuck out of my apartment."

"Yeah, Chloey, get out," Gabrielle sneers.

"You too, Gabi," Birdie says, and I notice that she's holding her phone at a weird angle. Is *she* recording?

Gabrielle blinks, surprised. "What? You don't mean that."

"I do." Birdie looks like a scolded kitten, but within a heartbeat, she straightens back into Birdie Bay mode. "We are done. This friendship we had—it's fucked up. I want you out of my life."

"Because of this rat?" Gabrielle glares at her. "Don't be ridiculous, Birds. If you're trying to prove a point, you—"

"Because of you!" Birdie cuts her off, her voice sharp enough to slice through the air. "You said it yourself—I don't *know* Chloé. The fact that I let her get close enough to hurt me is on *me*. But you? I look at you now and can't understand why you're still in my life."

Gabrielle inhales sharply, as if Birdie just slapped her, and for a long moment, the two of them stare at each other in silence.

"They're right about you," Gabrielle finally spits. "You're a mess, just like your addict of a father."

Birdie takes the blow better than I would have thought. She lifts her chin, calm and steady. "If that means I'm nothing like them—and nothing like you—then I'm fine with it."

Gabrielle makes a low, bitter sound in her throat. She lingers for a beat longer, maybe hoping Birdie will take it back. Then, without sparing me a glance, she brushes past, opens the door, and walks out.

I stay where I am, leaning against the wall beside the scattered packages. A drop of what I assume is blood slides down my forehead. Judging by the pain, there must have been at least two beauty fridges in that pile. Not knowing what else to do, I crouch to gather the mess when my eyes catch on a pair of shoes on the floor. They look out of place in Birdie's perfectly kept apartment, and it takes me a moment to register them—dark green imitation Loro Pianas. My stomach twists at what their presence might mean.

"What are Daniel's shoes..." I start, trying to meet Birdie's gaze, but she's staring at the ceiling.

She says nothing. The throbbing in my head deepens, and I'm not sure it's from the hit.

We just stand there in silence. She's breathing like she's just come back from a hike.

"I wish..." My throat burns as I speak. I don't know when exactly I started crying, but I am now. "I wish we could be friends again."

Birdie's eyes shimmer, and she inhales sharply. "Chloé..."

For a heartbeat, I think she might say she wishes that too, but instead she crosses the room and opens the door. "The truth is, I'm not sure you ever were my friend. Please, go."

I want to apologize again, to offer her something—anything—that might make it right. But I don't even know what that would be.

So I just bite my lip and leave.

34

Alone in my apartment, I find solace in the darkness, the curtains drawn tight to keep the world out. Time slips away unnoticed, and when I finally stir from the couch, night has already swallowed the city.

You'd think you'd recognize the exact moment your life fell apart, but it's never that clear-cut. As long as I stay offline, as long as I don't open Instagram to see whatever Birdie or Gabrielle might have posted, I can pretend everything is still fine. So I choose denial. I blast the music Daniel hates (Eminem), scream the lyrics off-key, and dance the way people do when no one's watching. After a few minutes, someone's pounding on the walls, but I don't care. I turn the volume higher, climb onto the couch, and sing until my throat burns.

I'm spiraling. Kind of wish I were high, but no—this chaos is all me. I'm the cocaine in my own bloodstream.

I step out onto the balcony and stare down. My vision blurs for a moment, then sharpens again. The truth settles in: life keeps moving. People hurry by, laugh, live. The sun does what it always does. In the grand scheme of things, no one cares about your disasters.

I glance toward Birdie's windows, but her curtains are drawn, her apartment dark. Maybe she and Daniel are out for dinner. Maybe he took her to our favorite bar's terrace for drinks. She'd look stunning there, glowing at sunset.

They make an interesting couple, Daniel and Birdie—I can give them that. A teacher and an influencer, drawn together by the shared sting of betrayal. I don't even blame them. I wouldn't go so far as to say I wish them well, because I haven't forgotten that they met while Daniel and I were still together, but I won't do anything to ruin what they have.

Besides, she's Birdie Bay.

No further explanation needed. She's the sunny West Coast warmth, the kind of girl everyone turns to look at when she walks into a room—the one you can't help but want to please, because her smile is contagious and her approval is everything.

I can't compete with that.

What's left is this dull ache, a small wound buried deep inside me. It's funny how I didn't realize, not until we were over, just how much I loved Daniel. And now he's gone for good.

The thought rattles through my mind for another second before I let it go. I look down again and pull myself over the wrought-iron guardrail, one leg at a time, until I'm perched on the edge, suspended above the street with only my hands gripping the rail.

I close my eyes and let the night air wash over my face. Summer's finally over. It was both the best and worst one of my life—the highest highs and the lowest lows. I open my eyes, and I'm so high up now that if I let go, I'd die. It would be so simple. The simplest way out.

But I never wanted to die. If you ever thought I did, then you weren't paying attention. What I wanted was the rush, and I got it, again and again.

When Daniel exposed me on his pathetic little account.

When Birdie said my name and her eyes slid to the phone in my hand.

When Jess screamed at me in that club, in front of everyone.

And all the smaller moments in between, each one cutting and somehow making me feel so important.

I'm not afraid of falling. I've already been on the ground before. What terrifies me is never getting any higher.

So I climb back onto the balcony and stumble inside on shaky legs.

Oh, I am many things. A backstabber. A two-faced bitch. Maybe even a bully. I don't care. But I'm not a quitter.

Gabrielle didn't post anything. In fact, I can't find the @Eolhc account anymore. She must have deleted it.

Birdie did, though. Right after I left her place, she shared an audio recording in her stories. Turns out, I was right—she hit record the moment she realized where the fight between Gabrielle and me was headed.

And let me tell you, it's some prime, juicy material.

Gabrielle's voice, sharp with fury as she screams at me, declaring I'll never be worth anyone's attention. And there's me, shouting out my confession for all to hear:

"Yeah, that's why I created @FauxEver!"

I can't quite name the feeling that runs through me, slippery and strange. So I replay the audio again and again, letting the weight of my own words sink in. Then it hits me like a ton of bricks: I'm *jealous*.

Jealous that I wasn't the one to post it first on @FauxEver.

This confession should have been mine to share. Diane was right—I had the mother of all scoops in my hands, and I let it slip away.

Birdie posted something else an hour later. A photo of two hands entwined—hers and a man's. That tiny scar above his thumb made it unmistakably Daniel's. A kitchen accident from when he was a kid. I remember how he joked about it at one of the family brunches. Birdie didn't write anything under the post, letting her followers speculate. Clever move. A distraction, steering attention from the drama to something easier to digest—a new romance. But I can't shake the feeling that it wasn't just that. She posted it for me. Her own version of Ariana Grande's *"The Boy is Mine."*

A cute "fuck you," Instagram edition.

I scroll through the comments. It looks like Birdie's been vindicated.

Claiming her power back

Birdie the phoenix

Queen B

The support is overwhelming; she's swiftly reclaimed her role as their role model, their favorite girl, the most amazing human on the planet. It's as if the scandal never happened, a distant memory swept away by the whirlwind of adoration.

And I can't help but smile at that. I'm happy for her, genuinely. She's back where she belongs, tucked safely into the hearts of her followers—whether their love is real or not isn't mine to question anymore.

My lips curve upward, and I close my phone. Maybe tonight, I'll finally sleep.

Two days later, I'm standing in line at the airport, waiting for my drink, when a message from Tobias pops up on my phone.

> It's out! You're gorgeous.

> Sending you a file with pictures for you to choose from for your own post. Don't forget the hashtags!

The Magnolia Swim pictures. Timely. This goes to show that there is always a way to surf on someone else's hype. I take a deep breath and open Instagram, turning a blind eye to my follower count or the flood of notifications.

As I navigate to the brand's page, I'm momentarily disoriented. I scan the images, searching for the shy, insecure brunette I once was. It takes a beat for my brain to catch up—I'm staring at my own face. But it's not the same timid version of myself; here, I'm confident, radiant, hot. My eyes sparkle, my freckles add a touch of charm, and not a single stretch mark mars my skin—Photoshop and its magic, no doubt.

It's a seismic shift from the image I held in my head: I look as good as any other girl featured in the campaign.

As if I truly deserve to be there.

I chuckle, and the person before me in line turns and

gives me a questioning look. I don't care because it's such a relief I could cry. Comments crucify me, as expected. Some call me a backstabber. Others say I'm a freak. The onslaught of tags directed at @FauxEver turns Magnolia Swim into the most commented post to date. Yet, there's nothing new there. And that's the silver lining of a social media shitstorm, I guess: once the most terrible things were said about you out there, you just stop fearing words.

From the corner of my eye, I spot two girls whispering to each other, shooting me not-so-furtive glances. Wonderful. I tug my cap lower over my head. They start circling closer, and I wish the barista would hurry up—but haven't you noticed? At airports, customer service is basically optional. If you're not happy, there's nowhere else to take your business anyway.

"You ask her," one of the girls says.

Her friend nudges her forward. "No, you go."

"*Bonjour*, are you the girl from @FauxEver?" They look younger than I first thought, but with all that makeup, it's hard to tell. Fourteen, maybe fifteen.

I throw a desperate look toward the barista, but he's too busy flirting with a guy who just ordered a vanilla matcha.

"Could we get a picture with you?" one of the girls asks.

I hesitate. I look like hell—red mark on my face from the fight with Gabrielle (two stitches, probably a scar)—but I remember what Birdie told me when we first met: gotta work on that affection ratio.

"Mmm, yes, okay," I say, forcing a smile that sends a wave of pain through my left cheek. "But only if you put the picture in black and white and tag my personal account, not @FauxEver." I smooth down my Alo Yoga sweatshirt.

The girls exchange a look, and one of them raises her eyebrow. What a brat.

"Yeah, whatever," the other one mutters, rolling her eyes.

The past weeks flash before my eyes, condensing into one single thought: I'd wanted so badly to be seen by the world that I was willing to be seen as anything—Birdie's best friend, Jess's sidekick photographer, the mean girl behind @FauxEver. But now I don't want to be anything. I want the world to see me on my own terms.

I want my control back.

"You know what?" I say, straightening and stepping away from the counter. "Actually, I don't want to take a picture."

The girls stare at me, wide-eyed, but I don't stick around to hear what they say. I grab my suitcase and head toward my gate.

I'm going to see my dad, and that's all that matters. I'm going to have a couple of days away from everything and everyone, time off to think about what's next for me. And it's thrilling, that feeling of having all the doors open.

Maybe I'll stay in the countryside and teach at a nearby school. I might meet someone kind, someone who's never heard of Birdie Bay, FauxEver, or Henriette-whatever-her-last-name-is. Then I could live a quiet life, one filled with simple contentment.

Or maybe I'll give photography another shot—join a support group, take a few extra classes, make new contacts. There are many ways to find success, so why couldn't my passion be mine? PM's words keep echoing in my head. I could live a life doing something I truly love.

Or maybe I'll just fly somewhere I've never been. I heard the matcha in Bali is amazing. I could drift around the world like those travel creators I used to admire, trying foreign foods and discovering new cultures and mindsets. I could live off new experiences.

A text from Diane appears on my screen.

> I found a top-notch IT guy for the FauxEver app. Do you want to meet with him? 😊

Or... maybe I'll go back to Paris and milk FauxEver for all it's worth. Team up with Diane, swallow my pride, and finally share what happened from *my* perspective.

I could make sure everything I did wasn't for nothing.

Just before boarding, I take out my phone and hit record.

"As I said, sometimes the grass only looks greener because it's fake." I smile into the front camera. "These past months have been wild, and the last few days? A full-on rollercoaster. But here I am, Chloé Warner. And I hope you're all eyes and ears, because I'm about to share my side of the story. Stay tuned."

I upload it to @FauxEver and press *publish.*

Acknowledgments

To my husband and my son—thank you for letting me write in (mostly) peace and quiet on weekdays, weekends, vacations, and even in restaurants. Every time I start a new story, I think the idea will fade—and every time, it ends up swallowing entire weeks of our lives. I'm endlessly grateful to you both for not making (too much) fun of me while I look like a gremlin in my writing cave.

To Alice Martell, who believed in this story so fiercely I sometimes wondered if she loved it more than I did—thank you for that summer call and the encouragement I didn't know I needed until you gave it.

To my brilliant beta readers—Sarah, Cate, Jas, Danielle, Jona, and Jennell—thank you for your honesty, insight, and support. You made this book better in every way.

To my family and friends, who patiently endured my talk of revisions and editors—I finally have something to show for all your relentless "So when does the book come out?" questions.

And finally, to you, dear reader—thank you for picking up this book and diving into the glittering chaos of influence. I hope you laughed, cringed, and maybe saw a little too much truth in it. May your likes feel genuine and your attention span mercifully long.

xx Elle

About the Author

Elle Grand loves stories—reading them, writing them, and hearing them from the people she cares about. She's a self-confessed phone addict and an overthinker by Virgo nature, which means she's always three steps ahead of the plot. Her friends call her for advice she knows they won't take, but she listens anyway.

When she's not deep into writing another book she's "completely obsessed with," Elle can be found spending time with her family or making yet another pros-and-cons list about adopting a cat.

instagram.com/authorellegrand

tiktok.com/@authorellegrand

goodreads.com/authorellegrand

www.ingramcontent.com/pod-product-compliance
Ingram Content Group UK Ltd.
Pitfield, Milton Keynes, MK11 3LW, UK
UKHW040759091225
9458UKWH00031B/247

9 782839 948852